The Painter's Boy

The Painter's Boy

An Historical Caprice

Andrew Wilton

FARRINGTON PRESS

Cover illustration: Richard Dadd, *The Curiosity Shop* (detail), water-colour, 1854, The British Museum

For my friends and colleagues in the
Turner Society

and

in memory of
Geoffrey Ashton,
who made the original suggestion

Author's note

Some years ago I was asked to provide a screenplay for a film about the great landscape painter J. M. W. Turner in which Peter O'Toole was to star. It was immediately clear that Peter could not be cast as the artist himself: two more different physical types could hardly be imagined. Looking for an appropriate role for him, I set about thinking of Turner's life and times, his existence as a public and a very private man, and of the people with whom he mixed professionally and in the course of his everyday doings. I was equally anxious to construct a plot that would be both entertaining and exciting, reflecting what I knew from long and intimate experience of his life and art, not too constrained by historical minutiae but set firmly in the London of the late 1840s when he was in his seventies. This story is therefore not a faithful history either of Turner or of the London of his time, but it is, I hope, true to the spirit of both.

I was not a professional writer for the screen, and was hardly surprised when my script disappeared without acknowledgement. But I felt that my narrative had some merit as entertainment, and redrafted it as a novel. That novel is what this book contains. The portrait of Turner himself is intended to be accurate. Most of the other characters are historically identifiable, though much greater licence has been assumed in depicting them, and most have little, if any, resemblance to their prototypes. A few are freely extrapolated from the circumstances described, in the interests of the story, and chronology has equally been adapted somewhat to suit narrative ends.

Readers will perhaps notice that I have tried to make up, in a very modest way, for what I regard as one of the most regrettable absences in English literature – one that might so naturally have been remedied in the years between Turner's death in 1851 and the death of another great artist of the age, Charles Dickens, in 1870.

I would point out that while, many years after the novel was written, the name of its anti-hero has become internationally famous, if not notorious, and is known as an anglicised German one, it is nonetheless a good old English surname: the musicologist Cecil Sharp, for instance, noted a folk-song, 'The Red Herring', performed for him by a Mr Trump of North Petherton in Somerset in 1906. On the other hand 'Villikins and his Dinah' is a cockney song very popular throughout the early nineteenth century.

A.W.
Chislehurst, April 2019

Chapter 1

LONDON. Dawn on a raw spring morning in the year 1848. It will be a year of revolutions and revolutionary manifestos. Half Europe – half the world – seems to be up in arms. Across the Channel, the French have just unceremoniously deposed their king in favour of a republic. Here in murky London a sense of division, of impending strife, pervades the swarming population. In the by-ways and ditches lurk strange, ragged fugitives from the potato famine that has half-annihilated Ireland, repulsive yet poignant reminders of a nation's indifference, intentional or unintentional, to its responsibilities. There is a nervous stand-off between haves and have-nots, wealthy and poor, Establishment and Chartists, owners and owned. People are looking over their shoulders at continental rebellion, and are decidedly uneasy.

In one of London's murky, uneasy thoroughfares, not far from Oxford-street, there is a barber's shop, its window full of wigs on stands, china jars of pomades and powders on shelves, lucent bottles of coloured unguents to soothe and refresh newly shorn male jowls: a battery of placebos and disguises for the anxious, inexorably thinning and balding male population of the metropolis. Above the barber's door there's a spindly pole, its red-and-white spiral also recently refreshed, apparently, as is the green fascia with its careful cream lettering: 'Barber : J. SHERRELL : Wig-maker'.

The barber and wig-maker himself stands in his doorway, a cheery, youngish man, leaning against the jamb and staring with concentration at the hairpiece he's arranging into mellifluous curls while he talks to a youth in country clothes chewing on a bun. They are engaged in an earnest discussion, punctuated with occasional smiles and outbursts of laughter, though the younger one is plainly nervous. The barber drapes the wig over a stand and puts it on one side. He looks keenly at his brother.

'So you think you'll be all right, then? I dare say you will – but he's a queer fish and no mistake.'

The young man is taking in all he says with wide eyes, lips clenched as though he is envisaging trouble.

'You'll find he's full of strange jokes – they make no sense to me. There's a good deal about him I haven't worked out. But you're an artist and you'll understand him, maybe. You'll learn a bit.'

'That's what I want, so much.' The boy makes a decisive gesture with the sketchbook he is holding.

'Anyway, don't you let him frighten you. Get those vittles down you and be off. He's always up betimes, and likely'll be stamping about waiting for you. Good luck, Frank!'

Frank swallows the last of his bun, shakes the barber by the hand with a nervous attempt at cheerfulness, and turns away down the street, dodging passers-by, crossing between horses and carriages, avoiding puddles and heaps of dung. The streets are drab, enveloped (to the eye) in a perpetual smoke shed from the ranks of chimneys that serrate the horizon, and pervaded (to the nose) by the choking smell of that smoke, and of horse manure spiced with the pungent reek of equine urine. He is almost too preoccupied to notice how the population is depressed-looking to match the streets. Not like the cheerful inhabitants of the seaside town he has come from. There, the fishermen and sailors are for ever singing shanties and telling stories, smoking tobacco and rejoicing in the bounty of the sea. Even the gales that pound their boats and rip their nets and flood their houses – even those are exhilarating. Here, no one seems so much as to notice the weather. Drably attired servants carrying buckets, baskets, packages of food, as if for a siege; footmen in discreet liveries; crossing-sweepers with their brooms; beggars with their pathetic hand-written signs – 'Orphaned and Hungry', 'Pity the Blind'; navvies in corduroy trousers breaking cobbles with pick-axes.

Frank threads his way through this forlorn humanity, and at length finds himself in side-streets where the crowds jostle less insistently, and the cries of traders and hawkers can be distinguished individually above a more subdued hubbub. This is the relatively civilised neighbourhood of Marylebone. On one little-frequented corner a man with a wooden leg is selling broadsheet ballads under a tattered umbrella, warmed by a small brazier. Frank stops for a moment to look at the sentimental, patriotic, sometimes gruesome rhymes with their crude woodcut illustrations. But he knows he is late, and hurries on. At last, consulting a scribbled note at the back of his sketchbook, he steers himself towards a particularly gaunt and depressing street, lined with a mismatched clutter of buildings, some grand, some plain, some of stone, some of brick. One is even shabbier than the rest, an austere grey brick façade lowering over an almost brutally plain entrance. The panes of its inexpressive windows are thickly grimed over, the woodwork of the front door almost paintless.

He gingerly approaches the door (no grand flight, only one low stone, not much worn) and hesitates to take the irreversible step of tugging on the bell-pull. The door is forbidding enough, flaking paint, tarnished knocker and all. He retreats to the pavement, and peers over the area railings. Deep down below, in the dank, flagged trench, a small woman is pegging a couple of dishcloths on a short line. She doesn't see him. He coughs, and she looks up. He has time to notice that her face is scarred with a large disfiguring mark, before, very quickly and with a scowl, she throws her apron up to hide it. He recoils in horror, but then, summoning up more courage, returns to the railing.

'Excuse me –'

'Eh? What do you want? You're not the cats' meat.'

'I'm sorry – no – I've come to –'

'We're not expecting anyone today.'

She goes inside, slamming the door. Frank waits, uncertain whether to go down, go away, or try the front door. As he stands there, he hears the bolts of that door being drawn back, and a key turning in the lock. The little woman reappears in the doorway, her apron still partly covering her face.

'You're not the young man from Margate? Barber's brother?'

He nods, trying to smile, relieved that she understands. But she scowls again discouragingly, turns and goes back indoors. Timidly, he follows her.

It's as gaunt inside as out. All he can make out is a dark hallway, not hospitably appointed. He recognises casts of classical sculptures round the walls, and the odd uncomfortable chair. The little woman leaves Frank alone, seated uncertainly on one of these and staring round him. Thin morning sunlight is beginning to filter through the dirt on the windows, casting odd splashes of brightness that illumine only dust and frugality.

Suddenly a large, hideously ugly cat with no tail jumps on to the back of his chair and rubs itself against his cheek. He gets up, startled, and moves as far away from the animal as he can, only to trip over another one lurking in the shadows. In a few moments at least a dozen

3

unsavoury cats are milling about his feet. He tries vainly to disentangle himself from them, dropping his sketchbook. It falls open on the floor, in a patch of light filled with the specks of dust that its impact has stirred. The cats swarm round it, over it. He stoops to rescue it, and as he does so a shadow falls across it. Two feet in unkempt boots appear in his range of vision, and baggy trousers in deep wrinkles round the ankles. He looks up, half terrified.

It is the artist, the great painter who is to be his employer – Mr Turner: short, with greying hair brushed forward in the Wellington style, and a weather-beaten face, bony-nosed, emerging from a bulky, messily tied cravat. His expression is frighteningly sombre, but there is a humorous trembling in the muscles round his mouth, and the eyes are a bright, inquisitive grey. Frank makes a grab for his sketchbook and stands up, breathless.

'Good – good morning, sir.'

Turner jerks a thumb at the sketchbook.

'Them your drawin's?'

Frank is mildly surprised by the soft Cockney accent.

'Yes, sir.'

'Hmph! I don't hire you to draw. No one draws in my gallery. These are my pictures. I won't have 'em stolen.'

'Yes, sir. I'm sorry.'

'You're here to work. What time is it?'

'Am I late, sir?'

'In this house, the work gets done in the morning. All the chores. I'm generally through with 'em by the time the likes of you are out of bed.'

'I'm sorry, sir.'

'Sorry? No need to be sorry – yet. You'll be doing penance enough from now on. It's you can do the chores for me now. I'm too old for 'em. Seventy-three tomorrow. Yes, it's time the younger ones took on some of the drudgery.'

'Drudgery, sir?'

'Drudgery! What d'you think a painter's life is like, if not a round of drudgery? What d'you think we've been doing all these years, if not to hand on the duties to the youngsters when we're past it ourselves?'

'I don't know, sir.'

'No. You don't – not yet. But you'll find out. That's what a painter's life is all about. Hard work, hard – hard work. Look at me.' He extends his horny, paint-stained hands, one thumbnail left to grow

4

extra long. 'Those aren't the hands of a lazy courtier, now, are they? Artists and courtiers – two different species, wouldn't you say? Artists are workers, you know. Why d'you suppose I've paint on my hands, eh?' The grey eyes give Frank a quizzical glance. 'Nobody else does the job for me, you see?'

'I understand, sir.'

'Do you, my lad? Let's hope so. And will you shake hands with all this paint?'

Frank takes the offered hand. He feels – or thinks he feels – a surreptitious bolt of energy pass from that calloused palm into his own. Turner moves to lead him out of the hall, then stops.

'Wait a moment –'

He disappears through a dark doorway. Frank hovers, nervously looking round for the cats, which have vanished. He examines his book, and brushes off a few paw-marks. There's a long silence, so long that Frank begins to feel he has been dismissed, and looks at the front door with half a mind to escape. Then the little housekeeper bustles out from the kitchen, retreats from him a pace or two and stands awkwardly with her face half-averted.

'You may go upstairs if you like.'

He blurts out 'Upstairs? Why – ?' But she has gone again, disappeared into the recesses of her sooty kitchen.

With trepidation, Frank mounts the creaking staircase, which is as dimly lit and dusty as everything else. At the top there is a double door, firmly shut. He hesitates yet again, but eventually finds the courage to turn the handle. He pushes the door open, alarmed by the loud squeak of its hinges, and with a final effort flings it wide. He gasps in astonishment, and stands rooted to the spot, amazed. Then slowly, wonderingly, he walks into Turner's picture gallery.

It's a long, red-walled room, flooded with light from a big, broken, grimy skylight that extends the whole length of it. All down the walls are stacked brilliantly luminous landscape paintings, large and small, framed and unframed, sometimes as many as six deep. He stops again to summon up the courage he needs to start looking: to examine each canvas in turn, kneeling to look at some, gently, reverently touching the paint of others.

He hears the floor creak behind him as Turner treads heavily across it.

'That's it. There they are. My children, eh? You didn't bargain for all this, I'll be bound.'

'They're beautiful!'

'Pooh! What about the square footage? Too much, ain't there?'

'Oh no, sir!'

'Too much for you to tackle, I mean. Your brother didn't tell 'ee you were to be turned into a manacled slave, now did he? But that's about what it is, my lad. Slavery. Night and morning, morning and night, from cradle to grave.'

Frank is beginning to be worried, and can't help glancing towards the door.

'Aye, you'd best be leaving now, if ye're frightened of hard work. Nothing came without labour, lad – nothing at all.'

'I'm willing to work, sir.'

Turner brings his face closer to Frank's and speaks in a confidential undertone.

'You see,' he says, 'the fact is I've not been as fit as I like to be. Me doctor is telling me to take life a little easier for now. So – if you want to work, you'll be able to help me.'

The jangling of the front door bell comes up from below. Turner grins broadly.

'And maybe – well, maybe I can play for a change!' He gives Frank a wink. 'Yes – I can dally with the fine ladies, eh? Flirt, ogle a bit. D'ye like that, boy? Eh? D'ye enjoy the ladies? Wait a bit and ye'll see some.'

There is a flurry of voices down the staircase, and Frank finds himself becoming agitated as the noise of conversation comes nearer. Turner goes to the door, opens it and waits on the landing for his visitors to ascend. The voices stop as he appears, and he watches them approach in embarrassed silence. There are four people coming up the creaking stairs towards him: a well-dressed man in his forties, obviously attached to a tall, plain but commanding woman; and another man of about the same age, preoccupied with encouraging a pretty, much younger woman, who wears an expression of permanent delighted amazement. Turner greets them all in his usual gruff manner.

The girl's companion speaks with a faintly American accent:

'You're acquainted with my good old friend James Lenox of New York, Turner. May I have the pleasure of presenting his niece, Miss Harriet Lenox, of the Bronck's? Mr Lenox has asked me to look after her while she's in England and I, in my turn, am asking Miss

6

Rigby here to guide her through the mazes of modern London, where even experienced men like myself have been known to go astray.'

Turner makes a little bow. 'I should say Miss Rigby would be the perfect – chaperone.'

'I know London well,' Miss Rigby puts in. 'I think I may say I am well qualified to act as *cicerone*. And dear Mr Eastlake has undertaken to help me.' She touches her companion's arm and the two look tenderly at one another for a moment.

The visitors promenade round the long room, admiring the pictures, Miss Rigby talking rather loudly but intelligently, Turner mumbling something occasionally. Eastlake is slightly pompous, self-consciously on his dignity. After a while, the other man contrives to get Turner on his own.

'I'm not here simply to introduce my charming young friend, Turner. You might guess I'd not venture inside your Gallery without a business proposition in my hand.'

'Aye, that's what I like to hear, Leslie. A good business proposition!'

'Harriet's uncle Lenox is still hankering after another of your pictures. Still a shade – suspicious, shall we say, of the "indistinctness" in the last one he bought of you. Pretends he understands it, but – well, I think he'd like something a touch – less fanciful.'

'If he wants one o' my pictures, he must take it fancy and all. He can't extract the fancy and leave it on one side, like the mustard on 'is plate.'

Leslie laughs.

'Well, Turner, may I choose something for him?'

'Why not let his niece choose? I'll wager she's a better eye for what he likes than you have, Leslie.'

Leslie laughs again, and they go up to Harriet, who is looking eagerly at everything.

'Mr Turner's a wise old gentleman, Harriet. He says you must choose a picture for your uncle. Will you?'

She looks startled.

'I? But I know nothing...' She looks round, at a loss, and catches sight of Frank, who is trying to be inconspicuous. With American candour she goes straight over to him. Uninhibited by any sense of impropriety, she has taken off her bonnet and holds it dangling from the strings. Her yellow-gold hair is revealed, brushed back in a long shining stream, crinkled enchantingly like water flowing swiftly over small pebbles. Miss Rigby is watching this display with an expression that suggests disapproval.

'Do you live here?' Harriet asks Frank, smiling her smile.

'No. I – er, I work here. At least, I shall, I hope.'

'Oh! And what shall you do?'

'Well – I am to help Mr Turner. Look after his pictures.'

'My! How very interesting!'

Miss Rigby's voice carries across the room to them.

'Harriet!'

She has to call again, for Harriet is sincerely interested in what Frank has been telling her, so much so that the firm tones barely pierce her consciousness at first. Then she turns, sees Miss Rigby's stern face, and goes over to her.

'Harriet!' in an emphatic whisper, 'In England, Harriet, well-bred young ladies do not speak to young men to whom they have not been introduced.'

'Oh! Then I'll introduce myself.'

'Not at all, if you please! I do not think this young man is quite – you mustn't –'

But Harriet has already walked back to join Frank.

'What's your name?' she asks him in all innocence.

'Frank – Francis Sherrell.'

'I'm Harriet Lenox. You can help me. Will you? I must choose a picture for my uncle – he lives in the United States of America.'

'But I couldn't do that – I know nothing about –'

'You know more than I do. Come on!'

And she puts her hand into his arm, and drags him off, to the manifest disapproval of Miss Rigby. Leslie, too, watches them together.

'That's a very sensible idea,' he says.

'It's most improper.'

'American girls – young ladies – are brought up on a slightly freer rein than their English cousins, you'll find, Miss Rigby. I give you full permission to train her as you think fit. But don't be hard on her. She's young, and means no harm, I assure you.'

'I don't doubt it, Mr Leslie. All the same... you've already agreed that London has its pitfalls.'

'Is that young man a pitfall?'

She doesn't go so far as to say what is in her mind, that all young men are rightly regarded as pitfalls. But she must defend her position.

8

'He might be.' She looks at Eastlake, and they nod meaningfully at one another, looking across to the two youngsters. Then, *sotto voce*, 'You know what they say of this household. No one knows who – what sort of a family the old man has.'

Leslie examines her face curiously.

'And you believe the boy is…?'

'I believe nothing. I only know that there are rumours. Unsavoury rumours.' But the old man himself is approaching. She says brightly: 'The pictures – are they not magnificent? What is that? The end of the world?' She points at one of the larger and more terrifying-looking subjects.

'That, I think, is Hannibal crossing the Alps,' says Eastlake. 'Am I right, Turner?'

'Aye. What else?' He seems reluctant to be drawn into a discussion of his work.

'I believe you showed it at the Academy in – a long time ago now, it must be twenty years…'

'Nearer forty,' Turner supplies laconically. 'And there's some have been here far longer than that.'

Miss Rigby can't help noticing that these pictures have been propped in their piles all those years under leaking panes in the skylight. Strange that their inspired author has no wish to protect them from the elements. And in so many cases the paint is cracked and peeling off in ribbons… She and Eastlake continue their inspection, sufficiently distracted for Harriet and Frank to proceed with their own tour of the higgledy-piggledy display without further interruption. As they stand together in front of one explosion of golden light, Harriet whispers,

'Aren't you afraid?'

'Afraid? Why?'

'I've heard them say he – Mr Turner – is a strange man. Hard and cruel – do you think he ties people up and feeds 'em on bread and water?'

'Ties them up?' He ponders the idea for a moment. 'Do you mean, in manacles?'

She nods and grins, gloating at the romantic notion. Suddenly, Frank does indeed feel frightened. But she is already thinking of something else – transfixed by the painting in front of them.

'Here it is! Uncle's picture! Don't you love it, Frank – I mean Mr Sherrell? Won't Uncle James like it?'

9

'It's splendid, but I don't know about your uncle.'

'But you think it's a fine picture?'

He nods enthusiastically.

'Mr Leslie!' she calls. Leslie comes over to them. 'Mr Sherrell advises me that this is a fine painting. I'm sure my uncle would like it.'

Leslie shakes his head.

'But it's perfect. Isn't it, Mr Frank?'

'I – I really don't know. It's very beautiful, but…'

'You're right, young man,' Leslie says firmly. 'Harriet, I thought you were taking the young man's advice. Your uncle won't want another dose of the vapours! – and certainly not the mists of classical antiquity. He's an American, remember. Something modern, I think. Try something modern. Look at this one – a railway train. That should surely appeal to an industrialist of the New World.'

'But look at the fog in it! No! I love *this* picture! He must have it! Mr Turner, Mr Turner – please tell Mr Leslie.'

But Turner grumbles into his cravat, looks sideways and shuffles off, leaving Harriet surprised and baffled. She approaches Frank again, but he is now hugely embarrassed and nervous, and jumps when she addresses him.

'Mr Sherrell,' she announces to him, solemnly, 'if Mr Leslie refuses to take that one, I shall – steal it!'

'What?'

'And you shall help me! Mr Turner! Mr Sherrell and I are going to steal this picture – it's so beautiful. Shan't we, Mr Sherrell?'

Frank overcomes his shyness.

'I'd be very tempted.'

Turner is there again, beside him.

'You'll do no such thing, I hope. Now lad, kindly show the visitors to the door, would you?'

'Yes, sir.'

As they troop out, Turner puts a hand on Leslie's shoulder.

'Why don't you call again to choose Mr Lenox's picture at leisure, Leslie?'

To Frank's embarrassment, when they reach the bottom of the stairs, Miss Rigby places a coin in his hand.

'Thank you,' she says. 'I understand you are employed by Mr Turner?'

'Yes, Ma'am. I'm to help restore the pictures, Ma'am. I only arrived this morning.'

'Did you now?' She surveys him carefully for a few moments. 'So you really are new here?'

Before he can even nod confirmation, she has turned and swept out with the others, to a waiting carriage which quickly moves off.

As soon as she has settled herself against the hard ticking upholstery, Miss Rigby voices her thoughts, though quietly, since Harriet is sitting opposite her.

'Did you believe him, Charles?'

'Why, yes, Elizabeth. I think I did.'

'Hm. I wonder. I certainly haven't seen him before. But nothing would surprise me.'

Harriet has been straining to hear what they are saying. She can't help herself interrupting.

'Surprise you?'

'Mind your own business, Miss.' Then, less sharply, 'Now, did you enjoy the pictures?'

Harriet looks at her, at first blankly; then slowly a radiant smile spreads across her face, and she nods thoughtfully to herself.

Chapter 2

TWILIGHT is thickening rapidly, the obscurity it brings intensified by fog. Inside a large tavern overlooking the Thames at Wapping, lamps are glowing orange, and many people are making merry. Tankards are passed over the heads of topers, somewhere a squeeze-box and fiddle are eking out a thin tune. At a corner table a tall, shock-headed man is putting words to the same melody, in a passable tenor voice.

'It was a rich merchant in London did dwell,
And he had but one daughter, an uncommon fine young
      gel,
Her name it was Dinah, scarce sixteen years old,
With a wery large fortun' in silver and gold –

Aye,' he interjects, breaking off the song, and speaking half to himself, half to his two companions. 'A wery large fortun', that's about it. That's what I'm in need of just now. There's those in the world would like fair shares for all, but where are they, here in beautiful England? In London? There's neither equity nor charity here.'

His companions make no comment on this general condemnation of contemporary mores beyond a corroborative grunt. One of them is a very tall, bulky, fair-haired man whose blunt visage is distinguished by a broken nose and two cauliflower ears, in which he frequently inserts a finger for the purpose of rotating it very hard, and examining it carefully on withdrawal. He is blessed, in addition, with all the other prescribed accoutrements of the bruiser, including an exuberant dragon tattooed on his neck. The other man is a small rotund fellow with a rabbit nose and hectic cheeks. He wears an incongruously colourful waistcoat and an untidy dark wig, which lend him an air of half-apologetic swagger.

The shock-haired songster takes a gloomy swig of his ale, and looks sideways under his lids at a table on the other side of the tavern, on which he has been keeping an intermittent eye all evening. It is half obscured by the partition that marks off the space it occupies as a private snug, with a balcony over the water. He can glimpse through the partition a group of men in black frock-coats and white cravats, their top-hats balanced on pegs and nearby chairs. They are crowded round the table, whose surface is covered with bottles and plates and the remains of a whitebait supper. The singer and his morose friends are too far off to hear what is being said, but the conversation is lively.

'Go on, Pick!' one of the gentlemen cries, in a light Scottish accent. 'We want to hear the end of this.'

Pickersgill gets up from his seat and arranges a plan or diagram among the cutlery by means of salt-cellars and pieces of lemon rind.

'You know the ending, Roberts,' he says. 'I told him there was no other place to hang it. The picture had to go *there*,' banging a pepper-pot on the table, 'there, between mine and Turner's.' Pick brings a salt-cellar and a spoon into line beside the pepper. 'The man was indignant. "What do you mean, sir?" he cries. "Your picture is too dark, and Turner's too brilliant. I shall be insipid between the two of you!" I told him he should consider himself fortunate to be placed among such luminaries. But no, he would not admit the benefit. It was a conspiracy, no less. The Academy was infested, it seemed, with villains whose only wish was to destroy his career. I was at a loss. Then...'

Turner has quietly left his place beside Roberts and walked over to the window, where he is leaning out, watching night descend on the Thames, the lights reflected in the water lapping over the mud, the barges lifting intricate patterns of tackle against the brownish sky, a rowing-boat creaking past. After a few moments Leslie joins him; behind them, Pickersgill's voice can be heard.

'Leslie, where are you going? It was Turner who calmed the man by offering to have his own picture taken down! Tell 'em yourself, Turner. You know what happened.'

Turner goes on staring at the water, shaking his head as Pick's story continues.

'He ordered the men to remove his picture, and then offered his own place to our disgruntled friend. Sly old devil! Immediate embarrassment, contrition, of course he wouldn't for the world...'

Leslie starts talking in a low voice at Turner's elbow.

'Turner, that picture I'm asked to find for Lenox. You know what the man's like. Wants to admire, but doesn't really know where to begin. Can you – would it be possible for you to paint something –'

Turner rounds on him.

13

'Something he can understand? Ha! He complained of me indistinctness. I told you, that's my shortcoming. Some people would say it's my only talent. If you don't like it, you must – but wait.' He pauses, a glint in his eye. 'Maybe for that niece of his, I might make an exception.' He is gazing steadily out over the river. 'She makes me wish I was a boy again.'

'You old –' Leslie gives him an affectionate nudge. Turner's eyes twinkle. He walks rapidly back to the table.

'It was only a ruse to keep my own place, ye see. He couldn't agree to my suggestion, could 'e? And as for Pick here – he wanted an end to the argyment. But I did hint that maybe – maybe – that there picture of his would look the better for a touch of madder in the drapery. He looked at me then, he did, and says, Why, Turner, I wonder but you're quite right! O' course I was right.' The whole table roars with laughter. 'The next mornin' he'd done as I told 'im. And he put my picture in the shade, and Pick's too.'

'No one could put you in the shade, you old humbug!' This from a wild-haired, wild-eyed man, who they all know is a phenomenal dab at painting animals. Landseer. Leslie, with an impetuous shake of his dark cow-lick, takes up the challenge.

'Humbug? Turner? If there's one man who doesn't know what that word means, he don't!'

'Come now, Leslie,' Turner interrupts him. 'Enough of me and my opinions. Where's the boy? You're in need of more claret. Hey, there!'

The boy brings another bottle. The merriment increases, with Turner at the centre of the laughing knot of men, all swapping anecdotes about their beloved Academy, its rivalries and jealousies, the barely suppressed hostility of some Committee meetings and the incapacitating sickness of the President, which is a worry for them all.

But then they return, as they always do irresistibly, to the odd occurrences at varnishing days, just before the Academy's Summer exhibitions, when they can all make last-minute improvements to their work once it has been hung. Turner is notorious for sending in blank canvases and painting them complete, there and then, in their frames. After a while Pickersgill and Leslie glance at one another, and move discreetly away to a corner where they confer in whispers, looking back occasionally at Turner's grey head. Then they return to the group.

14

'Well Turner,' says Pickersgill, slapping the old man on the back. 'You made short work of that bottle. I provide the next. And I'll wager you can't drink this one so fast!'

Turner stares quizzically at his glass.

'The wine don't agree with me nowadays,' he says. 'You mustn't give me any more. Rum and milk is my tipple – or ought to be. '

'Another glass won't do any harm,' Pickersgill says jovially, and summons the boy again, for a further bottle. Leslie picks up Turner's glass, and Pickersgill pours a generous quantity into it. Then Leslie replaces it under Turner's nose. Both men look on, a little anxiously, while he sits there, toying with the stem as he goes on talking. His speech is beginning to be a little slurred. In a pause, he takes a swig, then another. Pickersgill pours again, and Turner drinks again, egged on by the others, who for some reason seem to have temporarily lost their appetite for the wine.

It is an hour or two later that the cronies emerge from the tavern, noisily, and begin to walk off. As they pass a wall nearby, they do not notice three shadowy figures standing in its shelter, watching them. After a few moments one of the three, a man with a shock of dark hair, creeps after the party, and finds an opportunity to pull Turner by the sleeve, unobserved by the rest. At first Turner ignores him, but at last is compelled by the man's persistence to stop and attempt to stare him into desisting. Then, accepting the inevitable, he slips away from his friends and hurries with the man behind the wall, where the two other men are loitering. One of them, he can make out, is a giant, a towering hulk that, even in silhouette, conveys quiet menace.

'Don't take any notice of them. That's Chaz. He's only here to protect me. And Sammy O'Reilly, the big one – yes, he's very big, but he means no one any harm. If you don't hurt him, he won't hurt you.'

Turner ignores these introductions. The chill air is already beginning to sober him up, and this encounter focuses his mind sharply.

'Mr Turner, I must speak to you.'

Turner's lips tighten, but he replies,

'Well. If you must. Speak.'

'You never come this way now, and I can't talk to your man. He won't listen to me. He's a cruel man, Mr Turner.'

'Cruel? What d'you mean? He's my rent-gatherer and that's all there is to it.'

'Aye, a rent-gatherer. Rent-gatherers are cruel men.'

'Not to them as pay, by no means.'

'But to them as can't pay –'

'D'you expect me to discuss a mere business matter now? Leave it till the morning.'

'No, Mr Turner. It can't wait any longer. I'll have justice now, sir.'

'Justice, Mr Trump? What sort of justice will ye have at eleven o'clock at night, in Wapping, eh? There's more justice in the world at nine in the morning, than ye'll ever find at this hour. Wait till then.'

'No. Listen to me. I can no more pay your rent than I can sit in the new House of Parliament. You must…'

His pleas are interrupted by Turner's friends, calling for him from down the road.

'Wait, Mr Turner. You're a hard man. You may like to spend your evenings in liquor with your pals, but some of us won't see our good money washed down your greedy throat, and that's about it.'

'*Your* money!'

'Aye. It's our rents you're drinking. Where else does the money come from?'

Turner pulls his arm away from Trump's clutch.

'Let me go. You owe me more than six months' rent. I tell you, if you won't pay, you must quit the premises.'

Trump raises what Turner at first assumes to be a stick. But he doesn't strike, and after a moment Turner sees that it is an umbrella.

'And suppose I refuse to leave, Mr Turner?' The umbrella hovers in the air, an incongruous threat. 'Chaz!'

The smaller of Trump's friends shambles up. The huge Sammy remains propped against the wall, apparently indifferent. Turner surveys the little one – even shorter than himself – who gives him a superior leer and a shake of his wig. He is not cowed.

'There are such people as bailiffs in this world, I think.'

Trump lowers his weapon.

'And there are such people as Mrs Sarah Danby in this world, too, ain't there?'

This time Turner is visibly taken aback.

'What's that? What do you know of – Sarah Danby?'

'I know she's another poor creature that's learnt about your cruelty, that's what. I know what you owe *her* in the way of – rent, as you might say.'

16

'Rent?'

'It's only a manner of speaking. But I think it's a manner of speaking that you very well understand. Now suppose I was to say I won't pay *you* no rent until you've paid *her*? What would you say to that? And then – there's a certain George-Anna Danby, too, ain't there? Or is it George-Anna Turner?'

Suddenly, Turner is angry.

'Don't mention that name! Silence, you scoundrel!'

'Ah, there, Chaz, you see where we touch him? That's the way! Now George-Anna's a good friend of mine, Mr Turner, and I think she'll know how to make you see my point of view. Shall I speak to her about it?'

Turner has recovered his sang-froid now.

'Speak to whom you like. Only pay your arrears, or by God, I'll see you in gaol...'

At this moment, Leslie and Pickersgill, breathless and anxious, appear round the wall.

'Turner! Are you all right?' Leslie gasps, then rounds on Trump. 'Leave this gentleman alone, rascal!'

'He's doin' me no harm, don't you worry,' Turner interrupts calmly. 'But he'd better watch 'is step. I could do *him* some harm, if it came to that.' He looks intently at Trump for a moment. 'Think about it! Now, good-night!'

'Yes, sir,' responds Trump, irrepressibly. 'And maybe *you*'ll think about it, too. Good-bye – for the time being.'

As Trump and his companions disappear into the night, Pickersgill gives vent to his concern.

'Good gracious, Turner! What on earth – ?'

'Nothing, Pick, my friend. A poor rogue. I felt quite sorry for 'im. But thank 'ee for putting an end to our conversation. It's too late, and too cold for such chat. Let's be going.'

And they stumble off, arm in arm.

It's a longish walk back into the West End of London, and the party gradually disperses on the way. At length only Turner, Leslie and Pickersgill are left, huddling together for warmth in the wide, cold, empty streets. They hail a hackney-cab, and Turner is bundled into it by the others.

'That's it, Turner,' says Pick. 'Are you comfortable? Now, driver, take this gentleman to – what's your address, Turner, now? To –'

But Turner puts his head out through the window.

17

'Don't mind that. I'll tell 'im where to go. Thank you, Pick, Good-night Leslie. Driver!'

The cab rumbles away into the darkness. Leslie and Pickersgill look at one another wryly, then shrug their shoulders and shake their heads. There's nothing to be said: their little ruse has been foiled, as always, by the innate cunning of their amazing but mysterious colleague. They amble on, slowly and ruminatively, up the street until they too separate to their homes and beds.

Chapter 3

IN THE SUNLIGHT that pours in through the front-room window of a little artisan's house close to Lisson-grove, Sarah Danby is sitting lethargically, sewing a glove. Long ago, it seems now, she made gloves for a living, until she met a musician, an organist and composer who transformed her life into a perpetual round of harmony. They and their children would sit of an evening at the table in the parlour, and sing catches and glees, play the flute or the violin, and John Danby himself would perform his latest anthem or motet on the Broadwood pianoforte. But very little remains of that life, save the piano which she keeps reverentially polished, an incongruous note of elegance in a room that is remarkable only for its simplicity and lack of refinement. There's not much sign of polish or any other kind of household care in the scratched drop-leaf table and the few upright chairs that surround it.

Sarah, in an easy-chair, is the worse for drink, elderly and scrawny, her clothes respectable enough but old and worn like their owner. In an adjoining room someone is preparing food, making a clatter. Eventually that person appears with a tray. She is a woman in her late thirties, tall and dark, not unattractive, but with strong features and an aquiline nose. There is a certain untidy nobility about her. She puts the tray on the table and lays out cutlery and plates. The old woman stirs herself a little to watch her as she does this.

'Well, George, you're a comfort to me in my declining years, that I'll say. If I've no one else, I've got you. What are you giving us for dinner today?'

'You're absurd, Mamma. I'm sure I don't know why you will go on saying you're all alone.'

'And I'm sure *I* do. When you've reached my time of life, you hope to have your family about you, children and grandchildren, all in order, little and large, trebles and altos, tenors and basses. The whole choir. And what have I got?'

'A solitary mezzo-soprano. I'm sorry, Mamma. I never could sing well enough to be a true Danby. But then I'm not, am I? Not a real Danby. I'm a Turner really. The last of the line, you might say, with my sister gone off and married a Frenchman; she cares not a tittle about us – Lord knows where she is now.'

She sees that her words have only made her mother more gloomy, and attempts to console her. 'I'll try and sing after dinner, Mamma. We'll have a little glee-session together.' She goes to Sarah and tries to pluck glove and needle from her hands, but she resists, clinging tightly to them as though they were a protection. 'You must stop sewing now. Your eyes are tired. Come, we'll eat.'

As they are settling themselves at the table there is a knock at the street-door. George goes to open it.

'Ben Trump! What brings you here? Come in, and have something to eat with us.'

'No, I thank 'ee. I'm well, and need no vittles. But I'll speak with you if I may. Is your – your mother here?'

'She's here. Of course.'

Trump lounges into the parlour after her, and stands before Sarah, who peers up at him myopically. In the bright sunlight she sees a less sinister figure than the one that accosted Turner in the dark last night: a tallish man, approaching fifty, still handsome with a mobile face and black eyebrows, his plentiful black hair tinged with grey. He is shabbily dressed in what were fashionable clothes twenty years since – a lot of knotted cravat under his chin, and a stand-up collar on a narrow-waisted coat: the remnants of a never very refined or distinguished dandy. He balances his umbrella against the wall by the door, and wags a finger at it, warning it not to fall over.

After a moment, George-Anna returns to the back room.

'Ben,' mutters Sarah, looking him over slowly. 'Is it you? Where have you been?'

'Down in the docks. You know where I've been.'

'The Ship and Bladebone, is it?'

'How could I afford to spend any time there? Not as long as *he* keeps a-turning the screw on us. I'm thankful for a square meal at home, I am, and sometimes Meg brings me a pint of porter to my table.'

She grunts acquiescently, and absently picks up her sewing again, hardly noticing that the glove is dragging in her plate of food.

'Ho, no! I'll not be paying money twice into his pocket, when I can't hardly find the rent. But I'll put up with it no longer, Sarah!'

He grasps her arm, making her prick herself with the needle.

'Keep off, you clumsy fool! Look what you've made me do!'

'Clumsy yourself. Put that work down. I'm a-talking to ye.'

George-Anna has heard the exclamations and come back into the room. They don't see her, and she stands there, listening unobserved as their conversation goes on.

'I can hear you well enough. What is it?'

'You must help us, Sarah. Tell us where he hides himself.'

'How should I know?' she answers with a shrug. 'Does anybody know?'

'I reckon he knows himself. And you — well, you were close to him once, eh?'

She lets the glove drop into her plate and stares upward, her eyes unfocused.

'Long, long ago. I haven't seen him for years. I might be dead for all he knows or cares.'

'But you know his house, for sure.'

'Once I did, but —'

'Don't you pre-varycate with me, Sarah. I'll find it out. Now, where was his house in those days, those far-off days of youth and love, eh?'

''Twas close to Wigmore-street, in Mary-bone —'

'Well?'

'What will you do, Ben? I shan't tell you if you're planning any wickedness!'

'Sarah, woman. You don't care any more what happens to him, do you? That I won't believe.'

She looks at him dubiously, her eyes clouded with distrust and reminiscence.

'Why should I care about him? What was he ever to me save a —'

'A what, Sarah?'

She fires up.

'He used me, like a harlot he used me! I bore his girls, but would he ever be a father to them — or a husband to me? I was a mere lump of flesh to him — female flesh, for the asking. I was a fool.' Her voice is hard, her eyes dry.

George-Anna's face has gradually lengthened in horror. Now she retreats once again, rapidly, to her back room.

'Come Sarah,' Trump persists. 'Tell me.'

Her anger is directed at him now.

'I tell you I don't know! I don't know!'

Trump's face turns nasty in response to this attack. But he modulates his expression, changes his tactics, and moves to the piano. A volume of music and some song-sheets are lying on it. He picks up the book.

'Very well, Sarah, very well. What have we here? "The Skylark", eh? Well, you certainly were one in your prime, Sarah, a veritable song-bird.' He flicks through the pages, and starts to read and sing at random.

'Faint and wearily the way-worn traveller
Plods uncheerily, afraid to stop,
Wandering drearily, a sad unraveller
Of the mazes t'ward the mountain's top… '

'Stop, Ben! Stop!' Sarah has banged her hands over her ears and shut her eyes, as though the music were penetrating her brain by all the senses, not just one. 'I won't have you sing that. Stop!'

'Why, what have you against that fine old ballad? Here am I singing Agnes and Sadie both for you. You should take Sadie's part.'

And he begins again,

'Doubting, fearing, as his course he's steering –'

'Come on now, this is your part! –'

'Cottages appearing, as he's nigh to drop…'

'No!' Sarah screams at him. 'I won't have it!'

'Now this is a strange objection. I think I need to sing you out of your ill-humour.'

'Sing by all means, Ben. But not that.' She sees he is offended. 'It was one of *his* favourites,' she explains. 'We used to sing it together. I was Agnes, he was Sadie – it was comic – I can't bear to remember it. Don't go on, Ben, I entreat.'

He gives her a perplexed look, then continues thumbing the leaves of the song-book.

'Well, then, how about "Glorious Apollo"? And here's "To Anacreon in Heav'n" – why, you can't disapprove of these. Ah, they remind me of times long ago, when we enjoyed ourselves together. Now, Sarah, I'll give you your note!'

He opens the piano and props the book on the stand.

'George-Anna! We need your assistance!'

He plays a chord and begins to sing, but no-one joins in. He gets up and walks into the room next door, where he finds George cowering in a corner, her hands fretting at her apron. He puts an arm round her shoulder.

'Won't you come and sing, George? You've a sweet voice, my girl, and 'tain't exercised half enough. Come!'

She continues to stand there, shoulders hunched as though to repel him, head drooping, face drawn tense. He pulls her, and she resists. There is a struggle, in the course of which he tries to kiss her. She makes a feint at pushing him off, but it is not quite convincing. Sarah calls from the sitting-room:

'Ben Trump! What are you doing?'

'Whipping up a little support for my glee club. Minx!' he whispers to George. 'You'd like nothing better than a little sing-song with me, wouldn't you?' Once more he tries to kiss her, and this time she lets him, relaxing into her tight corner, her back pressed against the wall. Then he gently leads her by the hand to the piano.

And so the three of them sing 'To Anacreon in Heav'n', their voices blending well enough, for although none of them is very sweet-throated these days, they know the piece of old, and have harmonised together on many an occasion, long ago.

'May our club flourish happy, united and free-e-e-e—
And long may the sons of Anacreon entwine,
The myrtle of Venus – the myrtle o-of Ve-e-nus –
   with Bacchus's vine!'

While they sing, Ben moves close to George, and tries to fondle her. Eventually she lets him hold her hand. Already mollified by the music, Sarah sees this and her expression softens. When they have come to the end of the piece, she turns to him and says grimly:

'I'd do it for no one else, Ben Trump. But *you* – you know how to wheedle a stupid old woman. I'll take you there – if I can remember.'

Chapter 4

IT IS THE FIRST warm spring day. The Thames is in flood and the sunlight glitters playfully on the water. Trees along the bank are coming into leaf, and the steeple of Battersea church can be glimpsed through the budding branches. Bell-ringers are practising, and the sound carries cheerfully across the river. By the water's edge a tallman in his twenties is idling, sullenly playing ducks and drakes. Behind him is a wide tow-path along which a procession of carts and pedestrians moves into and out of London. The road is flanked by fields, with occasional outcrops of building: there is a row of low artisans' houses with small square gardens in front, planted with lines of useful flowers and vegetables, a few of which are about to bud. One of the cottages is surmounted by a curious iron balcony, and below, in its doorway, a well-built middle-aged woman is shaking out a tablecloth.

'John!' she calls. The idle young man takes no notice. 'John! You might come and help with the weeds in this garden.'

John continues to throw stones. He sees a small pleasure-boat going past, and deliberately aims at it, hitting the planking on its side. There's a pretty girl on board, who immediately notices the impact.

'That man has hit our boat with his stone!' she cries. John can hear her quite plainly: her voice has a decided twang – could it be American?

'Yah!' he volleys at her – at the boat in general.

A stern-looking woman surveys the damage.

'It's nothing, Harriet. Ignore it.'

The man who is with them is entranced by the scenery.

'Look at the light on the water. What a glorious spring afternoon, after all the greyness. The reflections are magical. Do you know what they remind me of?'

'Of course,' the stern woman says. 'Turner's water-colours. He can make paint just as translucent, as shimmering, as rainbow-coloured. Now, Charles, do you think that you could do that?'

'I, my dear? Oh well – of course, my subject-matter is rather different.'

'I know. Far more serious. Greek gods and so forth. But answer my question. Could you do it?'

Her companion can't think of a suitably dignified reply. Meanwhile, John has been staring at Harriet, enraptured. His mind entirely fixed on her, he has begun to wade out to the boat, deeper and deeper. Eventually he flounders in, splashing and spewing out Thames water. Harriet laughs, her giggles carrying like the church bells across the river.

'Silly boy! He was looking so hard at us that he fell in.'

'At any rate, *you* should not be looking at *him*. And he is hardly a boy – quite old enough to know that such behaviour is unacceptable. A vulgar, low fellow.'

'Not like that nice young man we met at Mr Turner's.'

'Which nice young man do you mean? Oh, you are referring to the – I trust you will never see him again, Harriet.'

Eastlake, pursuing his own train of thought, interrupts.

'Leslie tells me that the old man has promised to paint Lenox a picture – provided that Harriet asks him!'

'He is outrageous.'

Harriet is pondering the interesting question.

'I? What should I say, to persuade him?'

'You need say very little, I imagine. You must simply – look charming.'

'Disgraceful!' – Miss Rigby's comment, of course.

'Then,' pursues Harriet, 'I am invited there?'

'Not to my knowledge,' Miss Rigby says. 'We must wait. Harriet, learn patience, modesty and restraint. They are English virtues which may stand you in good stead.'

By this time John has waded back to the shore, where his mother is standing ready to scold: a shrewd, homely woman whose vaguely rustic accents betray an origin some way from the capital. She carries on where she left off a few minutes back.

'John! Come out, stupid! What d'you think you were doing? I saw you ogling that young lady. What do you mean by it? You should have more sense. Now, come in and get dry.'

She tries to hustle him into the house, but he is fixed to the spot, watching the boat drift on. He goes back to the road to see it out of sight, and only when it has disappeared from view does he come indoors, where his mother is holding up a large towel.

It is a poor, simply furnished place, though there are one or two quite nice things including a pair of Wedgwood urns on the chimneypiece, and a plaster relief showing a classical scene on the wall. Sophia Booth takes the towel to her son's hair, rubbing firmly and unsympathetically.

'One day I'll be rich enough to court a girl like that,' he says from under the towel. 'I'll have all the money I want.'

'And how will that be, my son?'

'Ah – you wait! You're not short of a sovereign or two, Mother, and I shan't be neither.'

'Why, do you think I'm going to leave you rich? When I'm having to spend, spend, spend keeping up this place, and – and – *him* –'

'Ah, you waste your money on 'im. Why d'you do it? You get nothing in return. You're a fool, Mother.'

'You blasphemous boy! Didn't I teach you your ten commandments? But no, you've never honoured your mother, though she does look after you like her ewe lamb.'

He straightens up, looks at her aggressively.

'Me? You don't care about me! I don't get a look in. All you think about is how to waste more and more of your money on *him*. The old scrounger! I wonder you don't see through him. A swindler, a cheat, that's what he is.'

'Don't talk so. That's wicked!'

'Not so wicked as a mother that hates her own son.'

'I – hate you? That's terrible!' She bursts into tears, burying her face in the towel. 'Oh, you're a bad child. I don't know what'll become of you! When I've given you a nice comfortable home, and you never have to do a day's work.' She turns to face him, her hands on her hips. 'It's time you went out and looked for a living, John. '

· 'Aye, I will too. You don't want me here no more. You and *him*. I'll find my own way.'

He rushes off, tearing the towel from her, and disappears upstairs. She dries her eyes on her apron and goes into the back kitchen, tut-tutting. She can hear him moving about above, the timbers of the floor betraying every movement. What's he doing? She can't make it out. Usually, when he goes upstairs he flings himself on his bed, and she hears nothing more for an hour or two. Today, there seems to be an unwonted deal of creeping about.

John changes rapidly into some dry clothes, and spends a few minutes carefully brushing his hair and admiring the effect in the dressing-table mirror. Then he tiptoes on to the landing to listen. Hearing nothing, he creeps into another room, and the door swings behind him. His mother can't hear the sound of a chair being carefully moved within, a drawer being opened, or the rustling of papers. For the little room is full of papers – pile upon pile of papers, some of them blank but many of them drawn on, or painted on, in brilliant colours. There are jars of paints and boxes of water-colours, trays of pencils and chalks. At one end is an easel, though there is nothing on it except a wooden board. From one side to the other are strung lines to which sheets of paper have been pegged in rows. These sheets are washed with the most delicate hues, indigo, umber, ochre, soft pinks and yellows: water-colours in the process of being moulded into landscapes of the subtlest atmospheric effects. John doesn't seem very interested in these indications of creativity, but having rummaged among the piles he quietly opens the door again and reappears on the landing, carrying a thin, roughly wrapped brown-paper parcel. When he gets down into the parlour he assiduously hides this from Sophia, then strolls into the kitchen.

'I'm off, then.'

His mother puts down the kettle.

'What d'you mean?'

'I told you. I'll get myself some work – gainful employment. You can spend all your money on *him* – I don't care.'

While he is talking he surreptitiously takes a long knife from the drawer in the kitchen table and hides it in his clothes. It's a sharp knife, as he knows well, for his mother insists on a well-equipped kitchen, and *he* – the old man – enjoys nothing better than to be grinding her blades on the carborundum he uses for honing his pencils and chalks. He stands around, nonchalant, for a few minutes longer, then makes to leave. She tries to keep him from departing so abruptly.

'Now wait, John –'

But he has darted off before she can stop him, adroitly picking up the package as he goes out of the house. She runs to the door, calling him. In a little cage that someone has hung just outside the door a tame blackbird is whistling softly. She stops to run her fingers companionably over its bars, as if that provides solace to her anxiety, before she goes back inside, shaking her head and beginning to cry again.

Chapter 5

ELIZABETH RIGBY takes her duties as *cicerone*, as she calls it, very seriously. She has, after all, a dual responsibility: to introduce the young American girl to the memorable sights of the metropolis, with all that that entails in explaining the history and institutions of the country; and to instil into her decidedly untaught mind the rudiments of civilised behaviour, as understood in this very epicentre of civilisation. There have been drives to many of the most interesting sights, and a trip on the Thames, but the more perilous activity of simply walking through the streets has to be avoided as far as possible. Nevertheless, there are inevitably moments when, with the carriage stopped in the road, they have to brave the crowd in the Strand or Piccadilly, in order to visit a mantua-maker's emporium, or an art dealer's gallery. Harriet has set her heart on buying a box of colours, for water-colour is an accomplishment Miss Rigby and her new English acquaintance all recommend. So a visit to Ackermann's in the Strand is on the day's programme. Then Howell & James have some irresistible Indian shawls to admire, and McLean's, in the Haymarket, has some American paintings on display that Elizabeth is anxious to see. She congratulates herself on being able to show Harriet something of interest from her own country. Short though the distance may be between the vehicle and the safety of a milliner's or a haberdasher's, she is nervous lest her susceptible young charge should somehow go astray. She prefers it when the girl's hand is tucked safely in her arm.

In spite of Elizabeth's continuous, and fascinating, description of the sights they are passing, Harriet seems abstracted, preoccupied with her own thoughts. She will stop unexpectedly in front of a shop window, or break away to stare up at a turret or gable. In Regent's-street the throngs of people make any sort of dialogue difficult to sustain, and Harriet is sometimes invisible for moments on end behind pedestrians and vehicles. Then, when they reach Oxford-street, they are engulfed in such a dense crowd that, to Elizabeth's alarm, she disappears altogether. After some moments of patient waiting, and then of alarmed searching, she realises that they are hopelessly separated. This is what she most feared. The silly girl has no idea how easy it is to become lost in these crowded streets, and how dangerous it is to be unprotected.

Harriet, sublimely indifferent to these difficulties, has quite deliberately given Elizabeth the slip. She has taken advantage of the shelter provided by a passing 'bus to hide behind a marzipan-seller's stall until her companion has walked on a few yards. Then she darts off down a side street. Pausing for breath under a wall hoary with torn playbills and advertisements for patent medicines, she asks a crossing-sweeper for directions. He is not very communicative, but stares at her with wonderment from a dirt-smeared face. She imagines his curiosity is simply that of a Londoner encountering a foreign visitor, but he is really puzzled by the sight of an obviously well-bred young lady wandering the streets on her own. When she asks again, he can only point mutely, and with a word of thanks she hurries off along the route he has indicated.

One or two more cross-roads and interrogations, several more shocked stares, and then she is standing on a scruffy doorstep, ringing the rusty bell. She can hear it dimly clanging within. Eventually the little domestic pokes her sadly scarred head up from the area.

'Good morning,' Harriet says in her open, candid way. 'I've come to see Mr Turner.'

A curt mumble:

'He's from home.'

'Oh. When will he be back?'

'How should I know? He doesn't vouchsafe to *me*, I'm sure.'

'Will he return soon?'

'I can't say. Probably not.'

There is a pause. The domestic seems unwilling to pursue the conversation, but doesn't actually go away. Harriet is determined.

'Is, er, Mr Sherrell here?'

The little woman becomes more animated.

'You're the young lady as came with Mr Eastlake, aren't ye?' Harriet nods. 'Wait.'

She disappears now, and Harriet can hear her calling, 'Frank!' indoors. There's another longish wait, and then the front door bolts are drawn back, and Frank appears on the step.

'Mr Sherrell!' Harriet bursts out at once. 'I've come back – to ask Mr Turner to paint a picture for my uncle. I know he's not here just now. But may I – might I come in and – look?'

Frank's brow registers perplexity.

'I don't know what Mr Turner would say. He doesn't like visitors coming in without his permission.'

'But he wants to talk to me – I know he wants to talk to me about my uncle's picture.'

'I see,' says Frank, though he doesn't. 'How can I help?'

'You must tell me what to ask for! I'm sure you know best.'

'Oh, I don't –'

She is standing in the hall now.

'We shall go upstairs and look at all the wonderful paintings, and decide. Let's!'

In the shadows, her back to the kitchen door, the little domestic is watching them.

'Oh, Mrs Danby, please don't tell the master!' Frank begs her.

She grunts, and turns back into the kitchen. The two youngsters go up the stairs, which creak all the way.

'Who is that?' Harriet whispers.

'Mrs Danby – Hannah, her name is. Mr Turner's housekeeper. She's very shy.'

'Poor woman! With that sad face.'

'Poor woman, yes. But she's a kind heart under her grumpy manner.'

He pushes open the door at the top of the stairs and once again the two of them are spellbound by the Aladdin's cave of wonders stacked up in Turner's neglected, leaking gallery.

Meanwhile, in the high-ceilinged drawing-room of a house near Fitzroy-square, Elizabeth Rigby, still wearing her walking cape and bonnet, is pacing up and down anxiously. Charles Eastlake stands by the fireplace, a newspaper in one hand, looking concerned. She has only just returned, after a frantic but obviously futile search along the pavements of Oxford-street.

'You must tell Mr Leslie that we can no longer undertake to look after his young friend, Charles. She is utterly – utterly intractable. Positively delinquent. I had thought that a few weeks of my chaperonage would set her in the right path, once and for all.'

31

'But you've only been in that position a week! She needs more time perhaps.'

'What is the point of my offering to spend time with her if she takes every opportunity to run away from me? I'm desperately worried. Anything might have happened to her – anything! Charles, you must take this matter in hand. Summon the police –'

'She is an intelligent young lady. I have confidence in her presence of mind. She has almost certainly found her way – where did you say you lost her?'

'In Oxford-street. Near Marylebone-lane.'

'Then I suspect that we can guess where she has gone. It's my belief the young minx allowed herself to become lost quite deliberately. She must certainly be disciplined, I agree as to that. But I think she is quite safe.'

'Safe? How can you know that?'

'I'll wager she has done what she was so eager to do, and would not stop talking of doing. She has gone to call on my esteemed colleague, J.M.W.Turner.'

'To Queen Ann-street! We must go there at once.' She makes impetuously for the door, but Charles restrains her.

'My dear, calm yourself. I shall go there presently. I have business with Turner, too. Please stay here, and – practise what I heard you preaching only the other day: patience and restraint? Trust me. I shall bring her back safe and sound!'

And in Queen Ann-street, Frank and Harriet are standing side by side, gazing at the pictures. One after another, they contemplate the golden glories, the bursts of effulgence, the men and angels of Turner's imagination. Then she stops, looking for one in particular, an image that hasn't left her head since she saw it on that memorable first visit. It was an explosion of colour and light, an Arcadia, a Paradise... what was it called?

'Wasn't it this one?' Frank asks, stopping at one of the most idyllic of the landscapes. I don't know what its title is. But it's – a vision of Italy, I suppose.'

'A vision, yes! A picture of Heaven on Earth – how I adore that place, that Italy of Mr Turner's, Mr Sherrell!' She pauses, then goes on in a voice that, for her, is almost hushed. 'It was such a strange moment, when I came before. I'm afraid I've fallen completely in love with that picture.'

'Fallen in love?' echoes Frank.

She turns towards him and sees him looking earnestly at her. She is suddenly embarrassed, blushes, and walks rapidly towards the door. He follows.

'I didn't mean to upset you, Miss Lenox. Please forgive me.'

She tries to look stern.

'Miss Rigby was right. I ought not to have come here by myself. I'm sorry, Mr Sherrell. I'd better go.'

'But Miss Lenox, I don't understand…' He trails after her as she makes her way purposefully down the stairs. Surely she will stop in the hall, give him a chance to speak and perhaps provide an explanation? But she marches on, opens the front door and walks out into the street. He makes to follow her, worrying for her safety alone in the London mêlée, but is overcome by shyness, a sense that he has no right to presume to assist her. He follows her with his eyes a little way, then slowly closes the door and stands behind it, digesting what has happened. Then he goes down the dark corridor that leads to the rear of the house, and opens another door into a big room dominated by a single large window, with under it a table, its top crammed with glass jars filled (or half-empty) with bright powdered pigments. There is a model ship in a box painted so that the inside is a seascape with clouds and a distant rainstorm. There are two easels, on both of which are half-worked canvases. Along one wall is a shelf of notebooks, most of them carefully titled on labels pasted to their spines. And strings are stretched from one side of the studio to the other, with clothes-pegs on them here and there; but no washing, or anything else, is hanging up.

Frank goes to work, stacking pictures that lie around in untidy heaps, examining each in turn with a fascinated eye. When he has finished a pile he goes to a table at the back of the room and leafs through a portfolio of loose, unmounted water-colours. His admiration for these miracles of delicacy and wise observation knows no bounds, and he has difficulty tearing himself away from them to get back to his proper task. Then there is a long jangling ring on the front-door bell. At first he ignores it, but it is repeated insistently. No one seems to be answering it, so he puts his head out into the passage and listens. Silence, and then another jangle of the bell.

'Hannah!'

No response. He walks into the kitchen, gloomy and dank and stone-floored, like its companion area outside. There is no one there.

He goes back to the hall, and heaves open the front door. Mr Eastlake is standing there with two other gentlemen, one of them very tall and distinguished-looking. With a jump of the heart Frank thinks that it must be the Duke of Wellington himself. But the tall gentleman introduces himself.

'Good morning. My name is Jones – George Jones. These are my colleagues, Mr Eastlake, and Mr Landseer. We should like to speak to Mr Turner if he is at home.'

Eastlake says, 'Is your master here, pray?'

'He's not, sir. I'm sorry, sir.'

'Will he be in later?' asks Jones.

'I couldn't say, sir. He's not been here this week, sir. I don't know where he is. Perhaps Mrs Danby, she would know. But –'

'May we speak with Mrs Danby then, please?'

'She's out, sir. I don't –'

'The devil!' Landseer interrupts, his hair flying. 'Is there nobody here, then? We left word to say we should call this morning.'

'Mr Turner won't have got your note, I think, sir. He's not been here for –'

'So you say, boy. Now, wait a moment.' Landseer whispers to the other two, and they all nod. 'Should you care to run an errand for us, young man?'

'Well, sir –'

''Tis a matter of some urgency.' Landseer holds out a coin. Frank looks embarrassed.

'I don't mean that, sir.'

'But I do. Will ye take this note to Mr Turner at once?'

'But I don't know where he is, sir.'

Landseer is close to losing his temper completely.

'For Heaven's sake! Does he keep his very household in ignorance of his whereabouts?'

'I'm only here to help restore his pictures, sir.'

'Indeed you are,' Eastlake interrupts, to calm the debate. 'We have met before, have we not? I came here the other day, with a lady – with two ladies…'

'Indeed, sir. I remember very well.'

'Perhaps,' Eastlake continues, pointedly, 'perhaps you have seen one of those two ladies more recently?'

Frank hesitates only a moment before replying.

'No, sir.'

'She has not been here this morning?' – giving Frank a close, penetrating look. He is proof against this, however.

'Certainly not, sir.'

'Strange. I would have sworn… This is disturbing.' He rubs his chin with a gloved hand, looking worried. 'I must leave you, Jones – Landseer. Pray excuse me, gentlemen.'

Without further explanation, Eastlake hurries off, leaving the other two bewildered.

'Now, young man,' Jones resumes. 'I realise that you do not know how to help us at present. But might I take the liberty of asking whether you would be prepared to put yourself at our disposal – on another occasion – in connection with Mr Turner?'

Frank looks doubtful.

'You will of course require to know exactly what it is that we wish you to do. I can assure you that it will be a matter in which you will be assisting friends of Mr Turner's who have nothing but his good at heart. In fact – we wish him to do us the honour of acting as President – that is, as Acting President – of the Royal Academy during the illness of its true – I mean, of our present – er, President who is at present – not to put too fine a point upon it, at Death's door.'

Landseer has been biting his lip and tapping his foot while this little speech is in train.

'You understand, lad?' he asks impatiently.

'I'll try to be of service, sir. But here's Mrs Danby now,' he adds with relief.

Hannah is coming up the street on her way home from marketing, carrying a modest basket of provisions. She recoils when she sees the gentlemen and hurries on down the area steps. She deposits the basket at the bottom and looks up, half covering her face with her shawl. Jones peers down at her over the railings.

'Mrs Danby? We are searching for Mr Turner, but I understand he is from home.'

She grunts.

'Aye, he may be.'

'Where might we find him, pray tell us? He's not been here for some days, I think.'

Another grunt.

'Nay.'

'Would you be so kind as to let us have his present address? We need to speak with him on urgent business.'

There is a brief pause, then Hannah answers.

'Can't do that.'

'And pray why not?'

A further pause, then she blurts out very rapidly,

'Because I haven't the foggiest idea where he is.'

She disappears in at the basement door, which slams after her.

Landseer is on the point of following her down.

'By God! This is intolerable!' Then, thinking better of his impulse, he turns to Frank. 'Boy, come here!' Frank obeys nervously. 'Now listen. There'll be a handsome reward for you if you trace your master to his lair, wherever it is. We've tried in vain to find him. Perhaps a limber youngster like you will be luckier.'

Jones takes him up in a more placid tone.

'Such information as we can give you, we shall supply. But I fear we are all, more or less, equally in the dark. Meanwhile, here...'

He holds out some money, but Frank puts his hands resolutely behind his back, shaking his head.

'Thank you, but no, sir.'

'You won't help us?'

'I'm not sure, sir – I'll see, sir.'

Landseer is incensed again.

'Puppy! Do as you're bid!'

'No, Landseer, no,' Jones placates him. 'Let him come to his own decision. Young man, I assure you that we have the highest regard for your master. We wish him only happiness. Our exertions are all for his sake.'

Frank looks at this kindly, well-intentioned and rather impressive-looking man, and can't help feeling sympathetic towards him. The scowls of Mr Landseer are off-putting though. And he remembers Mr Eastlake, and his important connection with Miss Lenox. He suddenly thinks of his defiant lie about Miss Lenox, and realises that there is a lot to be said for a course of action that will not compound that crime.

'Very well, sir. I'll help if I can. But I won't take your money. Though perhaps...'

'Perhaps what, boy?' Landseer demands, ready to be incensed again.

'Perhaps Mr Turner doesn't *want* anyone to know where he is.'

The two gentlemen men exchange significant glances. Jones clears his throat.

'A man in Mr Turner's position is not altogether a private individual. There are times when he is answerable to – to – the public. And to his colleagues, of course. The Royal Academicians.' The two of them can't help looking slightly self-important now. 'This escaping down his own secret burrow is all very well, but...' He mumbles something that Frank doesn't catch. 'Very well. Thank you, young man. We shall speak with you again.'

Chapter 6

IN THE LIBRARY of Elizabeth Rigby's house time passes all too slowly. The light on the farther wall has shifted steadily over the gold-tooled bindings that cover it, and a maid has come in to make up the fire. Beside it, Elizabeth is seated with a book unread in her lap. Leslie is with her, walking up and down, occasionally plucking a volume from the shelves and glancing at it cursorily, then putting it back with a little push that betokens frustration as well as boredom.

He pauses in this routine, hearing a noise from the hall. He looks briefly towards the door, and watches Harriet come in. With an innate adventurous intelligence, and by dint of enquiring of the ballad-seller and sundry street-side hawkers, she has found a cab and got herself home. It is a personal triumph, and she is smiling as always, but her arrival is greeted by a frosty silence. Undaunted, she makes her way across the room and, picking up her embroidery frame, seats herself opposite Elizabeth. There is a significant pause.

'Well, Harriet,' Leslie says. 'It's time we cleared this matter up. You've been disrespectful – *most* disrespectful to dear Miss Rigby.'

'Of course, I apologise!' she concurs immediately, smiling her broadest. Her expression is so cheerful, her manner so unforced, that they are both taken aback.

Elizabeth leans forward and puts out a hand.

'You won't – will you? – ever do such a thing again?'

'Oh – I don't know!'

This, and her insouciant way of saying it, shocks them to the core.

'What! – What do you mean, Harriet?'

'There are some things I simply want to do on my own.' She delivers this unheard-of sentiment without emphasis, as a matter of ordinary fact about herself. 'I'm sorry, I don't mean any disrespect, Miss Rigby. You're very kind. But I wanted to see those pictures alone.'

Elizabeth bridles.

38

'I'll wager you were not alone, Miss. That young man – was he not there too?' She fixes the girl with an interrogative stare, and Harriet cannot help herself blushing and looking confused. 'Aye, I thought so! This deception really is too much.'

'But he works there!' she bursts out. 'How could I avoid him?'

Leslie may not realise that the smile he casts towards her betrays a good deal of fondness.

'But he doesn't distract you from looking at the pictures, eh?'

She doesn't have to respond to this little sally, for at that moment Eastlake rushes into the room, taking off his greatcoat as he does so.

'What!' he exclaims as he sees Harriet. 'You are here, Miss! Where have you been?'

'I'm sorry, Mr Eastlake. I've been wicked. But you can't imagine how exciting it is for me to be here – in London! I just had to see for myself!'

'See – what?'

Elizabeth feels some explanation is called for.

'She has been to Queen Ann-street – to Turner's house. Consorting with that young man, I fear.'

Eastlake stands stiffly upright for a moment, then confronts Harriet.

'Is this true?'

She nods, so awed by his fierce expression that her smile is almost obliterated.

'Then the boy is a liar.'

'Charles!' Elizabeth says faintly.

'I'm sorry to say it. A liar. That is indisputable. I have been to Queen Ann-street, and he has categorically denied seeing Harriet today.'

Harriet looks distressed.

'He did it only to protect me, I'm sure!'

'If he told you that, Charles,' Elizabeth pronounces, 'he has told you the most egregious untruth. Harriet. Come here.' She points to the floor in front of her. Harriet gets up and stands before the minatory figure.

'You must have nothing, I repeat *nothing* more to do with him. He is clearly dishonest. I shall make sure that Mr Turner knows of this. You will not go there again, under any circumstances.'

'But I must ask Mr Turner to paint my uncle's picture, must I not?'

'Did you have no time for that today?' Elizabeth asks. Eastlake answers her.

'Turner was from home, of course.'

Elizabeth purses her lips.

'That makes your behaviour still more scandalous, Harriet.'

Leslie takes over, in a placatory tone.

'You must wait until we have ascertained Mr Turner's whereabouts, Harriet. Then we shall all go and speak to him together.'

Eastlake says, 'We shall never persuade him to paint what he doesn't wish to paint. He's highly jealous of his independence.'

Elizabeth looks at him admiringly while he says this, and can't resist adding her own rider.

'You might say that everything he paints is a manifesto of his liberty!'

Leslie, ignoring these evaluations, goes on mulling over his proposal.

'Our greatest difficulty will be to find him at home, I suspect. But might we not use Harriet as – as *bait*, shall we say? Put her in his way, and see if he bites?'

Elizabeth can't help being amused by the analogy, yet can hardly approve.

'You are preposterous!'

'Yes, we Americans are preposterous to you English. Don't forget, my dear Miss Rigby, that the same may be true of the reverse relationship.'

'What?' She looks uncomfortable, then laughs. 'You're right, of course. But when in London, do as the Londoners do. That you cannot contradict.'

Chapter 7

IT'S A FINE afternoon, but Ben Trump is carrying his umbrella as he walks beside Sarah Danby along the streets of Marylebone. He is looking about him as though he expected rain to pour out from the surrounding houses, to pelt them from the gutters. All these stern-fronted buildings are potentially threatening, and he may need to hide. Sarah too has her reasons to be wary. She is leading him through the maze of roads that once were familiar and now are only a haze of painful memory – a haze that mercifully numbs the worst of that pain, and makes it possible for her to relive that distant past. It has taken a few weeks to summon up the courage to honour her promise to Ben.

They stop briefly on a corner to confer, and ask directions of the one-legged ballad-seller who has his pitch there. Then, rounding another corner, they find themselves in full view of Turner's house. Sarah points it out to Trump, and for a moment or two neither of them can speak. For quite different reasons they are both filled with emotions that choke them. Then he puts the umbrella up, so that they can survey the place without being seen – or at any rate identified. Ben stands staring, taking in details, noting the neighbouring buildings, measuring with his eye the width of the street, the distance from one corner to another.

Sarah slowly regains awareness of her companion. She nods towards the house, and begins to tell him what she remembers.

'He built it himself,' she says. 'He always liked building houses, for some reason. I remember he said once, he'd have been an architect if he had his life over again. He had a little house in Twickenham, that he designed himself. But couldn't be bothered to live in it for long.'

'Did you ever live there?' he asks her.

'Bless you, no! He'd finished with me long before. I've never seen the place. I only came here once or twice. He found some lodgings that we shared for a bit. And he sent me away into the country when the girls were born. He was terrified of anyone

41

discovering us – me. I was an embarrassment to him, that's all I ever was.'

'But you remember what this place is like, inside?' Ben prompts her.

'I remember what it was like then. But he's made changes – built himself a gallery for his pictures and goodness knows what else. I doubt I'd recognise it now.'

'So you won't be much help to me, will you?' He sounds hurt, disappointed. She is surprised by his aggrieved tone.

'Help? Aren't you grateful to me for coming all this way for you? Do you think I want to be here, walking over all this old ground?'

They are on the other side of the road, and as they pass the house the front door opens and Frank emerges, to go off along the street. Trump turns to Sarah with a questioning look.

'That – ?' she begins his question for him. 'Maybe – oh, I don't know, Ben – but I wouldn't be surprised. Knowing Billy.'

'Ah, you know him, don't you, Sarah my old love? You've a pretty shrewd notion of what goes on in *his* life – in *his* house.'

'I used to know, but maybe I don't any more. Don't rely on me, Ben. Yet – who else would that be? He never employed an assistant, wouldn't hear of it. He let his Daddy do the chores in the old days, cooking for him, tending the garden, stretching his canvases. But he died, what? – twenty years ago, I guess. So what's that lad doing in the house? You may say, how could he keep such a secret? Yet – he's a great one for secrets, that I *can* tell you. I'd say, his nearest and dearest don't know what goes on in that dark heart of his – save that he has no nearest and dearest, I think. He's rejected us all.'

They have been watching Frank's progress, and he suddenly turns and looks back.

'We mustn't let him see us,' Sarah whispers urgently. Ben has lowered the umbrella, but now unfurls it again, bringing it down low over them both.

Round the next corner they turn into an alley, where Sarah stops again, and shows him the back of Turner's premises, the big studio window, the low roofs of outhouses. He asks her a great many questions, and she does her best to answer. But her memory is patchy and she keeps pointing out changes that make it impossible for her to recognise things. Ben becomes more and more impatient with her, but manages to prompt her into giving him a few more details, and at last he has satisfied himself he understands everything she can tell him.

Suddenly she says, 'I'd like to have a word with Hannah,' and returns to the front of the house. She stands by the railings, looking down into the area.

'Hey, what are you doing, woman?' Trump asks her roughly.

'I never see Hannah these days. It would be a good chance to find how she's keeping.'

'Hannah?

'My niece. My husband's brother's child – you never met her, but you remember her father. He was often at home when we made music in the old days. She's a poor sad soul, and she looks after him better than he deserves.'

'She lives here?' he says. 'Well, what about that! Why don't we enlist her help?'

'Never! She'd never allow anything to harm him. You must do this on your own, Ben, and you must make sure she knows nothing about it, whatever you're plotting.'

'In that case, you won't want to speak with her now, will you?'

'You mean – ?'

'You know what I mean. No point in making her suspicious unnecessarily. Leave her be.'

'Ben, I wish I knew what you've got in mind. I don't think I like this.'

'Bah! You're not his well-wisher, and don't tell me you are. Leave your wretched niece alone. Let's be off. But first –' and he looks over her shoulder, into the area. 'And that door?' he asks, pointing down.

'Straight into the scullery, if memory serves.'

'Hm.' He nods and strokes his chin.

She looks once more at the house with what seems like a shudder, and, pulling the umbrella down over both of them, she hurries him furtively out of Queen Ann-street.

They have barely turned the corner, the umbrella well down over their faces, when they almost collide with someone coming towards them from Welbeck-street. They side-step, mutter apologies and hurry on without recognizing George-Anna. After they have passed her, she realises who they are, and turns to speak. But then it occurs to her that it would be an odd and awkward meeting in that spot. Better let them go. And she has business they needn't know about until it has been accomplished.

As she comes near, she sees a little man with a tanned face surmounted by a rather squashed top-hat appear at the other end of the street. It is her father, carrying a large portfolio. As he comes closer, she calls in a quiet voice,

'Dad! Thank Heaven you're here. Where do you get to these days? Even Hannah don't know how to get a-hold of you.'

Turner casts a sharp glance up at the house, then takes her arm and pulls her into a corner out of sight.

'I keep my own counsel. You keep yours, my girl. I don't like you looking me out here.'

'Yes, I understand. But listen. I've urgent news. You must be careful. That Trump – Ben Trump –'

Her father stares into her eyes, which are a sharp grey like his own.

'Who's he?'

'Shadwell. Of course you know. A tenant of yours.'

'Ah – yes.' He scrapes the toe of one shoe on the pavement, and looks down at it thoughtfully.

'He's looking for you. He means you no good, Dad!'

Her father doesn't look up.

'Pooh! I don't fear men like that. He can't harm me.'

'I don't know so much.'

'Why, he's a poor idle fellow, don't know the meaning of hard work, that's his trouble. Let 'im work for his livelihood, like some of us – and then he'll be able to pay his rent.'

'But he's a musician, Dad. An artist. He can't get a living any longer. His voice is thin now, and cracking, his breath's short and weak. He used to play the oboe beautifully. Don't you see he feels he deserves a bit o' comfort now? He's not a labourer, to be condemned to the workhouse.'

Turner is struck by this. He looks at her with a spark of anger in his eyes.

'And how old am I? Seventy-three? And don't I work? Am I not an artist? Am I idle, lolling about with a tra-la-la on me lips when I might be hard at it, serving me fellow creatures? What's an artist for who won't work?'

'You're a hard man, Dad. They say you're cruel. Sometimes I believe them.'

Again he scrutinises her face intently.

'They say that, do they? I'm cruel, am I? And what would Mr Trump like me to do for 'im? Build 'im an almshouse, for the shelter of his old bones? Why, I deserve one as much as he does!' He pokes a forefinger at the buttons on her bodice. 'Tell him, from me, that hard work's the only way I know to be an artist.'

He suddenly turns away to stare absently up the street. 'But I'll tell you what. He can have another week. I'll give him that — because he's an artist, in his way. I shouldn't dare tell my rent-gatherer that. 'Twould be the ruin of me. Give him the message, and say that's the only leniency he'll see from me. It goes against the grain, but for you I'll do it, George. Now — be off. I've work to do.'

He brandishes his portfolio, and disappears down the area steps, leaving George to stand there for a moment, taking in the purport of their interview. Then, pulling her tippet across her bosom, she walks pensively away.

Chapter 8

FRANK HAS GOT into the habit of spending as much of his spare time as he can in Mr Turner's gallery upstairs. It has become a kind of obsession for him. Even when he is not working away on the repair of torn canvas and flaking paint, wedging loose stretchers to ensure that the fabric doesn't sag into unsightly folds, touching up the gilding on battered frames, he is looking at the pictures: looking, looking, endlessly peering into the mysteries of the artist's unfathomable technical mastery. He's obliged to spend time up in the long room, identifying difficulties and damages; but he goes there not just 'on business', as he describes it to himself, but because something draws him there, a magnetic attraction that he has no wish to resist.

He makes it his job to locate new leaks in the glass skylight, and to mop up puddles or place buckets to catch drips. He has tried hinting to Mr Turner that the glass needs repairing, but it's clear that no one is ever going to get round to that important task. One perennial problem is the Manx cats. They have made nests among the canvases and follow him about wherever he goes; their smell is all-pervasive; they wander at liberty in the studio and on the stairs, and no one cares when their muddy paw-marks make tracks across beautiful drawings that may happen to be lying on the floor.

Does he acknowledge to himself that there may be another reason why he is so drawn to the picture gallery? There's a part of his mind that wants to deny it, but another part – and it feels like far the largest part – longs to affirm it loudly: the room is always associated for him with the enchanting enthusiasm of the American girl. He knows it's absurd to hope for real friendship with her, let alone anything more. But the thought of her haunts his waking visions, and sometimes (he thinks) she visits him at nights, as he tries to sleep in the little bed that his brother has provided for him above the barber's shop.

It's nothing unusual for him to stay at the Queen Ann-street house late in the evening. Now that it's full spring the evenings are light, and when Mr Turner is away, as he so often is, Hannah doesn't mind if Frank lingers until dark. He takes an oil lamp and, slowly, as if in a trance, perambulates the room, walking round the walls and picking out one painting after another in the glow. It's a curiously exciting way to look at pictures, as though he were discovering each one for the first time as it emerges out of the gloom and comes within the radius of the light: and each in turn yields the multitudinous details of its magic with greater force and intensity because it exists alone, unique, in that small circle of radiance.

He has realised that a great many of the pictures are seascapes: ships moving calmly against bright skies, or small boats rocking on choppy water, men hauling at nets, birds wheeling above: the sights, the very tang of the air, of his own Margate. Those images arrest his attention for long minutes at a time. And he's amazed, again and again, by the contrast between these earthy – or watery – scenes and the melting gold of the imaginary vistas, the panoramas of a distant world that existed long ago, in an enchanted age, before noise and dirt and industry – before London.

One of the classical landscapes unveils itself, like a beautiful woman stepping into a limelight on a darkened stage. Yes, it's the Vision of Italy – a picture, he's discovered, painted in homage to Lord Byron. As he stands in front of it, enraptured, he is hardly aware of himself murmuring absently 'Harriet!... Harriet!'

As he proceeds from picture to picture, his footfalls echo on the bare planking of the floor. The door behind him is open on to darkness. In the distance a slight bang breaks the silence. Hannah's voice comes up brokenly from the kitchen, calling to him:

'Frank! Frank!'

He goes to the door and looks down the stairs. She comes to the bottom step, carrying a candle.

'Why aren't you gone home? 'Tis very late. I should have been in bed two hours gone, if it hadn't been for that goose I wanted to finish plucking. And so ought you.'

'Where's the master?'

'Don't you know, it's no use asking me. He must be coming soon, or he wouldn't have told me to get that goose. But I've no more notion of where he goes o' nights than you have. Now, go home, and good night.'

He hears her stumble off along the passage. A door slams distantly. It is very quiet now, and dark. He goes back into the gallery and squats in front of his favourite canvas, which he examines with eager curiosity, occasionally touching the surface as if to test the quality of the paint – or perhaps to receive from that film of pigment some ineffable vibration of the genius who placed it there.

He starts again as a faint grating sound reaches his ears, but then there is silence once more. He catches the rumble of a cart in the street. Then a long period of complete stillness and quiet. At last he thinks he really should be getting home. He's about to move when he hears a slight sound of shuffling, down in the hall. Almost inaudible at first, but then unmistakeably, shuffling feet on the stone floor. Has Mr Turner come home, at this late hour? But his footfall is always firm, the step of the confident householder. Not a guilty shuffle, the movement of an intruder. Frank is alarmed, and he stands up, tensely listening. He goes to the top of the stairs and holds up his lamp.

Shadows, impenetrable darkness, except for the muffled gleam of a gas-light coming through the narrow grimy windows from the street outside. Then he realises that in the blackness of the hall there are figures standing at the foot of the stairs, motionless. Struck with panic, he too remains immobile for a long moment. Then he starts down the stairs.

'Who are you? What do you want?'

Instead of answering, the figures move silently towards him, and for a few moments he discerns the faces of two of them. Then the lamp is snatched from his hand. It sputters out and there is nothing but darkness. He puts out a hand to steady himself on the stair-rail, only to feel fingers clamping themselves over it. He pulls away, but is caught, tight, and dragged steadily downwards. He lets out a cry of protest, and then something enveloping descends over him, muffling his shout. The darkness is replaced by a much hotter, closer blackness that suffocates and binds him, preventing movement or speech like the most agonising nightmare. He tries to call out for Hannah but can only produce a muffled groan. He is firmly pinioned, and pushed backwards until he falls on to the stairs, the edge of one of the treads sharp against his spine. Then his assailants, whoever they are, are hauling him upright, and he can do nothing but move stiffly in the direction they are dragging him. All the while they are giving vent to grunts and muttered expletives, and there is much laboured breathing. As they struggle with him one of them trips over a cat and lets out a cry that another tries to stifle.

Frank hasn't worked out how many of them there are. He thinks he glimpsed three, but perhaps there are more. Their combined force is too much for him, young and lithe though he is. One of them is very strong, a powerful body with long, muscular limbs that are wielded with ruthless force and determination. He tries to lash out with his arms and legs, but finds they have fastened some sort of rope or belt round the blanket so that he is effectively deprived of all movement. Even so, they're having trouble with those cats. There's an element of farce in this kidnapping, as men and cats tangle in the dark. Frank, under the blanket, is very frightened, but with an odd detachment realises that he can appreciate the comedy of what is happening.

Muscular arms are encircling him, dragging him – which way? They seem to be pulling him into the kitchen; he can feel the large flagstones underfoot. Yes, they've opened the scullery door into the area – no doubt Hannah left it unlocked. Or perhaps they came in by the window? And now they are heaving him out and up the area steps. Again, he can't help laughing to himself at the efforts they are making to force him up that steep and slippery flight. The absurdity of the situation somehow mitigates his terror as this band of bravoes manhandle him, cursing, through the area gate, and into a waiting van.

Chapter 9

THOMAS GRIFFITH is a successful man. He has done well for himself in the commerce of other men's creations. He has built up a comfortable business, and occupies comfortable premises in the very comfortable district of St James's, not far from the royal palace of that name. His rooms in Pall-Mall are well appointed – that is to say, lavishly hung with damask, and furnished with mahogany chairs, and bedizened with gilt frames in which pictures by the established masters of the day are displayed for the enticement of visitors to his august establishment. Thomas Griffith deals only in the best and most admired art of his time. To look at, he is hardly a match for the distinction of his 'stable': a stocky, bald man with a firm, kindly face. It is a matter of course that he is an intimate of J.M.W.Turner, whom he treats with great but friendly respect; and quite natural that Turner himself should be a frequenter of what Griffith would perfectly happily, laughingly indeed, call his 'shop'. Here they are, examining a portfolio, with a young enthusiast at their elbow – tall and auburn-haired, with pale, intense eyes. His name is John Ruskin. He peers with his pallid intensity at the works of art on display – on the walls, on easels and stands disposed about Griffith's handsome suite of rooms. He breathes rapturously as he progresses from one to the next, hands raised in amazement.

'Yes – yes, of course: masterpieces. He is an angel of light. I can't help saying it again – the greatest painter alive, greater than any Europe has seen for three hundred years. Now look at the delicacy – the subtlety – the grandeur – the *truth* –'

Much as he dislikes being the object of this kind of encomium, Turner can hardly escape it. He deals with it in his usual brusque and taciturn way, with a deprecatory 'Hrrmph.' But Griffith is not one to let pass a chance to promote one of his artists.

'Indeed,' he says eagerly. 'They're exceptional in every way. Quite beautiful. You've done more than I could have hoped, Turner. Yet – there's something about these recent water-colours of yours that I

50

confess puzzles me. This one, now. What an effect! But where's the town? Are these the people? And that cliff! Like a great wave, about to deluge everything.'

'Hrrrmph.' Turner looks abashed. 'Sorry, Griffith. Can't 'elp it. It's the way I paint.'

'But – different from your old way, Turner. Very different, you must allow. I admire, but I fear I don't understand. And do you imagine we can find buyers for such things?'

Turner shrugs. 'That's your business, not mine.'

Ruskin, who has been listening, all ears as well as all eyes, chips in eagerly.

'What I can purchase, I shall.'

'Not all, neither,' rejoins the painter.

'Perhaps not all, but I wager I shall be a better patron than any other of your admirers. My father is quite agreeable to my spending what I judge appropriate.'

'Aye,' says Turner with a sly look at Griffith, 'it's your father, not you, that buys my work, eh?'

Ruskin fires up.

'But it's I who make the decision as to which we shall acquire. He buys them for me, on my recommendation.'

'Don't 'e like 'em himself, then?' Turner seems to take pleasure in needling his admirer, to whom he is the first to admit he owes a lot. After all, it was the twenty-five-year old Ruskin who injected new life into his reputation as an inspired painter of landscape, in a learned and extraordinarily confident book, a survey of the history of landscape painting in Europe, from which he concluded that Turner, J.M.W.Turner, Royal Academician, was nothing more nor less than the greatest landscape painter of all time. The book made a huge stir, and people who had got into the habit of thinking the artist was past his prime had been forced to think again, to reassess their feelings towards his work. All of that has been very gratifying, to the artist and to his dealer. But the transformation was effected by a remarkable degree of confidence on the part of the author, an edge of self-certainty that Turner can't help wanting to deflate, very gently. Ruskin is piqued.

'My father is your greatest admirer – excepting myself. I've made sure of that.'

'I'm glad to say,' Griffith puts in, 'that you've made sure of a good many more than your father. But tell me candidly, Ruskin. What do you make of these? How many of these will you subscribe to?'

Critic and dealer go into a huddle, fingering the rainbow-coloured sheets. Ruskin makes no attempt to suppress ecstatic little cries from time to time. Turner paces the shop, glancing at the pictures on the walls, peering out of the window, and then going to the street door, which he opens. He stands there, comfortable in the warm sun, looking down the crowded thoroughfare. Among the milling throng he notices a tall and vaguely familiar figure, coming towards him. But before he has had time to disentangle it from the mass and give it a name, he hears Griffith calling him, and he turns back into the shop. The figure in the crowd goes instantly out of his mind.

'Now see this, Turner,' Griffith says as the painter re-enters the room. 'You told me there were ten drawings in this portfolio, did you not? But there are only nine, it appears.'

'Nine?' Turner hurries over to the table and leafs rapidly through the pile. 'Dammit! I know there were ten in there. Which one is missing? The Lake of Lucerne – no, here it is. The Pass of St Gotthard? No, that's here. Moselle Bridge – where's the Moselle Bridge? Hm. I'll find it, gentlemen, or paint you another one. But no,' he says with emphasis, after a moment's thought. 'I'll do no such thing. Ten there were, and ten there must be. I know the culprit. Leave it to me.'

Without further ceremony he quits Griffith's shop leaving dealer and critic aghast, and walks rapidly away down the street.

Chapter 10

AS THE SPRING DAWN makes slow inroads into the cobwebby dimness of the house in Queen Ann-street, Hannah sleeps on in her cubby-hole near the studio, and will not awaken until it is light, though that, of course, will not be long on this late spring night. For a long while after the struggling, blanketed Laocoön has departed the house is silent, but for the inanimate creaks of panelling and planking. Then the cats begin to stir again, and the light peers blearily through the dusty windows. Hannah rises at her usual hour, and goes to the kitchen to begin the round of daily tasks. She gets herself going with a glass of beer and a crust of bread. She is used to the simplest diet, and requires nothing more. The morning passes in the usual chores, feeding the cats, sweeping the flagstones in the kitchen, washing out dusters. She wonders where Frank Sherrell has got to: he has usually rung the front-door bell long since. Then towards noon there is a great banging: the front door slams, and the master of the house bursts agitatedly into the hall. He stands in his hat and overcoat, carrying a portfolio under his arm, and listens.

'Hannah!'

Silence. He stumps off along the passage to the kitchen. Hannah is there, at the central table, preparing the cats' dinner. She stops to look at him, wiping her hands on her apron.

'Hannah! Where's that boy? Where is he?'

She shakes her head.

'Not come in yet.'

He rushes into the studio. It is empty. He bangs his portfolio down on the floor, goes to the table under the big window and scrabbles about among the papers on its cluttered top. He then searches in various other places, more and more agitated.

'Sherrell! Are you there?' He hauls out a large watch and consults it. 'Should 'ave been here hours ago. So that's it. He's...' He finishes his mumbled ruminations inaudibly, and goes out into the passage. Hannah meets him there.

'He's gone!' he shouts at her. 'The damned rascal!'

'He's not been in this morning yet. Sick, d'you think?'

'Sick! Never. He's a thief, that's what 'e is. Taken one of my things. But he won't go far. No one can fail to spot it. Ha! They may not recognise the subject, but they'll recognise my hand. Nincompoop! Does he believe my stuff can be spirited away without the world knowing? It will be discovered in five minutes. And he calling himself an artist!'

Hannah is indignant.

'A thief? Fiddlesticks! No such thing, I'll swear. Sit down, now, and – take a glass of brown sherry.'

'Sherry? Sherry? What do you mean, woman? This is no time to be wasting expensive liquor. Hurry up, you must notify the police, and quick about it.' He gives her a rough push, and she retreats to her kitchen to put on bonnet and shawl. He continues to brood, chuntering to himself. 'Of course that's what he's done. I might have guessed. Why couldn't I tell? His wide-eyed innocence, his anxious-to-please manner. All too good to be true. Ain't it? Ain't it? Artist indeed!'

Hannah is ready now, standing before him and looking disapproving. He gives her a searching look, as though he has seen something for the first time.

'No. I'll go meself. How can you describe what's missin'? Lord bless you, Hannah, how could *you* describe one of my water-colours? Eh?' He gently takes her shawl from her shoulders and unties her bonnet-strings, smiling into her bewildered eyes. 'Don't you fret about it. He won't come back. Won't dare, the rogue. Go and sit down, and maybe –' he stops, considers a moment, then gives her a warm grin: '– have a glass of brown sherry. Sit you down. I shall be out a good while.'

He pats her shoulder affectionately, and leaves the house by the scullery door, almost bounding up the area steps in his anxiety to find the criminal.

His first port of all, naturally enough, is the barber's shop. Sherrell the elder is shaving a customer. It is none other than the eminent Royal Academician Charles Eastlake. The shop door is flung open abruptly and a draught flaps the white napkin tucked round the distinguished neck. Eastlake looks round to see who has come in.

'Watch out, sir!' Sherrell admonishes him. Your nose nearly caught the end of the razor.'

But Eastlake has glimpsed the newcomer from the corner of his eye.

'Turner! You're in a mighty hurry, man.'

Turner is grim. 'Aye. I'm chasing a thief.'

'No one's been in here, sir,' says the barber. 'What's taken?'

'Only one of my pictures, would you believe it? The thing I can't believe is me own stupidity. What did you mean by it, Sherrell?'

'Mean by what, sir?'

'Sending your brother – he is your brother, ain't he? – to work in my house. What mischief do you get up to when you're not wielding that blade, eh? Ye're not Sweeney Todd, by any chance, are ye?'

'I'm sorry, Mr Turner, I don't understand.'

'Your brother Frank! He's a thief. Taken one of me drawings. That's what he's done.'

'Never! I swear it. He'd never do such a thing.'

'Well, who else has the freedom of my house, my studio, I'd like to know?'

Eastlake asks, 'Are you referring to the young man who was helping to restore your pictures, Turner?

'That's him. Been showing visitors round, too, I gather – without my permission. That young friend of Leslie's, the American girl, Eastlake, you know her. Are they in it together, now?'

'Harriet Lenox? Impossible! But it's true she went to your house. I'm sorry. She's a headstrong thing. And what's more, the boy lied about it. Said she'd never been there.'

'Where is he, Sherrell? I'll have the law on him!'

The barber is nonplussed, standing with his razor idle in his bewildered hand.

'You're mistaken, sir! He's as honest as – as I am.'

'And how honest is that, I wonder?'

Sherrell is indignant.

'Sir! Barbers are an honest breed.'

Turner looks at him keenly. For a moment he is arrested in his vindictive fury, and passes a reflective hand across his brow.

'I believe you, Sherrell. I know a good bit about the barbering trade. I can remember when barbers were surgeons into the bargain. They'd bleed you as well as crop you. You don't go in for bleeding your customers, do you, Sherrell? No; barbers are decent, hard-working folk. I'm inclined to trust them. But of course there's exceptions...'

Sherrell doesn't want to hear any more in this vein.

'But he's not here, sir. I was thinking he'd been with you last night – didn't come home at all. When did you see him last?'

'My woman Hannah, she saw him last night before she went to bed. She was up late, plucking a goose. What he was doing at that hour I can't imagine. Or rather, I can.'

'He's told me how much he likes looking at your pictures, sir,' the barber interposes hoping to mollify him. 'Says he'd be happy to stay all day, and all night too, just looking.'

'Just looking, was he? Yes, looking and deciding which ones to make off with. Skulking about the place, he was, and Hannah should have known he was up to no good.'

'He's missing?' Sherrell is becoming increasingly concerned.

'Aye. What could be more suspicious?'

'I don't believe it for one moment, Mr Turner, sir. And I'll undertake to prove you're wrong. But first we must find him.'

'Find him, and turn him in,' Turner grunts. 'And don't imagine you can protect him, Sherrell. If he's hiding here, you'll be the first to feel the wind. Harbouring a suspect, accessory after the fact I think it's called. And when that gets about, however innocent you plead, it won't do your trade any good, mind. As for your brother, transportation is the mildest penalty for his offence, I believe. If the scoundrel appears on your doorstep, your best proceeding will be to hand 'im over to the authorities, at once.'

'You're too hasty, Sir,' Sherrell pleads with him. 'You've judged him before he's had a chance to speak.'

'Oh, he'll have his chance – when he's safely in custody. Why, I'll speak to 'im meself. As long as he likes. But don't go putting yourself in trouble by harbouring 'im, Sherrell. If he pitches up on your step, just fetch the constable. That's your first duty.'

'Even more pressing, though,' Eastlake interjects, 'you must finish shaving me, Mr Sherrell.'

The barber sets to work on him again, distracted and rushing it.

'Careful, man! I should like to retain my ears, if you don't mind. No *bleeding*, if you please. And – er – just a little of that toilet water, when you've done.'

Turner is watching this in grim silence, and muttering to himself.

'Fop! Me drawing's stolen and all he can think of is how 'e smells. There's your modern artist for you!' Then, aloud: 'I'm going round to the Academy, Eastlake. We must alert the dealers, everyone in the business. And you, Sherrell. Guilty or not guilty, I'll thank you to find that boy and bring him to me. Shut up shop, and look sharpish! And –,' going close to the barber and lowering his voice – 'if I'm wrong, and he ain't got the drawing, I'll let you pour that smelling stuff over me, and Eastlake here – *and* you can charge me for it.'

Chapter 11

BEN TRUMP'S rented home is a small semi-detached cottage in Shadwell, far away over to the east of the City. It's one of a row of low buildings in a narrow and sunless street, permanently in the shadow of a long, high wall of yellow London brick that flanks it on the opposite side. Behind the wall are goods yards and the wharves of the docks, alternating strips of busy quay and ship-filled water, stretching away for miles, punctuated by the masses of tall warehouses with their accoutrements of gantries and cranes. The sky is patterned with the masts of many hundreds of ships, their tops and cross-trees netted with a filigree of rigging among which gulls tirelessly wheel, uttering their penetrating cries.

The wall creates a barrier between the unceasing bustle and clamour of stevedores, harbour officials, warehouse managers, seamen, boat-builders, chandlers, all engaged in the trade of a huge empire, on one side, and the almost deserted, dreary road with its poky, dark, uninteresting houses, on the other. Trump's house is just like all the rest. It has a very plain doorway flanked by a single window, another window above it. In the low-pitched roof a little dormer is hardly high enough to afford a view over the lowering wall that stretches from side to side in front of it. At the rear, the offices are cramped, and there is a tiny paved yard.

On this warm morning, Trump and his two boon companions Chandos — otherwise Chaz — Grimshaw and Sammy O'Reilly are lounging outside the door. In the ungentle light of day Grimshaw looks as decayed as Trump, but without his air of lost gentility. His manner, though, is self-conscious and slightly histrionic, and he affects an idle, swaggering gait to match. His first name sits oddly beside his last, a sort of verbal toupée, a theatrical embellishment that parallels the ill-fitting wig he wears. Sammy, the most threatening of the shadows Turner glimpsed that night in Wapping, loses none of his menace in daylight, though he seems prone to a certain type of wry-mouthed smile, as though relishing the prospect of some succulent bullying in a moment. The three of them are talking in low voices, and they occasionally look up at the small dormer window in the roof.

'Now, Ben,' Chaz is saying, 'now you've got the little precious; what'll you do with him?'

'Why, make him work for me. You realise who that boy is?'

'Come, how should I know? He might be Master Betty himself for all I've seen of him, in the pitch dark.'

'That's a good 'un! But I don't think I like the sound of that. I seem to recall you taking quite a shine to Master Betty all those years ago. You actors are all the same. Won't have you interfering with this one, you old bugger. He's too useful to me. He's the key to my fortune, Chaz, that's what he is! Being heir to one himself.'

Sammy pricks up his ears.

'Heir to a fortune? Why, 'oo is he, then?'

'Haven't you guessed yet, you dunderhead? You know where we were last night?'

Sam looks puzzled.

'Why, was I supposed to rekernize the place? I'm no great shakes at such things – rekernizin' where I am – and in the pitch dark…'

'It's as well our carrier friend, Bob of the van, was sharper than you,' Ben interrupts him impatiently. 'He succeeded in his mission, at all events, for he took us there, and he brought us back – with a welcome addition to the party.'

Sam sees Ben's grin of triumph and imitates it. He gestures at his two companions, and then at the attic window, as though their joint presence in that spot were the result of some conjuring trick Ben is to be congratulated for.

'But you ought to have remembered, Sammy. I told you…'

'You did, Ben. You told me we were paying a visit to the house of your landlord, old Turner.'

'And so…'

'So you're saying this young 'un's his son and heir? I don't believe it!'

'Believe it or not, that's the fact. I have it from someone as should know. His own wife.'

'I thought he had never married,' Chaz says.

'Wife – kept woman – it's all one… As near as makes no difference.'

'You'll be telling us she aided and abetted you in stealing the boy. Her own offspring!'

'She did. But he's nothing to her. Not one of her brood. He left her – oh, years ago. Left her in misery, to bring up her daughters. The boy came later. The Lord knows who *his* mother may be. She – the wife – don't so much as know the lad's name. He's a dark horse and no mistake, is that Turner. But she knows what he's like. He didn't stop womanising when he threw her out of bed. There can't be any doubt about it. And – he's a lad, d'ye see? The old man abandoned the girls along with their mother. While his favourite, his darling, his pride and joy, is – here, in that attic! *Now* do you take me meaning?'

Sammy glances with a knowing smile from Ben's face to the attic window, to show that he's followed the intricacies of the argument. But Chaz is thoughtful. He waits a moment. He likes to time his darts precisely.

'But what shall you do with him?'

Trump groans and looks heavenward.

'Use your imagination, Chaz, my friend. Do you think I shall fester away here any longer, poor and pestered, with such a prize in me hands? I tell you, that child shall work for me – and work hard! And to work he must be fed, I suppose. I'll fetch him his vittles. Perhaps you'd like to take 'em up? No, on second thoughts it's best if Sammy goes. That will show the youngster he's not to play any tricks.'

He pushes Sammy inside, leaving Chaz staring up at the window, scratching his ill-shaven jowl.

If the cottage is modestly appointed, the attic is almost bare. There's no curtain at the window, and on the bare planking of the floor are a single upright chair and a small wooden bedstead. Frank is lying on the bed, with only a blanket between him and the lumpy, meagrely stuffed mattress. He opens his eyes painfully, and presses a hand to his head. He looks around, and listens.

Heavy footsteps are coming up the stairs. The last flight, from the first floor to the attic, is particularly noisy, every lumbering step accompanied by a daunting creak. Frank gets off the bed quickly and tries the door. It is locked. He peers out of the window, and hears the key turning in the lock behind him. A huge man he thinks he has seen before, but barely recognises, comes in with some bread and a small knife on a plate in one hand, a pewter jug of water in the other. Having locked the door behind him, he cuts the bread into chunks and hands these on the plate to Frank, putting the jug beside him on the floor. Frank is too hungry to question anything, and devours his breakfast wordlessly, propped against the edge of the bed. Sammy sits himself on the frail chair, which creaks complainingly as he does so.

'Well?' Frank demands as soon as he has quenched the most searing of his hunger pangs. The giant twists his mouth up mutely and his little blue eyes glitter with some unexpressed amusement. 'Well? What am I doing here? Please let me go.'

Sammy shrugs his huge shoulders.

'These ain't my quarters. Don't blame me if ye're not comfortable.'

'I don't care about the comfort. I want to be let out.'

Sammy peers at him with a faint curiosity.

'You weren't expecting this development, I'll lay.'

Frank, his mouth full, says nothing. The observation seems too self-evident to merit comment.

'I'm not the guv'nor', Sammy explains. 'Don't ask me no questions, if you please.'

'Then bring your "guv'nor" up here so that he can explain – and let me out.'

'You just eat yer vittles, and then I can leave yer in peace.' Sammy indicates the remaining fragments of bread on the plate with a casual thumb. 'That's it. Now, with your leave, I'll be takin' these down again.'

He stoops to pick up the empty plate, but Frank, driven by sheer frustration, kicks them out of his reach and pushes his head hard down, on to the floor. Then, giving Sammy as hefty a kick in the flank as he can manage, he makes for the door and turns the key.

He is half-way on to the little landing when Sammy's great forearm reaches out and drags him back into the room. He is thrown on to the bed, and the huge man stands over him, his mouth still working silently, the tip of his tongue protruding and slowly moving over his lips. The twinkle has departed from his eyes, and his face wears the look of an outraged animal. His great fists clench and unclench themselves. Frank is terrified, but knows that he mustn't betray his sense of panic. He pulls himself up from the bed, and tries to stand facing Sammy, though there's no space: the backs of his legs are pressed hard against the wooden bed-frame and he is leaning awkwardly backwards, breathing fast, his own fists tight against his thighs.

Then the blow is launched. He receives it full on the cheek, and falls sideways, half on to the floor, catching his hip painfully against the edge of the bed, which bangs against the wall. He suppresses a cry of pain, but can't help putting his hand up to feel the damaged cheek. It is sore, and in a minute begins to throb. The giant has raised his arm again. But at that moment there's a shout from below.

'Hoy, there! What are you about? Sammy, you aren't causing trouble are you?'

Sammy looks sheepish and turns away from Frank. There are rapid footsteps on the stairs, and Ben Trump is hammering on the door.

'Let me in, Sam! Hurry!'

He finds the door is open, and bursts in.

'What the devil did you mean by leaving it unlocked?'

'He couldn't get away,' Sammy assures him brusquely. 'I've got him cornered.'

That is evident at a glance. But Trump is not pleased.

'Have you hurt him? Fool!'

He comes over to Frank, and pulls the hand away from the now darkening cheek. He grits his teeth. 'Can't you even deliver his vittles without a fight?'

'But he – he tried to escape,' Sam blurts out, mortified to be criticised for his careful guardianship.

'Escape? Did he – ah, well. Then it's time I had a word with the young gentleman. You may go, Sammy.' He pauses to consider. 'You remain on duty, though – outside the house. It's as well he's learnt where your particular skills lie. He'll be less inclined to try another runner. Off you go.'

As Sammy thuds down the stairs, Trump sees the knife he has left behind on the floor, and quickly picks it up. He turns back to Frank.

'Now, you probably want to know what you're doing here.'

Frank gives an ironic snort. Trump continues.

'Well, let us try to be philosophical about it. Nothing happens without a reason. However, you must forgive these humble quarters. I would entertain you more lavishly, if I could – but that's not possible. And for why? You see, it's like this. A certain gentleman, a Mr Turner –'

'So he *is* behind this,' Frank mutters.

'Behind this? Oh yes, he's very much behind this. He's behind this miserable room, this bony bedstead, this fly-eye of a window – they're all his! And for why? Because they certainly aren't mine!'

Frank interrupts this apparently demented flow.

'Why did you bring me here? And where are we?'

'My first is your last, as the riddles say. But in truth, my first is Mr Turner's last. His very last and least and most unconsidered – his slum or hovel – this, young man, is my place of abode. Through pleasures and palaces, wherever I may roam, be it never so humble – that, to answer you, is where we are. And, you ask, why? If it weren't for him, you wouldn't be here.'

'I don't want to listen to you. I demand to be let out.'

'Not want to listen to me! And they used to say I had the voice of an archangel. But Mr Turner – he's no angel, as the likes of me can tell you. He's a dangerous man. He hounds and persecutes the innocent, he does, deprives 'em of their rights and steals the last crumb from their very mouths. Once you're in his power, he won't let you go until he's squeezed you to dust. Now, I can play that game too. And since I can't rightly find my way to squeezing him, you must do instead.'

Frank clenches his jaw.

'You shan't touch me.'

'Brave words, boy. But I think you'll feel more friendly towards me when you've heard me. Believe me, I don't wish to harm you. I'd much rather not –'

'And I shan't be intimidated by you, either.'

'Intimidate? Who said anything of that sort? Look here –' Trump makes himself comfortable on the chair, and leans towards Frank confidingly, making gestures with the knife to emphasise his points. 'I have a proposition to put to you, and it's like this. How does he treat you, the old curmudgeon? Do you see much of all that money he's hoarded up, the miser? Don't he keep you on short commons, working all day long? You might as well be his manacled slave! But, tell me –' Trump becomes even more confidential – 'do you really believe he'll leave you a penny of all his ill-gotten gains?'

He pauses to augment the effect of his triumphant conclusion, and then can't resist a little burst of song.

> 'I'll give your large fortun' to the nearest of kin,
> And you shan't reap the benefit of one single pin,
>   Singing tooral-i, ooral-i, ooral-i-ay!'

Frank doesn't know what to make of this. But Trump quickly returns to his theme.

'No! he'll be buried with 'em, I swear. Now, my young friend. Don't you think we could prevail on him to be a little – a little more amicable towards you? A little more, how shall I say – fatherly?'

'I don't know what you mean.' Frank stares at him, baffled.

'Come now, Master *Turner*. Don't feign such innocence with me.'

Frank splutters, 'You don't know what you're talking about.'

'O' course I do! I wasn't born yesterday. Don't you try to mislead *me*.'

'Indeed – indeed I don't.'

Trump's face twists into a sneer – a sneer crossed with a snarl. He gets up, and closes on Frank, bringing the knife close to his face.

'Now that I can't abide. I want this to be a friendly conversation; but I don't care for a flat lie to my face.'

'You bastard! I'm not lying. But you – you're a kidnapper and a scoundrel.'

Trump stands back a little and looks down his nose at Frank, the sneer more pronounced.

'How very unpleasant! Now, boy. Listen.' He brings the knife closer to Frank's chin. 'We may as well talk plain. I have a little business with your old man, and I need your help.'

Frank is not flinching.

'You shan't have it.'

'Well then, I must wait. And so must you. You've breakfasted? There may not be much more of that unless you come to your senses. I'll take the plate. And the jug.'

He bends down to pick them up, just as Sammy did, and as he does so, Frank again takes advantage and leaps on him, bringing him to the floor. Jug and plate clatter down. Trump utters a strangled expletive.

'Vermin!'

They struggle; the knife flies clear of both of them. Frank gets hold of the jug and tries to bring it down on Trump's head, but Trump dodges the blow, pushes Frank down again and rises, panting, with a foot on Frank's stomach. He feels for the knife on the floor behind him, and having found it raises it above Frank's face, leering down in triumph. Frank tries to heave the boot off his body, grimacing and struggling for breath.

'A tricky customer, I see. I'm truly sorry. But I don't despair of you, lad. You've shown some mettle. But I realise that I must be

64

circumspect. Not too much rope. No rope at all for a bit, I think. But,' and he adopts an engagingly reasonable manner, 'I shall be ready to discuss the matter again later – when you've had time to give it some thought.'

Frank watches as he leaves the room, locking the door and taking the knife, though leaving the plate and jug behind. Rising painfully, he sits on the bed. Then he opens the window. He can just get his head out through the narrow casement. The view is unpromising: an almost deserted street stretching a long way in either direction, with a few cottages on this side, and opposite the uninterrupted wall skirting the dockside for half a mile or more, with its intricate fringe of masts and rigging beyond. By craning his neck, Frank catches sight of a corpulent little man walking with mincing steps past the cottage. He picks up the plate and jug and, holding them well out of the window, clashes them together. The man below stops and looks up.

'Help!' Frank shouts. 'I'm a prisoner. Help!'

Chaz raises his hands in mock astonishment.

'My word, what a noise! Should you be making such an ungodly din, boy?'

'I'm being held prisoner here.'

'Prisoner? That's putting it strongly, isn't it? I seem to remember helping Ben Trump get you up the stairs – but I left you tucked up in bed and sleeping, if I may say so, very prettily.'

'You're mistaken. I've been locked in. If you can't get into the house will you please go to the police?'

'Police? Heavens, no! I avoid them like the plague. I can't help you there.' Chaz's manner becomes solicitous. 'I hope he's given you some breakfast? You'll be starving, poor thing.'

In increasing alarm, Frank speaks with fierce emphasis.

'I'm in danger, please believe me.'

'Oh, what we're asked to believe these days passes – well, it passes belief. You mustn't expect too much of me in that line. But what I will gladly do is come and visit you – later. That will be a pleasure. Put me down in your book, will you? Where *does* Ben Trump find them? And now, please excuse me. My attendance is awaited in the City. *Au revoir.*'

Frank watches the ridiculous little man stroll out of his vision. It's a pity that *he* wasn't sent up with the victuals. Frank reckons he could get the better of him quite easily. But for the moment there is nothing to be done, with the giant on sentry-go below. He retires to the bed, demoralised. There are quick steps on the stairs, the door is rapidly unlocked and Trump rushes in, grabs the plate and the jug, and retreats, locking behind him. He shouts through the door:

'None of that! No noise. No one can hear you. Well, only Sammy O'Reilly. And rest assured, it's no use trying to appeal to Sam. You know – you've felt – what he's worth. Or to Chandos Grimshaw, either. He's a good friend of mine. A great actor, once, he was. Come down in the world, like me. Yes, he sympathises with my lot, Chaz does. You won't find him much help. In fact, you'd do well to keep out of his way. He might take too much of a liking to you. And in this God-forsaken part of London there's nothing and nobody to help you nor any of us, and that's about it.'

Frank listens to all this in shocked silence. None of it makes sense. He seems to be the plaything of mad, arbitrary agencies who have no idea who he is. He certainly has no idea who they are. He retreats to the bed, sits on it and huddles into his jacket, frowning in agitated thought.

Chapter 12

JOHN POUND is slouching, an incongruously louche figure, past the smartly stuccoed façades of St James's, carrying his ill-wrapped parcel. Under his furtive brow, his eyes are alert, taking note of the passers-by and their stylish clothes, of the shop windows and their expensive contents. He stops indecisively in front of one of these, an emporium with a handsome frontage and one or two pictures in ornate gilt frames displayed on miniature easels. Peering through the glass, he can see the proprietor, a nattily dressed man with a grey fringe round his bald pate, showing a picture to a client, a pale-haired gentleman who is talking enthusiastically.

He lingers, looking up at the fascia, then at the door with its bell and knocker, and after an effort of will, gingerly turns the handle. As he steps inside, the dealer – it is none other than Thomas Griffith – and his customer both turn and stare at him.

'Yes, sir? What is it?'

John gulps, abashed. He stammers a few syllables, but is quite unable to reply, and hurriedly makes his exit. He continues his walk rather more briskly, eyes always on the look-out, always aware of what is going on round him, taking in details. He walks and walks. He begins to realise that he doesn't know quite what sort of a shop it is he's looking for. That one in St James's was too grand, daunting, and probably too close to home – to someone's home – for comfort. That dealer chap looked as though he knew a thing or two. Not worth the risk. But what's the alternative, then?

It is a good while later that he finds himself somewhere in the City, in a dim alley sloping down to the river, and comes across a seedy shop-front stuck all over with prints. Inside – there's not much clear glass to see through – there are dusty portfolios full of paper – more prints no doubt. And pile upon pile of old books, some them reaching up to the low ceiling. After more hesitation, he goes in. A bell attached to the door rings loudly, making him jump.

At first he can see no one. The place appears to be deserted. He goes up to a pile of loose leaves on a table and is just about to begin flicking through them when, from behind one of the columns of books, a greasy and dishevelled individual emerges, giving him another fright. But the greeting is quite friendly. The bookseller straightens his wig, primps his cravat a little, and speaks ingratiatingly.

'And what can I do for you, sir?'

He walks across to stand closer to John, who clears his throat and manages to come out with the sentence he's been rehearsing.

'I – I – do you buy water-colour drawings, sir?'

'Water-colour drawings? Water-colours? Hm. Maybe, young man, maybe. Have you one there?'

John begins to undo his parcel, with the shopkeeper peering over his shoulder, a hand on his arm. Eventually the layers of wrapping are pushed aside and the water-colour is revealed. John holds it up for closer inspection.

'Well, youngster? What sort of trash do you think you've brought me there?'

'Trash?' John is incredulous.

'Come, come. Don't waste my time. I'm a busy man. You want me to buy that? Absurd! A mere daub.'

'I thought... ' John is speechless. This is not at all how he imagined the interview proceeding.

'What did you think, eh? That you were in possession of some masterpiece?' The shopkeeper breaks into mocking laughter. But his other hand comes down on John's arm, making him feel distinctly ill at ease.

'I thought 'twas at the least a little bit valuable, sir. It's the work of a real artist – a Royal Academician.'

'Royal Academician, eh? So you know the painter's name, do you? Which Royal Academician would that be, now?'

John was hoping he would not be brought to this. But he makes up his mind. Might as well be hanged for a sheep as for a lamb.

'It's by Mr – Mr – Mr Turner, sir.'

The shopkeeper stares for a moment, not at John, nor at the water-colour, but out into some disconcertingly unspecific corner of space. Then he begins to laugh, and he goes on laughing until the tears come into his eyes and he is hugging John as tightly as though he had brought him a fortune in ready money.

'Turner! Mr Turner! Ha, ha, ha!' Then, suddenly very sober: 'Now, how would you have come by such a thing, pray?'

'I swear it's genuine, sir. Only look at it. You've not looked at it.'

The shopkeeper stares into the picture, trying to make out anything at all.

'Well, I'll admit, now I look closer, 'tis boldly done. Can't make head nor tail of it, but I daresay an artist did it. But Turner, though? And yet – who else would be so – are ye sure you didn't do this yourself?'

John is astonished and indignant at this slur.

'Me? Ho no, I couldn't draw a jug o' water from the pump, I couldn't. Look at it, sir. It's a beauty.'

Even as he says it, he feels a repugnance at the thought of praising the man, though it is for his own gain.

'Very well. I'll give ye sixpence for it.'

'Sixpence! Never! For a water-colour by Mr Turner! They do say he's the greatest painter alive today. Why, he charges ten guineas for something like this.'

'Does he now? And how might you know that, pray? Don't tell me you're another of his progeny.' This last in a low aside. But John probably doesn't know what 'progeny' means, anyhow.

'I've heard 'im a-talking –' John breaks off abruptly.

'You've heard him talking? So you do live in that house of his – with the cats?'

'No cats, no, sir.'

'Well, let's say half a guinea.'

John gives him what he trusts is a withering look, and begins to wrap the drawing up again.

'A guinea, then. Two.'

'Say five and you can have it.'

The shopkeeper agonises dramatically, hand to forehead, trunk twisting.

'Too much! Far too much. But –' he takes the package from John's hand and searches the drawing again for clues. If only it were signed! If only he could spot something, some little detail, that would tell him unequivocally – he curses his lack of knowledge. 'Well, my lad,' at last. 'I'll pay it. But I think I'm mad to do so. Here you are.'

The dealer scrabbles for the money in a trousers pocket, and then in a remote drawer of the litter-strewn desk, and with the greatest reluctance holds the coins out in his palm. John takes them, then tips his forelock.

'So. Now, you don't know me, but you can take my word for it that's genuine. No fear!'

He makes for the door, and is almost on the other side of it when the shopkeeper calls out.

'Er – wait! Would there by any chance be – more water-colours by Mr Turner where this one came from?'

'Any more? You can bet there's more! Plenty more! But you ain't seen me, you haven't. You never saw me in your life.' He swings jauntily out into the street, and starts to whistle as he stuffs the money into his pocket. The dealer calls again, but he doesn't so much as turn round. Going back inside his shop, Chaz runs a hand through his unkempt wig and gives a histrionic sigh. He is excited, yet something tells him he has embarked on a course of events that is fraught with danger.

Chapter 13

IN A SMALL tailor's shop in Holborn bolts of cloth are piled high on shelves round the walls; there is a wide board on which the tailor sits cross-legged to work, surrounded by a little crowd of silent witnesses to his industry: waistcoated, trousered and jacketed stands, some revealing their wooden bosoms to the world, others decently covered with shirts and stocks and frills. The tailor is a beady-eyed little man who attends to his customers attired in waistcoat and tape-measure, thick, small-lensed spectacles and pieces of white chalk. He is not cross-legged at work just now, but standing, arms folded, watching rather impatiently while John Pound examines a length of fabric, holding it up to his chest and strutting with it in front of a cheval glass, then throwing it over his shoulders and twisting round to assess the effect of the cloth across his back.

'Rather coarse, this stuff, considering the price you've quoted me,' John announces peremptorily.

The tailor is evidently offended by this disparagement.

'Coarse? Far from it, sir,' he ripostes. 'I've told you that is the highest quality worsted, and you contradict. Are you telling me I don't know my business? That worsted is more than the likes of you would normally be wearing, I think.'

'The likes of me? Who d'you think you're addressing, eh?'

'I think I'm addressing a young —' The tailor bites back the epithet he is about to utter. 'A young gentleman,' he finishes with perceptible distaste.

John ignores the hint of insult. Tailors are supposed to be the acme of deference. Why should such an insignificant little fellow take it upon himself to be impertinent? 'Shall I take my custom elsewhere?' he says primly, congratulating himself on not losing his temper.

The tailor is tempted to answer in the affirmative. But business is business.

'I'm sure you will be very happy with the suit that I can make for you, sir,' he says. 'I take it you will be in a position to pay?'

'Are you suggesting I might not be?'

For answer, the tailor closes his eyes and spreads his hands expressively. John draws himself up to his full height, towering over the little man.

'How dare you!'

The tailor can see what sort of fellow he is dealing with here, but maintains his deferential manner.

'I ask for a small sum on deposit, naturally, before I begin any order. I'm sure you will appreciate the necessity for that precaution – sir.'

John chooses to take further offence at this, and blusters for some time. The tailor fingers his tape, and waits for the tantrum to subside.

'Perhaps you would prefer to cancel your order, sir?'

He has spent a lifetime dealing with vain, arrogant and bullying customers, and has refined the art of adding insult to injury with the utmost suavity. John is uncertain how best to proceed. Should he stand on his dignity, or let the man's insolence pass?

He pulls a few coins from his pocket and thrusts them at the tailor, conscious of looking somewhat vulgar as he does so. The tailor looks at each sovereign quizzically, the successive bunchings of his eyebrows a series of implied doubts as to John's probity.

At last the cloth is agreed, the measurements are taken, and an appointment for fitting pencilled into a book. John, unwilling to seem overawed, wanders round the shop, pulling haphazardly at bolts of material and making evaluative remarks under his breath.

'Could I ask you to make haste now, sir? I've an important client arriving in a minute.'

'I'll take my time, thank you.' He turns his back on the man, and whistles with studied unconcern. He hears the bell inside the shop door ring, and turns to see a rakish gentleman amble in. The tailor trots up to the new customer and begins to fawn on him outrageously.

'Your honour, this is a privilege. Please to take a seat, sir. And forgive me one moment while I fetch your honour's suit, sir.'

He bustles off. John realises that he is no longer the centre of attention. The suspicion enters his mind that this is all a deliberate snub to himself. Unwilling to expose himself to further humiliation, he takes his leave, muttering audibly that he has a pressing appointment to keep.

That appointment takes him much farther afield. He has discovered a means to independence, and that independence must be embodied in suitable premises. Where should he set up his base for operations? He doesn't want to be too close to his new friend the dealer in the City. And he certainly doesn't want to be anywhere near Chelsea. The grander parts of the West End are out of the question – and besides, there's at least one person who frequents the West End that it would not do at all for him to meet. This is a moment when there is great virtue in anonymity and invisibility. What a lucky thing it is that he bears his father's name, that of John Pound the elder, Sophia Booth's first husband. There need never be any fear of his being connected with the ménage in Chelsea. He can disappear into the throngs of the capital and be his own man now, in earnest.

He walks along Fleet-street, and up Fetter-lane to Clerkenwell, where the great dome of St Paul's away to the south heaves itself high above the low buildings that spread out northwards, away from the City. He turns into a long road leading uphill out of London, and sets out along it, the dome always behind him, watching him. He walks on and on, trying to shake off the sense that he is being followed. And at last he comes to a place where the air is clearer, there are pleasant residences, fewer shops and fewer people bustling along the street – people, moreover, who have never seen him before, who can have no idea who he is. He feels he can relax a little, and strolls along, affecting leisurely curiosity, a young man in no hurry. But when he sees a greengrocer's stall on a corner, he stops and asks a question of the plump woman who is weighing potatoes into someone's basket.

'Why not try Mrs Jellyby next door? I know she often has a spare room. It's noisy, mind you – there are a lot of children about.'

John thanks her with a curt nod, and walks on to survey the next-door building. It's a small terrace house, two steps up to a front door opening into a passage. There's a deep area, from which childish screams can be heard. He puts his head over the railings, and counts at least six brats of different ages, squawling and pulling one another's hair.

He takes a long breath, and pushes open the front door.

Chapter 14

ALONG the interminable perspective of London stock-brick that is the harbour wall, a woman is trudging towards Ben Trump's little house. It is George-Anna, looking tired and more untidy than ever. As she reaches the door, Trump comes out and greets her.

'George! Now what are you doing here? Have you come to see me?'

'Ben. I've a message for you. From –' She is out of breath.

'From your mother?'

'No. From my –'

'A message from your own bright eyes. All the way from Marybone, just to see me! How charming! But – hush!' He glances anxiously up to the attic window, remembering the situation. 'We mustn't make a noise. There's – there's a baby in the next-door house, that simply screams when it wakes, so I wake it as little as may be.'

'A baby, Ben? That's nice. But what a place for a young family, I do think!' She casts a deprecatory eye round the bleak townscape.

'Aye, no fresh air, no green, no clear sunlight. What a spot indeed. It's only the dregs of society who have to make their homes here, I can tell you. Fancy you coming all this way!' He looks at her with a flash of the old admiration. 'Come inside, my love.'

He leads her into the poky, ill-furnished front room and sits her on an upright wooden chair, then stands with his hand on the back of it. He goes on talking very quietly.

'Well, dear, you take me by surprise. We're not well used to entertaining here. The accommodations are, as you see, simple. There's no room for so much as a clavichord. And I had to sell my hoboy to pay the rent a year ago. Barbarously we're treated, and a barbarian I become. So if we wish for music, my dear, we must make our own harmonies.'

He squeezes her arm meaningfully. But she stands up again.

'Ben! Listen. My – Mr Turner has told me to tell you –'

'So your message is from him, is it? Hah! What words of comfort do you bring from the old thief?'

'He's no thief. He says you may have another week to pay.'

'Another week!' Trump is outraged, flails his fists and bites his lower lip in fury. 'Now I must call him generous, I suppose! The impostor! The tyrant! The infidel!'

He is suddenly silent, and they hear the sound of banging from upstairs.

'What's that, Ben?' George asks. 'Who's up there?'

'Up there? What d'you mean? Ah – 'tis the child – my neighbour's infant, no doubt. What tantrums these children throw, to be sure!'

'Infant? I don't think so. It's too loud, and that noise isn't coming from next door. It's in this house, I swear.'

'Never! But – let me go and see.'

Trump goes to the foot of the stairs, and at that moment Chaz Grimshaw enters from the street. He is excited about something.

'Ben Trump! I have the most extraordinary news – But,' lowering his voice, 'you have company.'

There is renewed banging from the attic, and Trump begins to babble loudly, hoping to drown the sound.

'Why, Chaz, you! Now this is well timed. Sammy has had to go about some very important business – and I'm sure I can't imagine what it is – so I'm glad to have you by me. Now, George-Anna here thinks she hears a noise from overhead. I tell her 'tis not possible. 'Tis the babe next door, I tell her. But no, she will have certainty. I'm not anxious to leave her just now, so run up, will you, and look about. You'll find nothing there, I'm sure of that. But –' he whispers in Chaz's ear, 'here's the key. Keep the boy quiet, and don't let him hear us.'

Chaz puts a finger to his lips, pantomiming secrecy and confidentiality, and goes with exaggerated caution up the stairs. Trump shepherds George back to her chair and pulls it farther away from the door.

'And now, my dear, let us return to the real reason for the favour of this visit. You didn't come so far to announce a week's reprieve of my execution. When he's finished his errand above, I'll send Chaz out to the Ship and Bladebone for a pint of porter, and we'll be snug together presently.'

George is not so sure that this is what she wants.

'Well, Ben, I don't know –'

'But I do, very well.' He puts a hand on her knee. She pushes it off, but he is not to be so easily discouraged, and persists until they are engaged in a half-amorous romp, the two of them rolling on the floor and making quite a deal of noise. Ben has somehow forgotten his concern to prevent Frank from discovering that there is a visitor downstairs.

Frank for his part has stopped the regular banging by which he hoped to rouse attention to his plight and is listening intently for clues as to what is going on. He can hear faint voices, and some sounds of scuffling, of furniture being knocked and pushed. Then there are footsteps on the stairs, on the landing outside the door, and the key is turned in the lock. When Chaz walks in, Frank recoils and backs towards the window.

'Good afternoon,' Chaz greets him. 'We have met before – a most enjoyable conversation this morning, though we have not been properly introduced. But now we are more on a level, as it were, we can, I hope, become better acquainted. How very agreeable. Chandos Grimshaw at your service.'

He sits himself on the bed.

'And I do believe we met very briefly last night, too. Sadly, 'twas too dark to see much of anything at all. London streets are so badly illuminated, are they not? Why was gas lighting invented if we're still the people that walk in darkness? But by the gracious light of this blessed morning I glimpsed your head out the window as I – er, happened to be walking by, and says to myself, there's a pretty young fellow, if ever there was one. I'd welcome the chance to be better acquainted, and now, lo and behold, fate has granted my very wish!

Frank glowers at him, and then begins to stamp on the floor. Chaz jumps up in agitation.

'You must stop that at once.' Frank disregards him, and continues to stamp as loudly as he can. Chaz grabs his arms and tries to topple him. Frank opens his mouth to shout for help, but Chaz puts a hand over it. Frank frees an arm and wrenches the hand away, but Chaz keeps a tight grip.

'Oh no, I'm sorry, but that won't do. Upon my word there's no one to hear – no one, that is, who will pay the slightest attention. Save your strength – and what a strong young thing it is!'

Frank finds the situation increasingly repellent, and spurred to extra effort by a feeling of imminent nausea finally shoves Chaz away.

He stands panting and scowling in a corner in a challenging posture, fists clenched.

'Keep your distance, you vile monster!'

He pauses for breath, then, gritting his teeth, charges at Chaz and deals him a blow on the jaw that momentarily dazes him. Holding his face with one hand, Chaz makes an aimless swipe at the air with the other. Frank balls his fist and puts all his strength into a punch in the stomach. Winded, Chaz grunts and falls to the floor. His arms outstretched, the fingers scrabble in an attempt to clutch hold of something solid, to lever him to his feet. Frank puts a foot on the nearest wrist, and Chaz lets out a shriek. Bending down, Frank fumbles in the pocket of Chaz's coat for the key, extracts it with some difficulty and quickly lets himself out. Pulling the door to behind him he sees Chaz sitting up and rubbing his wrist and chin ruefully.

Frank creeps downstairs, briefly stopping to listen. At the bottom, he pauses in the tiny entrance-way to listen again. The door into the living-room is open, but no sound comes out of it. Then he hears a voice, a woman's voice that he doesn't recognise.

'Stop, stop a minute, Ben. No, I said stop! All that thumping, and now I swear I heard a crash. What is happening upstairs?'

She and Trump are on the floor in a tangle.

'Wait until you've a babby, my girl, and how I'd like you to have one – mine. Then you'll know how noisy they can be.'

'Baby! That was no baby. It was Chaz, I'll be bound. But what's he doing?'

'I told him to look for noises. Perhaps he's found one. Don't fret. He'll come and tell us when he's ready.'

He catches sight of Frank's head round the door-frame, and lets out a yell.

'Hey, Chaz, Chaz, you thundering fool! Why did you let him out?'

'Let him out? Who is it? Ben, who have you got there?'

Trump has struggled to his feet, and dashed out of the door, snatching up his umbrella and brandishing it, in pursuit of Frank, who has too short a lead. Trump grabs at him and pulls him down, then sets about belabouring him with the umbrella. George has followed him out and witnesses this fight with horror. She sees another man coming up to them, a great tall man like a wrestler, with long, thick arms and a bandy-legged walk. Frightened by this vision of uncompromising physical strength, she hurls herself into the fray, hoping to pull Frank away from Trump's blows.

'Stop, Ben! Let him go! Don't do that – don't!'

She tries to grab his arm, but he lashes savagely at her. She crouches in terror, hiding her face. Then a heavy blow on the side of her head fells her to the ground. She is still for a moment, then gradually recovers and picks herself up. She wipes a hand across her bleeding forehead and cheek, and looks around. Trump and Frank have both disappeared, but in a moment a great shadow falls across her. She realises that the giant is standing over her, looking at her with mild interest, an incipient smirk on his face. She tries to get to her feet. While she is off-balance he pushes her to the ground again, and brings another hefty blow down on her head. Dazed, she can do nothing but lie there, hoping the monster will go away. After a while, she dares to lift her head again. Now the big man has gone. George raises herself cautiously to her feet, and a sharp pain flashes behind her eyes. She puts a hand to her brow, and realises she is bleeding profusely.

She staggers to the closed door of the house and tries to open it, but it is locked. Banging on it with as much strength as she can muster, she raises a shout.

'Ben! Open the door! Let me in! Ben! Ben! Ben!'

Chapter 15

NOT FAR FROM Ben Trump's little house there is a tavern, famous in the locality of the docks, that goes by the picturesque name of the Ship and Bladebone. It is here that Trump and his few companions like to repair of an evening to while away the hours before retiring. Twilight is beginning to descend, and the publican is standing on his doorstep, scanning the street as though searching for potential customers. At tables just inside, topers are nursing their tankards of ale and discussing the events of the day. He exchanges a few words with them. He pauses in mid-sentence as an arresting sight meets his eyes. A tall woman with her face covered in blood is coming unsteadily towards him. He gapes in surprise.

'My lord, what's 'appened to you, Mum? 'Ad a haccident?'

'Please – let me come in,' George begs. 'I must sit down. Give me a glass of water.'

He helps her into a seat in the dim interior, and summons a dishevelled girl to fetch a drink.

'You look as if you need a pint o' porter, Mum,' he volunteers. 'That's the best thing in the world for a shock. There's not a stevedore in the docks as don't swear by it.'

'I'm not a stevedore,' George tells him. 'Let me get my breath.'

The girl brings a glass and a jug of water.

'Set it down there, Meg,' the landlord instructs her. 'Pour it, Meg. Give 'er the glass, Meg.' Meg obeys these instructions dutifully. 'Now, Meg, fetch a bowl of 'ot water. And a cloth. The poor lady needs a good wash, I'd say.'

'Thank you,' George says gratefully. 'Do you know a man called Trump – Ben Trump?'

The girl opens her eyes wide. 'Ben Trump? I'll say I do!'

The publican reprimands her. ''Twasn't you as was hasked, Meg. Yes, Mum, I know Ben Trump well. If 'e's bin drinking, 'e didn't get 'is liquor from me, 'e didn't. What's 'e mean by that, I hask yer?'

'He wasn't drinking. Do you know who it is he keeps upstairs – in his roof?'

'In 'is roof? Lord, 'ow should *I* know? Mind, I didn't never 'ear of 'im 'avin' anyone up in 'is roof. Did you, Meg?'

'Is it a lidy, Mum?' asks Meg. 'I 'ope not, 'cos I like Ben, and 'e's always nice to me.'

'It's a man. A young man.'

The publican interrupts. 'Now Meg, get that 'ot water and don't stand there haskin' 'pertinent questions.' Meg goes off as bid. 'Whatever next? A young man in Ben Trump's roof? Now what would 'e be doin' with one o' those, eh? Now if it was Chaz Grimshaw, that'd be another matter. But they're thick as thieves, them two. And bad customers. Not a pint of my hale 'as either one of 'em drunk in weeks.'

George can see that he is about to launch into a harangue, but he is cut short by a scream from Meg. She comes running back into the bar-parlour.

'A man! There's a man out by the pump! He frightened me ever so. Come out of the necessary-house, 'e did, and was creepin' past me when I sees 'im. Oh, I'm in a stite of shock.'

The publican is phlegmatic. 'And what's so surprising about a man comin' out of the necessary-house, Meg? Ain't that what it's for?'

'Ooh no. It wasn't like that. He wasn't doin' what men generally do in them places. He was 'idin', that's what.'

''Idin'? What d'yer mean, 'idin'?'

'He didn't want me to see 'im, I'm sure.'

The publican's spirit of leadership is kindled. 'Let me go and look,' he says resolutely. He is about to investigate when Frank puts his head round a door at the back of the room. The bruise on his face is dark purple, and pulsing painfully.

He comes hesitantly forward to them.

'There 'e is!' screams Meg. 'What did I tell you? It's a man!'

The publican is stentorian. 'You there. What do you want?'

'I want to speak to this lady,' Frank says, indicating George.

'Good heavens!' she exclaims. 'It's the lad from upstairs. I thought you were locked up again.'

'I managed to fight the brute off. He got me back into the house but I escaped. I've been hiding in the yard behind here. I wanted to thank you for trying to help.'

'But I don't understand,' George says, her face half-hidden by a blood-stained handkerchief with which she is trying to mop her wounds. 'What were you doing up there in that attic?'

'I can't tell you here. I must get as far away from here as possible, at once.'

'I'll come with you.'

'Wait!' the publican commands her sonorously. 'Until Meg's brought you your 'ot water. You need a nice scrub.'

'I can't wait. We mustn't waste a moment.'

She gets up, and feels dizzy, loses her balance. She almost falls, but Frank holds her firmly. They parry the reiterated invitations of the landlord, and with her arm in Frank's walk steadily towards the City. At first they proceed in reflective silence, each too bemused by what has happened to formulate a remark. But after a few minutes they strike up a conversation, tentative at first, then a flood of sympathy and mutual, puzzled enquiry. As they piece together the story of what has happened, a great red sunset spreads itself behind the towers and domes on the horizon. George hardly sees it, but Frank takes courage from it: it is a glorious banner of light that seems to beckon him on.

Chapter 16

SARAH DANBY is sitting in the parlour of her little house off Lisson-grove, poking the fire and gulping gin and water from a tumbler that she replaces with care on a small table after each swig. When she reaches the bottom of the glass she looks at it vacantly, then levers herself to her feet and goes into the next room to find something to eat. Her lethargic search yields only a couple of biscuits, which she takes to her place by the fire. She lights a lamp on the table, then goes to the window and after looking out draws the curtains. There is a fine evening sky, quickly darkening. A small patch of the brilliant effect is just visible above the chimneys, but Sarah has barely noticed it.

She sits down again, but seems restless, and after a short time gets up and goes to the front door. She opens it and looks up and down the street. She thinks of renewing her scavenging in the kitchen but decides against it. The condition of that room only confronts her with the stark fact that she has become an inveterate slattern. She returns to her chair. Her eyes closed, she gropes for the tumbler, and knocks it over. With a muttered curse she sets it upright, and closes her eyes again, her head lolling back against the chair. And so for a while she sleeps, an occasional snore erupting from her half-open mouth. As she sleeps, the evening darkens into night. Then there is a noise of footsteps outside, and the front door opens. She is startled into wakefulness, and gets up, surprised to see two people coming into the room.

'George!' She is shocked by her daughter's bruised and cut face, dried blood smeared across it. 'What have you done? What's happened?'

'Nothing, Mamma. Don't ask. Mamma, this is Mr Sherrell. He's had a very nasty experience. I don't understand it. Do you know – you'll never guess what his job is?'

'Well?'

'He's been working as studio assistant to –'

82

'No! To your dad? So the old boy has at last admitted he needs a bit of help, has he?' She laughs mirthlessly. 'And do you enjoy your job, Mr Sherrell?'

'But it's not that, Mamma. He thinks Dad has somehow or other conspired to have him kidnapped.'

'Well, we knew all along he was mad, just like his mother, poor soul. This only proves it.'

George is busy filling a bowl with hot water from the kettle. She brings it into the parlour and begins to wash her face. She gives Frank a cloth, too, and they ablute together. Sarah has noticed that Frank, too, is sporting a large bruise, but she continues to sit there, doing nothing to help.

'No, Mamma, that's not fair. Dad's as sane as I am. He's different, of course he is. Maybe we don't understand him. But he's not mad – and he'd never do a thing like that. Why should he?'

'Madmen need no reasons,' Sarah says, as though from the depths of a reverie, her eyes closed.

'Oh, you and your bitterness! You'll never be fair to him.'

'Fair! Was he ever fair to me?'

'Now, Mamma. Enough of all that.'

'He's selfish and cruel, always has been. Look at Ben, now. Reduced to misery by his eternal greed.'

'You must admit Ben's a feckless sort. He'd have ruined himself anyway. And Dad only charges a reasonable rent. Every landlord's entitled to do that. But –' She looks at Frank. 'Has that got something to do with Ben's kidnapping Mr Sherrell here? Perhaps –'

'Ben's the kidnapper now, is he?' Sarah interrupts her. 'What in heaven's name do you mean?'

'That's the long and short of it, Mamma. Ben is a bit crazed, I think.'

Sarah shakes her head over and over again, defeated by these revelations.

'The thing I can't understand,' Frank puts in, 'is why he thought I was Mr Turner's son.'

Sarah sits up and stares at him.

'My God. Are you the boy I saw coming out of Billy's front door the other week?'

He nods. 'I expect so.'

She begins to laugh hysterically.

'And really you're only his assistant?' He nods again. 'Then it's all my fault. The whole thing's my stupid fault. But,' she calms down, 'how are we to believe him, George?'

'Believe him?'

'When he tells us he isn't Billy's son.'

'Dad's – son? You mean you told Ben that Mr Sherrell was my brother?'

'Your half-brother, I suppose. I saw him leaving the house in Queen Ann-street, and thought he must be another child – by some other woman.' Her laughter has modulated to something like tears now.

'This is what comes of your wretched bitter thoughts, Mamma. If you'd put the business out of your head, 'twould never have occurred to you to suppose anything of the sort.'

'Put it out of your head yourself, my girl! Do you think such pain can ever be put out of my head?'

Frank thinks it diplomatic at this point to make his statement.

'I swear I'm nothing to do with Mr Turner except his hired assistant. Only been with him a few weeks. I'm from Margate, and my brother is Mr Turner's barber...'

'What did you say?' Sarah screams. 'Margate! Why, he's spent half his life in Margate. He had lodgings there for years. Who's to say what he got up to there?'

'Mamma, you're being ridiculous. Go on, Mr Sherrell.'

'I want to be a painter. It's an education just to be there when he's at work. He sometimes puts his hands in the great pails of paint and smears' em on the canvas - and when he's painting a water-colour he washes in the backgrounds with his fingers. Imagine!'

'Mad,' Sarah mutters. 'I told you so.' She turns confidentially to Frank. 'His mother was mad, you know. Died in Bedlam, she did.' Frank looks shocked, George embarrassed.

He glances at her, and thinks better of querying this statement. Instead, his enthusiasm carries him on:

'No, Ma'am, he's not mad. The pictures - they're full of the most wonderful details. In those large seascapes, the water churns enough to make you sea-sick, and yet every last halyard is exactly in place! And in the water-colours, he scrapes out the white gulls against the sky, even the drops of spray on the waves - with his long thumbnail. He's a genius!'

84

'Genius! Hmph!' Sarah settles back into her chair, pulls her shawl tightly across her chest and picks up the tumbler. Her daughter is thoughtful.

'I think I begin to see. You told Ben that Mr Sherrell was Dad's son. His only son. His heir, perhaps?'

'I never mentioned that.'

'You didn't need to. Ben could work it out – or guess. He knows the only others are mere daughters. Useless, pathetic females. And one of them living abroad... But a son – a useful bargaining counter, he thinks. A hostage. Or maybe he could be persuaded to share his patrimony, nice generous lad that he is. What did he threaten he would do?'

'He never really explained,' Frank says. 'Too agitated, I think. Just hinted that I could help him. Or –' he corrects himself, '– tried to persuade me I wanted to help him. That we both had a grievance. But – he also said it was Mr Turner's doing that I was there. I don't know what to believe.'

'Believe the worst,' Sarah advises him sourly. 'Then you'll most likely be right. The old sinner.' Frank infers that she means Turner rather than Trump. But George will not be bullied into disloyalty.

'We must believe the best. It's all a mistake. Ben's desperate. He's so short of money he doesn't know what he's doing.'

'But he hurt you terribly,' Frank says. 'I saw him.'

'Well, there was another of them who did the most damage. A huge bully of a lout, with fists the size of puddings. Poor Ben! What company he keeps! But he didn't mean me harm. 'Twas all part of his misery. And, you know, it's Father's misery too. I wish I could help them both. Explain things to them. Explain one to the other. The other to the one. But men are so obstinate. They never listen to common sense.'

'I believe you're soft on that good-for-nothing Trump. And he's years older than you. Made love to me in my day, he has.'

'He needs someone to love him. That's the trouble.'

'Aye,' her mother says dryly. 'We all need that. So you forgive him for knocking you down?'

Frank interrupts.

'He threatened me with a knife.'

George is genuinely shocked. 'With a knife? Oh God, Ben, you fool!' After a moment's reflection she adds, 'But he wouldn't use it. No – no.'

'I didn't like the look of him,' Frank offers.

There is a heavy knock on the front door. George gets up and goes to answer. On the step are three large policemen, in belted greatcoats, with truncheons raised aloft and lanterns slotted on to their belts. Their leader speaks gruffly.

'Mrs Danby? We're looking for a thief who we have reason to believe you are sheltering on these premises.'

George replies loudly and rather slowly, 'A thief? No. There's no thief here, I can assure you.'

This is evidently unsatisfactory, for he goes on, 'I'm afraid we shall have to search the house, ma'am. We have an eye-witness report that he entered the building half-an-hour ago, in company with a female. Excuse me.' He beckons with an elbow and his two constables come forward. George continues to stand firmly in the doorway. 'Make way, if you please.'

'No! Wait a moment, Mr Peeler,' George says, her voice pitched to resonate through the house. 'Tell me again what you've been told. I – a woman came into this house in company with a thief? What sort of thief?'

The sergeant consults his pocket-book. He has bushy eyebrows that seem to form a fringe between his eyes and the page. He squints painstakingly through them, stumbling over the words.

'Youth aged about twenty, light brown hair, drab jacket and trousers. Female aged about forty, tall, aquiline features, spoon-bonnet, dingy shawl.' He raises his eyes to her face and scrutinises her slowly from behind his eyebrows. 'That sounds like you, ma'am.'

'I can't deny it,' George says, confused. 'But I know nothing of this thief you're talking about. Mamma!' shouting back into the parlour, 'The police are here, looking for a young man they say is a thief. We don't have anyone like that here, do we?'

The policeman is determined to pursue his mission.

'I'm sorry, ma'am. We've a warrant to search the premises. We shall proceed now, if you please.' He extends his truncheon to push her aside, and the two constables follow him into the parlour. Sarah is still seated by the fire, looking rather ostentatiously surprised. Frank is nowhere to be seen.

'Excuse me, ma'am. Are you Mrs Danby, tenant of these here premises? We have a warrant to search for a youth, age about twenty, light brown hair, drab jacket and trousers. Is he here to your knowledge?'

Sarah regards him with a look that conveys, she hopes, unconcerned contempt. 'No. Certainly not.'

'We shall proceed with the search, men. Forward.'

They fall in, in quasi-military fashion, then break to rummage behind chairs, in cupboards and even, for the sake of thoroughness, into the pianoforte and under the thin mat on the floor. Then they go out of the room and their heavy boots thump up the stairs. George looks questioningly at her mother. In a hoarse whisper, Sarah says,

'He wanted to stay – said he knew nothing about it – swore he was completely innocent. Innocent!' She laughs silently. 'I made him climb out the kitchen window. Good riddance.'

After a few moments during which the two women maintain a tense silence, the policemen come back. Sarah asks insouciantly,

'What's stolen, officer?'

The sergeant brings himself instinctively to attention.

'A Mr Turner – the painter, you know, he's famous – has reported a picture missing. Says the youth stole it from his studio. We have investigated and found no other persons have had access to the property, saving a housekeeper for whom he vouches. We issued a description. Said youth was seen walking with a female – apparently this female – along the Strand. We followed them to this address.'

He turns to George.

'I'm afraid, ma'am, we must ask you to accompany us to the Station, seeing as how you are implicated, having been observed in company with said youth. You will be required to make a statement.'

'No!' George bursts out. 'I've nothing to say.'

The sergeant's eyebrows twitch slightly, as if they wished to express covert sympathy with her. But he is stonily unmoved.

'I'm sorry, Ma'am. We'll wait until you have put on your bonnet and shawl.'

George is in distress now. She pleads with him, and then with her mother, hoping for a word of sympathy, of extenuation.

'Best go with them, George,' Sarah says. 'Don't you worry – I'll look after things.'

Suddenly drained of fight, shoulders drooping, her head bowed, George submits to the sergeant's firm hand, and he leads her away.

Chapter 17

THE SUNSET that spread itself across the sky as George walked towards her incarceration has been watched by at least a few out of the hurrying mass that is the population of London. On the bank of the Thames near Chelsea, Turner is strolling, hands clasped behind his back, admiring the great flushed face of the sky, observing the nuances of its gradual obliteration in darkness. He is so absorbed that when a passer-by greets him with a friendly salute, 'Good night, Admiral,' he is hardly aware of the interruption.

As night thickens, he turns in at a gate. He walks up the short garden path and straight in at the half-open front door. There is a dim light in the downstairs room, and he takes flame from it to light a candle which he carries with him upstairs. After a few moments he emerges on to the iron balcony on the roof. He pulls a sketchbook from the pocket of his coat, and begins to draw, staring intently at the swiftly fading marks in the sky. When there is no more light to see the page, he goes on drawing until he has finished the train of thought prompted by the spectacle, then snaps the book shut and goes back down the steep narrow flight of stairs.

In the kitchen, Sophia is pouring tea from a huge brown pot into two cups. As he sits himself heavily in one of the wooden chairs drawn up to the table, she pushes a cupful towards him, and he takes it and sips.

'That's a sky, this evening,' he ruminates. 'I wish I was young again. I'd do it all differently. There are better ways to catch a sunset. I think I know now. After seventy years!'

His thoughts seem directed inwards, for his own benefit rather than for anyone listening. But Sophia adds her gloss on them: 'Seventy successful years, I should think.'

'Maybe. Maybe not. Success is achieving what you set out to achieve.'

'And you haven't done that, dear? Most people would think so, I'm sure.'

'What most people would think is neither here nor there. I'm the only one who can say whether my purposes have been fulfilled. And I say categorically that they have not.'

'But –'

'Aye. I've painted pictures – a few pictures – fit to hang with the old masters in our new National Gallery. But who cares? They don't want that sort of picture today. They don't want old men like me around. The Presidency, now. Would they think I ought to be the President of the Royal Academy? Some would, you might think, Sophy. But not they. No. It's young Eastlake they've got their eye on – Eastlake!' He packs much contempt into the repetition of the name of his colleague and admirer. 'Even old Griffith says he don't really like me things. By-the-bye, that stolen drawing. The police are dealing with it.'

She looks at him with a pleased smile. 'Well, they'll find him, make no mistake.'

'I hope so. I'll wring the brat's neck.'

'Wicked lad! It's not like you to be so deceived, Bill. You've a sharpish eye for roguery. Now, have another cup.'

She pours again. It is a cosy, unpretentious domestic scene, very different from the bleak austerities of the Queen Ann-street house. Sophia is a good, comfortable home-maker, though much younger than Turner, and he is obviously quite at ease and contented here. The blackbird outside the window whistles a few sweet notes, as if to join in the happy atmosphere. As the two of them sit quietly communing together, the outer door is pushed roughly open and John comes in, clearly more than a little drunk.

'John!' his mother says, relief in her voice. 'Thank the Lord you're back. Where have you been?'

He looks across at her with an insolent grin.

'I told you I'd make my own fortune, Mother. That's what I've been doing.'

Turner laughs.

'That's right, my lad. Hard work and perseverance. That's the way to make a fortune. Well, I'll believe you when I see you in a silk hat and a pearl cravat-pin.'

'Well, you will, and sooner than you think.'

'Now, Bill,' Sophia says, to smooth the little friction that has already arisen between the young man and the old one. 'I'm sure he'll do it. Well done, Johnny. And what is it you've found to do?'

John puts a finger to the side of his nose.

'Ah, you wait and see. I don't give away my secrets so easy. Besides – I wouldn't like you to be disappointed.'

'We'll wait, then. But I can't imagine what you can have – it is honest, Johnny, isn't it?'

'Honest? What d'you mean?'

'You know what your mother means, John,' Turner intervenes, heatedly. 'Money got by hard work – that's honest earnings. Money got without hard work – that's dishonest earnings.'

'Well, some jobs are harder than others, I suppose.'

'Of course, dear,' Sophia says emolliently. 'Now would you like some tea?'

'No thanks. I'm going out again now. Er – business.'

'Will you be back tonight?'

He looks resentful, as though the question were an unauthorised intrusion into his personal affairs. 'No. No.'

'Give your mother a kiss then, Johnny.'

But he has already left the room. She puts a hand on Turner's shoulder.

'What a son! Never know from one minute to the next – but it's nice he's got himself employment, isn't it?'

'I'd like to know what sort of employment it is.'

She sighs.

'We'll find out, soon enough.'

'And if he's got enough money for a drink, he should be saving it, not spending it.' Turner gets up from the table. 'Look, it's quite dark. I'm off to bed.' He makes for the stairs.

'I'll be up in a few minutes, Bill.'

As he creaks his way up to the bedroom, she potters about the kitchen, washing up tea-pot and cups, rinsing tea-cloths and hanging them on a rail near the dying fire. She pulls the table-cloth into a bundle and takes it to the front door to shake it. It's quiet in the garden now, and beyond the gate the river flows black, only a few lights flickering on the farther shore and reflected in brilliant zigzags in the water. She shakes the cloth vigorously, and folds it over her arm. She is about to go inside when she hears a sound, and stops to listen.

'Is that you, Johnny? Johnny? Are you there?'

But there is no one in the little garden, and no answer comes from the empty towpath outside. She goes back indoors. After a while,

90

the light in the kitchen is taken upstairs and the downstairs window is a black rectangle in a dark wall.

A silhouette gradually makes itself discernible among the dim shadows round the garden gate. John is watching and waiting. After what seems to him an age the light in the bedroom is blown out and the house and its neighbours settle into one great silent shadow.

He waits a little longer, curbing his impatience as best he can, then stealthily, cursing the cinders of the path under his feet for the explosive cracklings they make, creeps up to the door and lets himself in.

Chapter 18

NIGHT HAS FALLEN. Its shadows envelope the Marylebone police station, where the Inspector is standing behind a tall oak desk, writing in a big leather-bound volume by the light of a glaring gas-lamp that has the effect of making the surrounding gloom more impenetrable. Its glow blanches the features of George-Anna, who stands before him, white with apprehension.

'I tell you, officer,' she is saying, 'I know nothing of all this. There's no more that I can say. Why should I want to purloin my own father's work?'

The Inspector is young, keen, and talkative.

'Well, here you are, saying your name is Turner, same as 'is, when we know you're generally called Danby, and you're not married – not according to our records. That's suspicious for a start. But then, they do say he's a rum 'un. Makes a lot of enemies, even among his own kith and kin, I'm told. Secretive, miserly. They don't know so much as where 'e spends 'is nights, I b'lieve. That's rum enough for a start, ain't it?'

George is more animated now.

'But he's over seventy! He's a great painter. A Royal Academician, don't forget. Go and ask them there.'

'Artists – I don't 'ave no truck with such types.'

'Remember he's the person who preferred the charge in the first place.'

'So 'e did. But I shan't be surprised if it isn't a great ramp to fool insurance.'

'Insurance! My father would never dream of insuring anything. He's far too...' She checks herself.

'How do you know?' he needles her. 'He's canny, ain't he? Highly suspicious.'

'You've no proof...' she begins again.

'No, indeed we haven't. And that,' he says with an air of finality, looking up at her, 'that is why the prime suspect is you, Miss. We 'ave evidence against you, don't we?'

'No!'

He is surprised by the firmness of this.

'Oh yes, we do. Mr Turner accuses one Francis or Frank Sherrell, youth aged twenty, of larceny. You are seen in company with said youth. He enters your own domicile with you. He then – disappears. You are accessory after the fact, at very least. We shall 'ave to detain you until such time as you procure suitable recognizances.'

'My father – he'll vouch for me.'

'Oh, will 'e? When he hears what we know of your association with Sherrell?'

'I don't care. I demand the presence of my father's attorney, Mr Jabez Tepper.

'Mr Tepper, eh? If that will give you a more comfortable night, Miss, it shall be seen to. And now...'

He signs to a waiting sergeant, who rattles a large bunch of keys suspended from his belt, and leads George off along a corridor to a small cell. The corridor has blank stone walls, so that every sound echoes – the chink of the keys, the thump of the policeman's boots. George tries to walk absolutely silently, so that she makes no sound, no echo – as if by being noiseless she could somehow not be here at all. The policeman holds the door open for her respectfully and she slips inside, only to stand motionless as he at great length and with great care locks it again.

Long after he has disappeared, she is still standing there. Then she turns to survey the scene of her imprisonment. The floor is awash with filth, and the first thing she notices is a hunched figure, crouched among the effluent, and shrouded in dirty drapery, with its head bowed on to its knees so that the features are invisible, though a straggle of unkempt grey hair falls on to its shoulders from under a ragged bonnet. This creature makes no motion at the sound of George's arrival. George wonders why she hasn't chosen to sit on a chair, or lie on a bed – surely there are beds? She looks round the cell, to discover that there are no chairs, but that the single narrow truckle bed is occupied by two women who seem, incredibly, to have attained the oblivion of deep sleep. A further two listless and motionless figures are propped uncomfortably against a wall. There is nowhere for George to lay herself down, unless she joins the crouching wretch on the foul floor. And so she goes on standing there, her eyes dry and staring vacantly, her heart keeping up a protesting beat that makes her whole body throb. She stands like that, as immobile as any of the other inmates, for perhaps an hour. Then, slowly, fatigue overcomes her. Her knees collapse under her, and she sinks on to the floor against the rear wall, to wait for morning.

Chapter 19

IT IS A BRIGHT morning, and the motes of dust are thick in the sunbeams in the second-hand bookshop in the City. Chaz Grimshaw is sitting among his portfolios, scribbling in a ledger. His scribbles are not the carefully recorded figures of the accountant. They are random marginalia, little sketches of leaves and flowers, nosegays and garlands that ornament the pages more prettily than sums. This is Chaz's book-keeping, the discipline of his trade. It is an idle diversion rather than serious business, perhaps, but he prefers the details of his transactions to remain in the regions of flowery fantasy. There is much to be said for that.

He looks up when the shop-bell rings, and his heart jumps as he sees that the visitor is the young man who brought him a drawing – a drawing he said was by Turner the Academician – the other day. Chaz paid over the odds for that. He has looked hard at that drawing since, trying to persuade himself that his instinct was sound, that his gamble will pay off.

The youth is carrying another parcel.

'My young friend!' Chaz's greeting is both sincere and forced. He cannot decide whether he is glad or frightened to confront such a tempter again. 'And what brings you this way again so soon?'

'You did ask me if there were any more where the last one came from.'

'The last – ?' Chaz feigns forgetfulness. 'Ah, so I did. A water-colour, wasn't it? But I can hardly credit that you've already procured another. Is it possible?'

'Don't ask me. Just have a look.'

He tears open his parcel. There are three water-colours inside. Chaz thumbs them eagerly, hoping that this time a clear sign will be given him. He lets his hand glide down John's arm, then turns to look at him. He surveys John's unprepossessing attire with a frown, but notices an incongruously shiny new cravat, a brilliant scarlet picked out with sprigs of turquoise.

'I thought maybe you would have indulged in a new suit with all that lovely money I so generously let you have last time.'

'Oh, no – I've a poor mother at home, who needs it more than I do.'

'Now that's generous! What a son you must be to her. But I'm pleased to see that you have indulged yourself to the tune of a handsome cravat. You obviously like to dress up.' He watches John twirl the end of the cravat with a smirk of satisfaction. Yes, the boy is decidedly thespian by temperament. Encouraged by the observation he puts a tentative arm round John's waist, and John moves slightly away. Chaz clears his throat thoughtfully.

'You know, if you are really short of the needful, there are other ways in which you might earn a little.'

John looks at him, his curiosity, or at least his cupidity, aroused. Chaz gives him a gentle squeeze.

'Yes. I swear it would not be – unpleasant. I'm not very demanding. You would undoubtedly find the – work quite agreeable. And I'm sure the extra money would be very welcome for your poor old mother.' His hand has begun to wander away from John's waist, and is tentatively caressing him elsewhere. John looks dubious, and is about to put some distance between them, when he changes his mind and stays put.

Chaz takes courage.

'Would you like to think about it? On the other hand, ready cash is always useful, is it not?' He removes his hand and walks a little way off.

'Wait – ready cash?'

'The day is very warm,' Chaz goes on. 'I often seek a little repose on my bed these summer afternoons. I like to live above the shop, as they say. It's most convenient – for the City. Shall I put up the shutters for an hour? I'm expecting no one.'

John is uncertain how to interpret these apparently random remarks.

'I'd better go, then.'

'Oh no, stay! You would have no objection if we continued our business upstairs, would you now?' He has returned to John's side and his hand is active again. 'Come along – this way –'

Torn between disgust and fascination, John goes with him to the foot of the stairs, and follows him up. They stand together in the doorway of the little bedroom. It is a squalid, unkempt space, into which the dealer's stock has spilled from below, lying in stained piles between the bed and the dusty wash-hand stand with its chipped crockery ewer and basin. The bed itself has been perfunctorily covered with a darned spread. In the window, a thin curtain serves as a trap for flies, which are buzzing about in its sparse folds in their efforts to escape.

John becomes aware again of Chaz's interfering hand. He knocks it away, continuing to stare at the scruffy room, and particularly at the ill-made bed.

'So, then, you'll join me?' Chaz asks in what he hopes is an alluring voice.

'Well – how much?'

'You are a sharp businessman and no mistake. Shall we say a guinea?'

'Five guineas.'

'Little devil! Let us call it two and a half.'

Now John is standing quite still, as if thinking hard, his small eyes narrowed to slits.

'You wouldn't be wanting any of this to come the way of the police, would you?'

Chaz suddenly looks terrified.

'What do you mean? Why are you speaking of the police? What are you talking about?'

'You know what I'm talking about. Five guineas. No, we'll make it seven.'

'You can't mean –' Chaz is trembling now. John stands there, looking at him through his narrowed eyes. 'I'm sure you mean well. You're thinking of your poor mother, aren't you? Let us say seven guineas then. She will be so grateful. And we'll value the – er, the works of art later?'

'We can value them now, can't we?'

John has turned to the stairs and is making his way down again.

'But our little chat up here...'

'I don't think that will be necessary, will it? You'll give me the money anyway. It would be bad for your business if the police took too much interest in your – non-professional activities. I think you could swing, as a technicality of the law, ain't that right? And you won't need to assess the value of these things I've brought you. You'll pay for 'em anyhow, I think.'

Chaz has begun to tremble uncontrollably. John looks at him with disdain.

'What's the trouble, mister? You've nothing to fear – just so long as you keep up the good work, helping me care for my old mother.'

Chaz staggers to his chair, and slumps down in it, abject.

'You won't breathe a word to a soul, will you, boy? You wouldn't be so cruel.'

John puts out his hand, rubbing his thumb over his fingers. He remains in that posture for a long time as Chaz weeps silently into a large pocket-handkerchief, and then scrabbles in his drawer for money.

As he watches the abject, fawning figure, John is suffused with a most agreeable sense of power. It fills him with a kind of warm pride, and he begins to feel that, at last, real success has been granted him. With proprietorial ease, he flings himself into the chair behind the desk – Chaz's chair.

'So,' he says. 'I'll be coming by regular-like, to collect your payments from now on.'

Chaz doesn't dare to question this. But there's a look of terror in his eyes that boosts John's enthusiasm for his new role. He lolls back further into the chair, which creaks under his weight.

'But – now I think of it, why should I take the trouble to visit you here – when you might be saving me a tedious journey. Why don't you bring the needful to me?'

'What do you mean? Look, here it is – that will suffice, will it not?' Chaz pours coins into John's palm with as bold a gesture of munificence as he can feign. John looks down at the trickle of metal.

'Oh, that will do – for the moment. But don't forget I shall be looking forward to seeing you again very shortly. Now, shall it be here – or at number 48 Goswell-road? That would be so much more convenient.' With exquisite indolence, he picks his teeth and examines his finger-nails. He doesn't notice the change in Chaz's expression, the glimmer of brightness that flickers across his cowed face, and is as rapidly suppressed.

'But of course! It will be a privilege to save your honour the trouble.'

John isn't at all certain whether he should take this new deference at face value.

'I will present myself the day after tomorrow,' Chaz tells him – and his face wears what looks almost like a smile – 'with a further offering for your poor mother. And perhaps I may crave the privilege of meeting the old lady?'

John realises his mistake, and hastens to remedy it. He stands up, brisk and businesslike.

'Now I recall, I have business in this neighbourhood and it will be no trouble to me to call here again. You have no need to know my address. All that's required is that I know yours. Which I do. You will be seeing me again very soon, I assure you!'

Anxious to minimise any damage done, he gives Chaz what he hopes is an ingratiating grin, and leaves the shop. The bell gives a brief jangle of relief at his departure.

Chapter 20

MEANWHILE, Frank has been on the run. His first instinct, his great desire, was to confront Mr Turner and deny the charge against him. He ran all the way from Lisson-grove to Queen Ann-street, and stood in the dark before that blank, uncared-for front door. He stared at the unlighted windows of a house that he knew was deserted by its owner. In the basement, he also knew, Hannah was dozing in a kitchen chair; perhaps she'd already gone to bed. It was no time of night to be disturbing her. Urgent though his errand was, it would have to wait until morning.

His instinct, next, is to turn down towards Oxford-street and his brother's shop. There will be shelter there, and some reassuring advice maybe. All the while he is conscious that the police are looking for him, that at any moment he may be apprehended. He will have to hole up in his cramped room above the barber's, until he can decide on a swift and certain course of action. Instead of running, he walks evenly, making as little commotion as possible, an indistinguishable nobody in the night streets. And when he reaches the barber's, with its darkened shop-front and narrow side door, he knocks as quietly as he can.

He sees the glow of a candle becoming steadily brighter behind the fanlight, then hears the key turn in the lock, and his brother's head appears in the gap between door and door-post.

'Who's there? Who is it?... It's too late for callers.'

'It's me – Frank,' he whispers urgently. 'Let me in – quick.'

The door opens wider, but his brother is still standing across the passage, blocking his entrance. He has been giving the matter of his wayward brother much careful thought since Turner's visit.

'Ah, Frank, at last. Now you've got some explaining to do, and no mistake.'

'Aye, there's a great deal to tell – let me in, for God's sake.'

'Now wait a moment. Are the police after you?'

Frank is shocked by the directness, and the pertinence, of this.

'What do you know of that?'

'So – they are. I can't have a wanted criminal in my house, that's for certain.'

'Criminal! Do you think I'm a criminal? For the love of Heaven, let me come in.'

'I hope you're not, Frank, I'm sure. But what's that great bruise on your face? You certainly look as though you've been getting yourself into trouble. No, until the police are satisfied you're innocent, it's a risk for me to be harbouring a suspect. Do you realise you could be transported to Van Diemen's Land for this? I've already had the gossip bandied about in the shop, and where will my trade be if everyone hears of it?'

'You mean you won't give your own brother shelter, food... I'm starving.'

'Ah Frank!... That it should ever come about that I should deny hospitality to my own kith and kin. You must eat, of course you must. And that bruise needs tending. But I'm chary of having you under my roof until this business is cleared up. Can't you doss down somewhere for a few days?'

'What? You don't believe me, don't trust me?'

The barber scratches the side of his nose sympathetically, and looks kindly on his sibling.

'I trust you, Frank? Of course I do! But Mr Turner, he doesn't, I much fear. And until he's satisfied, and calls off the Peelers, I can't run the risk of my shop being searched – ransacked, I suppose – imagine what my gentlemen would have to say! It wouldn't be such a hardship for you – just for a day or two, would it?'

Frank fixes him with a stern gaze.

'I never thought *you* would betray me, Jack. But don't you worry. I shan't give anyone the chance to suspect *you* of anything underhand, no fear!'

He turns and walks off. The barber runs into the street, calling after him.

'No, Frank! No, that's not what I meant! Come and be fed! Come and rest, at least for a while!'

But Frank has rounded the corner and doesn't return. Although he is not running, he finds himself breathless. Then he realises he has been holding his breath, too angry to use his lungs. His indignation boils in him, he wants to exert himself violently, to distract himself from his own savagely thumping heart. He starts to trot, then speeds up to a run, and is shortly hurtling along the dark streets, muttering under his breath, careless of the attention he might be drawing to himself by his headlong progress.

When his anger has subsided a little he realises that the thought uppermost in his mind is that now he has direct proof that Mr Turner suspects him. Somehow the posse of policemen alone couldn't persuade him of that. But his brother's abject fear of contamination from contact with the object of the painter's fury – that has convinced him. The idea of the neatly kept barber-shop being threatened with a visit from those heavy-footed Peelers is so much more real and alarming than the apparition of the force in the unfamiliar and remote houses he has found himself in so unexpectedly today – houses that, for all he knows, are regularly visited by the constabulary.

Yes, he is now truly a refugee from the law. In a little while, when he has worked off his anger and confusion, and tired himself out, he considers the position. The fact is that his best course is to hide at once. The longer he's out on the streets the more likely he is to be seen and stopped.

He has no idea where he is. He looks about him. Tall buildings, in long continuous rows, their plastered façades occasionally splashed by the light of a gas-lamp. Surely somewhere there's a patch of darkness that he can nestle in for the rest of the night? A cautious review of the street to either side of him reveals no promising retreat. But then someone appears like a spirit out of the night air – a young woman, who seems to have glided out of the very walls he was peering at. She hurries off with her head down and her bonnet pulled over her face, as though avoiding anyone's scrutiny.

Frank is only momentarily intrigued by this incongruous character in such a deserted street; but it flashes through his mind that it was some benevolent spirit sent to guide him. He takes note of the place where she materialised, and walks towards it. Sure enough, he discovers a narrow crack of shadow, an alleyway between two shops, and slips into it. Immediately behind their imposing fronts, the buildings reveal themselves as old and crooked. Their walls lean intimately towards each other, closing off all remaining light from the street outside.

Eager to take himself as far from the thoroughfare as possible, he stumbles on in the dark, past the black shapes of houses and workshops, until the passage widens a little and he can see a strip of diffused and murky light from the night sky high above him. But it's still almost pitch black in the alley, and after a while he hits his shin on a bollard, or a tub, or something invisible standing to one side of the narrow way. He stifles a cry of pain, and puts out a hand to feel what's there. It's a wooden box – a packing case, or trunk. Something much resembling a tea-chest.

He is about to continue on his way when a thought strikes him. He pulls the chest on to its side, and something loose and soft tumbles out of it across his feet. A little squeamishly, he bends down to touch whatever has spilled there: some sort of material – cloth, rags. He holds a sample up to his nose. It smells clean enough. Maybe this will do for a bed tonight. The rags are soft, their container smells of raw, slightly fragrant wood: the distant odour of India, perhaps. It can only be a tea-chest. From somewhere along the way comes another faint smell, of fresh-baked bread. Frank's mouth waters. But the alley is deserted, with not so much as a window lit up. There's nothing to be done now about his hunger. He must sleep on it.

Feeling his way into the chest with arm outstretched, he finds a deep pile of the rags, and with a slight frisson of apprehension crawls inside. Then, to his horror, he feels something not just soft but warm and yielding – like flesh. Some animal is there in the chest, nesting among the rags as Frank wishes to do himself. But no ordinary domestic animal – no cat, no puppy, no tame rabbit: it's bare flesh he has felt, and not fur. He scrambles out of the chest, and in doing so disturbs the thing he has inadvertently chosen as bed-fellow. He hears a slight gasping sigh, a brief cry of wonderment.

He has woken a baby – a tiny child, abandoned among those rags. He stands up, staring into the darkness that is all he can see of the tea-chest and its contents. And the baby begins to howl.

Stricken with alarm, he instinctively puts a hand into the mass of fabric and attempts to stroke the infant. An arm, a shoulder, whatever he can locate, he touches and caresses, hoping to soothe it into silence. But its crying grows louder, becomes a long, terrified scream of bewildered anguish. He plunges both his hands into the chest, and picks up the baby. He is at once reminded of the little sister he took in his arms as a small boy, a sister who survived only a few weeks. This is a fragile, vulnerable thing, and the unexpected memory prompts him to pull the child to him, press it against his breast and then rock it gently to and fro, back and forth, muttering something to it between compressed lips.

He has heard that London's streets are nightly littered with unwanted children, the offspring of poor wretched girls too frightened to acknowledge their own progeny, reluctant mothers who have shuffled into back streets – just as he, Frank, has done – to deposit their guilty burdens in whatever dark corner they dare. He remembers the fleeting figure that emerged from this very alleyway a short time ago. What pathetic young woman was it who found this box and pushed her own babe into it, maybe cushioning it with a few tatters she had brought with her, maybe glad to find some adventitious bedding already here for it?

Then the awful truth dawns on him: he can't put the child back in the chest, abandon it as its mother has just done. He must take charge of it, and if only for an hour or two assume the role of a parent. He tries to make out the features in the tiny face, but there's barely light enough to distinguish the pale flesh from the dark rags. He is carrying an unknown human creature, unrecognizable yet inescapable. Its weight seems to increase as he clings to it, and, he realises, its cries have steadily diminished until they are now only a gentle whimper. He is unequivocally responsible for this new person.

The sensible thing would be to take it to a police station, but that's out of the question. Whatever duties this orphan demands of him, to give himself into custody cannot be one of them. Yet what else can he do with a foundling?

Frank is quite as exhausted by this conundrum as by his long and frightening day. The child is silent now, and he can think of nothing to do but follow his first intention and crawl into the chest to sleep. Fear of discovery is overlaid by so many other sensations, of concern for the orphan and of puzzlement as to his proper course of action, that unconsciousness creeps up and mercifully overcomes him. Curled up with the tiny warm body clutched tight against his stomach, he sleeps long and soundly.

When he wakes, it's broad day, and the alley is full of brisk early risers. Twenty yards off, two people are busy opening their shop, laying out goods on a trestle table, sweeping flagstones. Nobody takes any notice of him. The goods on that table are pies and buns and loaves: the night's baking, laid out in irresistible array. He stands staring at the fare, temptingly spread so close by. Where else will he get breakfast? No one will be suspicious of him if he buys a roll. He feels in his pocket, and for the first time realises that he has no money. He had a little purse at Turner's house, but it isn't in his pocket now. Did those brigands take it when they kidnapped him? Very likely. It hardly matters: he's penniless. The buns are unobtainable.

He considers going up to the stall-keeper and simply begging for some water, hoping that he will offer a crust out of pity. London is full of vagrants; he can hardly be conspicuous in that capacity. As full of vagrants as it is of foundlings. Then it occurs to him that his new charge may prove useful to him. He climbs back into his chest, and examines the litter of rags. Yes, they are the remnants of clothes. Among other things, a linen shirt, full of holes but soft and fine, and a pair of torn trousers: if he can dress himself in these, he will no longer be Frank Sherrell, Mr Turner's assistant, but a poor young man with a baby brother, lost and helpless in a strange city. In that new persona perhaps he can beg food and drink with impunity.

The baker is so intent on balancing his piles of loaves on a trestle that he hardly takes in the lad standing in front of the stall, looking longingly at some Bakewell tarts on the next table. But his wife comes out of the house, and immediately notices the baby.

'Would that little thing be your brother, young man?' she asks peremptorily, pointing at the tiny swaddled creature in the intervals of scratching a large mole on her left cheek, which quivers, whether with sympathy or revulsion Frank can't decide.

Her hair is drawn up tautly from her forehead into a bulbous little linen cap, so that her head has the outline of one of her husband's cottage loaves, above her plump, wrinkled face. Surely she is sympathetic?

'He's hungry. Please, have you some milk I could give him?'

'Is there no one to care for the two of you?' she asks with growing concern. He shakes his head. 'Poor wretches!' she goes on. Then, seeing her husband looking across at them, 'Well, it's none of our duty to feed the whole town, we're not so rich ourselves that we can give away all our hard work.' Then she smiles, and adds in a low voice behind her hand, 'But how could I let that waif out of my sight without givin' it a drop of something?'

She hands Frank a tart from her stall, and goes inside to find a ladleful of milk. The baker, as bulky a figure as his wife, with a broad flour-sprinkled apron, sees what she is doing and is indignant that she has fallen for so old a trick.

'Be off with you!' he flaps, as though Frank and the baby were importunate mongrel-dogs. 'Stealin' our livelihood – you ought to be reported.'

Frank is alarmed by this turn of the conversation, and is about to make himself scarce when the woman comes back and, remonstrating with her husband, holds the ladle to the child's tiny mouth. Much of the milk is spilt, but to Frank's relief a good quantity of it goes inside. The exercise accomplished, a large bubble emerges from between the baby's lips and it registers contentment. Frank is delighted. But only for a moment. The miniature features pucker into a frown, the mouth opens and it starts to wail.

'Ah, he needs 'is swaddling changed,' the baker's wife opines. 'Now, are you familiar with such matters, lad?'

This is an aspect of the situation that hasn't occurred to Frank. He is quite at a loss. But the kindly woman takes the child from him and unwinds its apparel, inspects it and takes it indoors.

'You'd best come with me, son. If you're intending to continue its guardian, you must learn a few motherly tricks.'

And, cheeks all aquiver with revitalised maternal feeling, she demonstrates how to clean and change the infant. He follows her movements with fascination, but some misgivings. Will he really have to perform this operation himself?

'He'll tell you when 'e needs your attention. Have you any clean linen?'

Frank remembers the remaining rags in the chest, and goes to fetch them. As he holds them out for the woman's scrutiny it occurs to him that they may have been left there for this very purpose. They consist mostly of several lengths of soft cloth torn into convenient strips.

'Aye, they're clean – they'll do,' she says judicially. 'But wait, I'll give ye some more. There's no end to it, you know!' Her laugh tells Frank that along with the new-found motherly instinct she has recovered a cordial sense of humour.

In a cupboard under the narrow staircase at the back of her tiny living room, she finds some folded napkins, and a few pins. He takes them with gratitude, and puts them up with the other scraps and his own discarded jacket in a bundle made from his shirt. Then he hoists the fresh and contented babe on to the other arm. The woman thrusts a mug into his hand, and in a conspiratorial whisper tells him to drink. He gulps down the milk, and they go out once more into the street. The baker has been distracted by some early customers, but seeing them emerge he begins to bluster about young thieves and suchlike criminals. His wife ignores him.

'There, now. You can go on your way fed and watered. Where shall you take the little one, lad?'

Frank looks vacant, and shakes his head again. 'I don't know this city,' he mumbles.

'Lost, are ye? And how did you find your way here? Where are you from? – But we've no time for all that,' she says hurriedly, catching a threatening scowl from her husband. 'With no mother, you can't mind the babe yourself, I dare say. But there's a place for foundlings, you know. An asylum that cares for the poor mites. They call it...'

The baker is impatient now, and signals with a threatening raised hand that she is to return to her proper responsibilities.

'Enough prattle, woman. That's time enough you've wasted. You've been lucky, lad,' he tells Frank. 'We don't make a habit of giving buns to beggars.'

His wife grimaces at him behind his back, and gives Frank a wink. 'Good luck, boy,' she tells him in a stage whisper. Then with exaggerated secrecy she thrusts a Bath bun into his trousers pocket. The baker, outwitted, pretends not to notice.

And now Frank sallies out on to the London streets in his new character, the orphan boy with his bundle of belongings and baby brother. At first he skulks in the shadows, creeping under scaffolding or down deserted alleys, fearful of attracting any attention. Rounding a corner, he almost knocks down a policeman who is standing there admiring his brightly polished gun-metal whistle. He has just put it into his mouth for an experimental blow when Frank collides with his substantial abdomen. A long shrill shriek emerges from the whistle before it pops out of his mouth like the bung from a fermenting cask. As he scrabbles in the dust for it, he finds breath to remonstrate.

'Where do you think you're going, youngster? Hurtlin' along without paying no attention – anyone might'a been in your way.'

But it's more a question of injured pride than serious damage, and after a moment he is buffing up the whistle as if the Queen was about to come by with her brigade of Life Guards to inspect it. Frank doesn't want to draw attention to himself by making too rapid an exit, but soon sees that he is of no interest to the constable whatever. Even so, the fierce whistle has reached the ears of some of his comrades, and a couple of them appear round the corner, ready to provide reinforcement in the event of an affray.

They take in the little tableau in front of them: their fellow officer, the boy with his infant brother, and a mood of ineffable tranquillity on the street corner. Nothing amiss here, evidently. Frank is rooted to the spot for a few moments, wondering if they will take notice of his face, which is still darkened by the bruise. But he reflects that whoever followed him and George to Sarah's house probably only saw him from behind, and in any case it was already too dark to make out his features. The bruise will surely not be on record as a distinguishing mark. At any rate, his injury attracts no attention now, and with great self-control he walks quietly away. The policemen don't so much as turn their heads in his direction. Frank Sherrell, the fugitive from justice, is no longer visible. Even if those Peelers had been detailed to look for him, they would have made no connection between the runaway they're after and this sad youngster in charge of a new-born child.

In addition to its merits as a disguise, the baby, he soon discovers, is a wonderful means of procuring sustenance. Every so often a passer-by takes pity on the poor little thing, and stops to offer it a sip of cordial, or a sugar-plum. The latter, Frank judges, is a trifle indigestible for one so young, but a morsel pinched off and administered on the end of a finger proves an effective way to soothe an incipient wail of hunger or bewilderment. He too benefits from this charity: candlegrease buns and Sally Lunns and all manner of sweetmeats come his way, as though the child exerted an altruistic magnetism on every kind of nourishment. If he thinks a particular benefactor has an especially kindly eye, he plucks up courage to ask about the asylum for orphans that the baker's wife has mentioned. But he gets no satisfactory answer. No one seems to have heard of it, or, if they have, they have no idea where to find it.

Despite these disappointments, he bears his burden almost cheerfully through the pullulating city. He feels liberated like a ghost, seeing but not seen, a wanderer content to explore, to wait and see what will happen. He takes the trouble to make the baby's acquaintance properly, to exchange smiles and giggles with it, to tickle its palms and bounce it on his knee. He awakens a heart-breaking little smile, but discerns a glint of fear in the creature's dark eyes that warns him to be always tender with it. When its weight becomes too great, he finds a bench and rocks it to sleep, or cups a hand under a fountain and dabs water on its mouth. He feels more protective than ever, and is filled with a sense, perhaps quite unjustified, that he is doing something noble.

The shadow that blots this strange euphoria is the gulf of misunderstanding that has opened up between him and Mr Turner.

And – he realises – this is all made somehow more unbearable because it removes him, too, from Harriet Lenox. If he can't go back to Queen Ann-street, how can he ever hope to see her again?

When dusk falls he is no nearer to solving the question of what to do with the baby. A light warm rain has begun to fall, and finding himself near the Thames, he looks for shelter under a bridge. A flight of stairs leads steeply down to the river's edge, and he descends it cautiously, clutching the child tight, to a great stone arch, the first of a gigantic file of them that carries a main road over the Thames to Surrey. And there, as his eyes grow accustomed to the gloom, he gradually becomes aware of a crowd of silent folk encamped on a wide stone platform above the tide-mark, standing and sitting and lying, huddled under blankets, some with pots on little smoking fires, some tearing at fragments of bread or meat that they have scavenged in the course of the day. At first the spectacle frightens him, but they ignore him, or if they turn their eyes in his direction it's only to stare blankly, as though they were dead souls watching new arrivals in the infernal region. There's a hellish stench, too, blended of foul Thames water and unclean humanity.

Moved by so strange a sight, Frank tries to communicate with the nearest of them.

'Well, at least it's good and dry under here,' he says cheerily.

'If it's droy you're wantin',' the thin man he has addressed replies slowly, 'if it's drouth you want, you're the lucky one. Some of us here,' he jerks his head towards the multitude behind him, 'could do with a drink.'

He holds up a bottle, shakes it and turns it upside down.

'Droy as a bone,' he laments, and throws the bottle to the ground.

'Here,' Frank says, 'someone gave me a bottleful of water just now. For the baby,' he explains, as though anxious not to be thought greedy on his own account. 'We could spare you some.'

'Water!' the thin man cries contemptuously. 'What would I want that for? There's water enough in the river.' He points to the fetid and stinking stream that runs sluggishly past them a few yards away. Frank is sickened by the association of ideas he conjures up.

'Then I'm afraid I can't help you,' he says, and turns away, hugging the child close as though to protect him from this new apparition of misery. In the course of the night it becomes clear that some at least of the thin man's companions are not entirely without refreshment. Loud bursts of singing, and then argument and shouting, make it difficult for him to sleep.

He lies there haunted by a vision – an angel of light that hovers over this tragic landscape of huddled despair. It seems to him that the angel looks like Harriet, and he is filled with shame that she might see him in this awful place. She has her arms outstretched, as though to signify that she understands and pities all these lost people, half-submerged in a deep and echoing gloom. And then the vision merges with another, which he gradually realises is one conjured up by Mr Turner himself, a picture he and Harriet have stared at in the gallery at Queen Ann-street. The two of them looked at it for a long time, and could make nothing of its strange glow peopled with apocalyptic figures. Now, it all seems to make perfect sense. The glow enters his heart, and he feels a new, warm wave of peace steal over him.

On the point of dropping at last into some sort of sleep, he is startled by a light flashing over his face, and he opens his eyes to see a couple of policemen staring across the sea of vagrants. One of them has a lamp fixed to his belt, and they are pointing out some familiar characters to a bearded man who is with them, evidently an interested outsider – a government inspector or some such, Frank guesses. He can make out a bright emerald silk cravat behind the small, spade-shaped beard. Are they looking for criminals on the run? These visitors would hardly be able to pick him out in that shadowy, hugger-mugger throng, but for a moment he's afraid of being recognised. Then the lamp is turned away, the visitors move off, and he returns to his fitful repose. The baby, thank the Lord, is oblivious of all and passes the night in the sweetest of slumbers.

Chapter 21

CHARLES EASTLAKE and Elizabeth Rigby have gone to visit Thomas Griffith at his shop, and have taken Harriet with them. She is rather left out of the conversation, but very anxious to catch as much of it as she can.

Griffith is astride one of his hobby-horses – the most distinguished horse in his stable.

'If only it were easier to pin the man down. Here one minute, gone the next! I love him dearly, if only for his art. But I vow I shall have to forswear dealing with him if he persists in such studied elusiveness. And I still have no idea whether he can attend my little outdoor *conversazione* at Norwood tomorrow. How can we bring him to heel? You say you have engaged the services of the young man he hires to stretch his canvases, Eastlake?'

'He had agreed to help if he could. But he seemed to know little or nothing himself, and Mrs Danby, the housekeeper, cannot tell him anything – she is kept equally in the dark, of course. And now the boy has disappeared as well. He is suspected of stealing that drawing of yours. It was a water-colour you had agreed to buy of him, Griffith?'

'Aye, one of a set – strange how he prefers always to work in sets. One is never enough, there must be a dozen, two dozen... What energy!' He has opened a portfolio. 'Look, here are the others.'

As they bend over the pile of drawings, they hear Harriet breathe her thoughts behind them. 'Frank Sherrell? No!'

Eastlake seems to take her up. 'I confess I thought him prepossessing enough, when we met in Turner's gallery. But people of that class – especially the youngsters – can be deceptive. It's a lesson you must learn, Miss Harriet.'

'I know enough to know that,' she says pertly. Elizabeth reproves her.

'Most rash, and most unladylike. I have told you before that you ought not to think of him at all.'

'How can I help it?' she asks ingenuously. 'Where is he now?'

111

'Run away,' Elizabeth pronounces with decision. 'We shan't see him again, I doubt. The rogue!'

'Run away?' the girl echoes forlornly. 'But he's done nothing wrong, I'm certain! He mustn't be punished!'

Griffith interrupts this futile discussion.

'Pray come into my office, Eastlake, and you, Miss Rigby, if you please. We must see how we can get to the bottom of his little mystery.' They move into the room at the back of the shop.

'Stay here, Harriet, my dear, and study some of these works of art. They will teach you the more enduring values, and perhaps bring you to realise that our passing emotions are of no significance whatever.'

Left alone, Harriet glances briefly at the works on the walls: landscapes with mountains, rivers and lakes, or ships in choppy seas, all bordered in gold, and set off by thick gold frames. But she soon tires of this, and wanders to the window, peering down the street with an anxious look on her face, as though she expected Frank to materialise there.

Instead, another young man appears, sauntering along in a state of high self-satisfaction. Perhaps John Pound is pleased with the sartorial effect he has achieved in the past hour or two, though to the dispassionate observer it is, to say the least, curious. He has purchased a new shirt and cravat, and, impatient to be seen in them, put them on. He has also splashed out on a high-crowned beaver hat, which he wears at an exaggerated angle. His suit will not be ready for a day or two, and so he is still wearing his old, creased coat and stained trousers. When he sees Harriet, poised like the prettiest of portraits in her own frame of the shop window, he stops, transfixed, then opens the door and stands on the mat staring at her. As she goes towards him he bows elaborately.

'Your servant, Miss.' He is now, all of a sudden, the man-about-town, with a clumsy 'educated' accent.

'And yours, sir,' she replies mechanically, very puzzled by his appearance. He seizes the opportunity and her hand, which he tries to kiss. 'Sir!' she protests, withdrawing it rapidly.

'Your devoted slave, in fact, Miss,' John pursues, undaunted.

'What...?'

'For long have I been your worshipper from afar. Excuse me, Miss – John Pound, at your service. I will gladly do anything you bid me. Any whim, any fancy of yours shall be my instant command.'

112

She surveys him coolly as he delivers himself of this rigmarole, then bursts into irrepressible giggles, which in turn become loud laughter. He looks surprised at first, but soon realises that he will cut a better figure by laughing too.

'But indeed,' she says when she can find breath for words. 'Indeed, I do have a most urgent wish.' John falls on to one knee, exchanging one ludicrous posture for another. She laughs afresh. 'Get up, do! You are ridiculous! But seriously – would you like to help me?'

He places one hand on his heart. 'You know I would.'

'Will you help me search for someone who is missing?'

He looks bemused. 'Missing?'

She nods.

'Well, who is this missing lady?' he asks.

'Not a lady,' she corrects him. 'No. A gentleman.'

'Ah.' He is slightly deflated.

'His name is Sherrell – Frank Sherrell.'

'Sherrell,' he repeats, trying to fix it in his mind. 'And where does he live?'

For some reason this question embarrasses her, and she blushes. John likes that.

'I don't know, I'm afraid. But – he's an artist.'

'Oh no!' he exclaims involuntarily. 'Not another! We don't need any more of *them*, I'm sure.' Then, cross-examining her sternly, 'What do you want to find him for?'

He sees that she has become misty-eyed.

'Because – I don't want him to come to any harm. I'm afraid he might. Now – *do* you think you could help me find him?'

Despite his mounting jealousy of this unknown object of the girl's warm feeling, John can't resist her hopeful smile. After a brief, silent struggle between jealousy and desire, he swallows and grins back at her.

'We'll see what we can do, Miss. Now, where do we begin?'

'I really don't know, that's the trouble. All I can tell you is that he works – or used to work – for the famous painter, Mr Turner.'

'I don't believe it!' John's astonishment and anger erupt, but inwardly: he daren't let Harriet suspect anything. She is telling him more.

'But Mr Turner thinks he has stolen one of his pictures, and...'

'Stolen a picture? The villain!'

'But he didn't!' she cries. 'I know he didn't! Please, please help me find him so that we can prove he's innocent!'

She looks eagerly into his face, but he is not responsive. John is thinking hard, looking down approvingly at his new cravat while caressing the nap of his hat.

'Well,' he says eventually. 'You don't set your admirers the easy ones, do you, Miss? It's like the fairy tales, eh? Do I have to fill a hundred sieves with water by sunset, or sweep the sea-shore clean of sand? No! My task is to find someone in London – one single solitary individual – in this great smoky metropolis. You're cruel, Miss.'

'Not cruel. Only – worried.'

'And, even more important – how shall I find you?'

'Oh, I don't know. You must write to me care of Mr Eastlake, here at Mr Griffith's. Can you remember that?'

'It's engraved on my heart, Miss – Miss what?'

'Lenox. Do try! I shall be so grateful. Will you help me?'

'For a smile and a glance from your beautiful eyes – anything.' He kisses her hand again. As he does so, the office door opens, and Elizabeth is looking at them across the room.

'Harriet! *Harriet!*' she calls. 'And you, young man, what do you mean by this impertinent behaviour?'

John adroitly skips to the street door and performs an awkward bow. 'At your service Ma'am. Good-day.' He makes what he hopes is a dignified, if rushed, exit.

'Harriet,' Elizabeth begins in low, earnest tones. 'I am becoming extremely concerned at your apparent negligence of all the decencies. It seems you cannot so much as see a young man without permitting him to make violent love to you. It pains me. Your American manners are out of place here in London. As long as you are entrusted to my care in this treacherous city, I shall watch you like a hawk.' The other men come into the room, and she turns to them. 'Ah, Charles. It is time we were going.' She takes Eastlake's arm. 'Harriet, come along. And *stay with me.*'

Chapter 22

CHAZ, HAVING recovered some of his aplomb after the shocks of John's visit, makes his way over to Shadwell, to show Ben Trump his latest acquisitions. John had considered retaining the drawings, since he had stumbled so opportunely on a more reliable and permanent source of revenue. But balancing the risks of returning the items to their portfolio against the benefits of being paid for them over and above his other transaction, he has opted for maximising his profit. And so Chaz puts a brave face on it and spreads his booty over Ben's table with something resembling triumph.

Sammy O'Reilly is there as well, and this doesn't improve Chaz's mood. He has always suspected that Sammy dislikes and despises him. It makes him uncomfortable to know that the huge man is standing immediately behind his chair as they open the paper folder with its precious contents. Ben and Chaz gloat over the haul, though Ben's pleasure in it is perhaps more unalloyed than Chaz's.

'Look at that!' Ben enthuses. 'Those washes of indigo, gamboge, viridian! The delicate hatching, the blushing, dribbling, oozing colour – every stroke of it solid gold! That's the only value of a work of art. Why lock it up in obscurity when it can be shining with the resplendent light of golden guineas?'

'Guineas?' enquires O'Reilly. 'If that's what they are, they're a dam' sight more int'restin' than yer stupid "indigo, gamboge" and what have yer. How do we turn 'em into cash, tell me that?'

'It's not quite as simple as that, Sammy. You must be patient.'

'If there's no money here and now, I ain't staying. You conny-sewers can get on with it on yer own. Just let me know when the guineas arrive!'

'Don't worry about that,' Chaz tells him. 'Of course we'll send you word at once. Rest assured – we value your assistance – infinitely.'

The tight little smile of self-approval hovers on Sammy's lips as he heaves himself into a dirty donkey jacket and takes his leave. Chaz breathes a silent sigh of relief.

115

'The gent I acquired them from tells me there are great stacks of these in the house,' he says. 'What can the man mean by it?'

'It makes me livid,' pursues Trump, 'that he can hound the likes of me for a few paltry shillings each week, when he's worth a fortune in drawings and paintings he refuses to part with! And you mark my words, it's all earmarked for that boy.'

'You were a fool to let him go,' Chaz accuses him. Trump retaliates angrily:

'You were a fool to let him get the better of you, Chaz. And I was a fool too, to leave you to deal with him. Oh, I don't know who's more of a fool, you, me, or the stupid, greedy, swindling, miserly bastard who –' he breaks off and grins. 'But this is the way to get our own back on him! Pay him in his own coin! Sell these, Chaz, and then there will be money enough for his rent.'

'Aye,' says Chaz. 'But why should I pay your rent?'

'What? I thought you and I were working together. I thought you were a pal of mine. Look here. You know I'll pay you back – but now you're rich you can afford to let me have a small advance.'

Chaz doesn't – can't – explain to him that he will probably not be as rich as he might have hoped. 'Pay me back? A small advance? And what rate of interest do you think would be appropriate?'

'You wouldn't charge me interest, Chaz – we're old friends.'

'But business is business. My rates are modest, but I can't afford to be unbusinesslike. Say twenty per cent?'

'Twenty per cent, you scheming dog? How can I repay you at twenty per cent?'

'I wonder how you can repay me at all. But that's my rate. The rent-gatherer is due, I think, tomorrow. And this is the last time of asking, I understand.'

'I take it unkindly, Chaz. After all these years. But what can I do? You see me now, poor, helpless, at my wits' end. And you take advantage of my – disadvantage.' Chaz grins unkindly at Trump's unintentional joke. Trump scowls. 'You wait! I'll be even with you one day, Chaz.'

There is a loud bang on the door.

'What in the devil's name is that?'

Both men jump up. Trump picks up the folder of drawings and after a moment's hesitation takes it out of the room as the banging persists.

Chaz looks round anxiously until he returns. Before Trump can get to the door a police officer has pushed it open and walked in. He is the self-same officer who interviewed George a night or two back. Four of his colleagues linger outside in the street, awaiting his summons.

'Now then,' the officer says in his usual portentous accents. His manner is rougher than it was with the women in Lisson-grove. 'I'd like a word with a Mr Trump, if you please.'

Ben identifies himself, his tone ingratiating. 'That's me, officer.' He and Chaz are both behaving as genteelly as possible now, remembering the manners they once deployed regularly. But Chaz's calm exterior hides an almost hysterical state within. He is convinced that the young man with whom he has recently done business has already betrayed him.

'And this gent?' asks the policeman, indicating Chaz.

'A friend, officer, just a friend.'

'Does he live here as well?'

'No, officer.'

'I'll just make a note of his name and address.'

Chaz, almost numb with terror, stutters, 'Excuse me – b-b-but is s-s-someone going to b-be arrested?'

'Is there anyone here that ought to be?' the policeman enquires, with the air of a man who has solved a Euclidian proof. He raises his eloquent eyebrows at Chaz, pencil poised above his notebook. Chaz opts impulsively to give a false name, and, his imagination having died altogether, says the first that he can think of.

'Er- O'Reilly, officer.'

'First name?'

'S-S-Samuel.'

Trump looks at Chaz, astonished, but says nothing. Pressed for his address, Chaz gives Sammy's, in Wapping, as far as he can remember it.

'Now then, Mr Trump,' the policeman says, turning back to Ben. 'You're acquainted with a Miss George-Anna Danby?'

Ben smiles. 'I think you'll find her real name is Turner.'

'Turner?' the policeman is satisfyingly surprised. 'Now that's a coincidence, ain't it?'

'Coincidence?' queries Ben. 'No. It's her father's name.'

'But you see, Mr Trump, the reason we're here is on account of a charge of larceny preferred by a Mr Turner.'

Chaz is jolted into an involuntary response. '*What?*'

'It's like this,' the policeman begins, settling into an easy narrative mode. 'Mr Turner is an artist. Painter, you know. Shows his pictures at the Royal Hacademy and such.'

'Really?' Chaz is fascinated by these titbits of information. The officer quells him with a glare.

'On Thursday last, the 28th, Mr Turner was happrised of the loss of one drawing executed by himself, subject Cob-lenst Bridge (I believe that is a German town), from a portfolio. He is hextremely careful, so he tells us, who he admits to his premises. The only person of unaccredited origin known to him to have been so hadmitted was one Francis, or Frank, Sherrell, employed by Mr Turner to mix his paints, or clean his pictures, or some such.' The policeman's air of certainty evaporates temporarily in the presence of these technical mysteries. 'Dusts 'em, I suppose, once a week – I don't know. Howsoever, by a chance too extraordinary to be coincidence, the said Francis, or Frank, Sherrell did upon that very day, Thursday the 28th, leave, vacate and absent himself from the aforesaid premises without so much as a by your leave. The hinference is obvious. Said Francis Sherrell purloined the said work of art. He was subsequently observed in the company of the said Miss Danby, the same you say is Miss Turner. If that were so, it would be egregious indeed. But the reason we are here, gents, is that said Miss Danby, upon being questioned, testified that she had met, encountered, and made the acquaintance of said Mr Sherrell in this very house. She seemed reluctant to produce this information. A circumstance natur'ly tending to arouse our suspicions that she was happrised of unlawful goings-on. Such as the receiving of stolen goods. Works of hart, perhaps?'

He pauses for dramatic effect. His two auditors are unaffectedly spellbound by his story. Neither moves; both have their mouths slightly open and are staring at his eyebrows. Their suspense is tangible.

'More interesting still is the fact that although we followed Sherrell to a certain address, when we conducted a search at that address he was not to be found. He had, in short, done a bunk, scarpered. This circumstance greatly increased our certainty that we were on the track of the felon or felons. And that track has led us – here.'

He looks round him, a pleased smile on his face, as though to check that his present surroundings are indeed 'here', as claimed.

Ben speaks after a moment.

'And so you accuse us of – larceny?'

'As to that,' the officer replies steadily, 'I shall bide my time. But I shall require you to answer a few questions.'

'Such as?'

Trump is fixed with a very beady, if partially occluded, eye.

'Where were you on the 27th and 28th ultimo?'

Ben and Chaz look at one another, aghast. Ben plunges in.

'Very difficult to say, officer, at this stage. Do you remember where *you* were, Chaz?'

'Er – I think you mean Sammy,' Chaz whispers between gritted teeth. 'I'm your old friend Sammy O'Reilly, remember, not – nobody else.' He flashes a hideous smile at the policeman.

'Sammy, damme, yes,' Trump says, clapping him on the shoulder and looking shifty.

'That's a question that can be asked again at the Station,' puts in the policeman. 'Here's another. 'Ave either of you gentlemen ever been in possession of a work of the artist Mr – er,' he consults his notes, 'Joseph Mallord William Turner?'

'It so happens that I am, in a very modest way, a dealer in books, prints and – er, suchlike,' Chaz babbles. 'It is therefore just possible that I –'

Ben kicks him violently on the shin. He doubles up in pain, but by a mighty effort of will refrains from bellowing aloud.

'No,' he finishes. 'No – I really think it most unlikely.'

'A hart dealer, eh, Mr O'Reilly? So you would know what these here documents are referring to. You might recognise such a hobject if it were passed under your nose?'

Chaz is squirming.

'Ah, dear me, that's another matter, of course.'

'Another question. Are there, at this moment, any works of art – of any description – on these premises? Now I should warn you that we intend to make a thorough search while we're here – I have a warrant –' he produces a piece of paper and waves it at them – 'so it'll be as well to answer haccurately.'

'No. Certainly not,' Chaz says quickly. Ben looks thoughtful.

'Accurately, of course. Accurately – well…'

'Well, what have you to say, Mr Trump?'

'The accurate answer is undoubtedly, yes.' Chaz looks at him, horrified. The policeman is unmoved.

119

'I see. And can these works of art be produced?'

'Yes,' Ben says. He doesn't get up.

'Well?' the officer repeats. 'Mr Turner may be a Royal Hacademician, but it wasn't what I believe is known as a hacademic question.' A rictus of policemanly mirth breaks across his face. Very slowly, Trump gets up, leaves the room, and after some moments returns with the portfolio. He puts it on the table in front of the officer.

'And what, may I hask, is this?'

Trump's actions continue in slow motion. He puts out a hand, and lowers it to the wrapper, and gently draws the top leaf aside. Beneath are a few grubby prints. Chaz, who has been holding his breath and sweating profusely, looks at him in amazement.

The policeman picks up a print by its corner and holds it up to the light, as though he were examining a bank note for signs of forgery.

'Is this a water-colour by Mr J.M.W.Turner R.A.?'

'Dear me, no,' says Trump. 'That's an engraving. They're all prints, you'll find, officer. Musical subjects. That's my line – music. Here we have The Musician's Muse, pretty, ain't she? And this one – this is Madame Pasta in "Medea in Corinth." You will of course be aware that that is an opera. And Madame Pasta is an opera singer. What a voice!'

The policeman looks sceptical.

'Are you sure none of 'em are water-colours? Any views of Coblenst Bridge?'

Chaz points eagerly at one of the prints. 'Could this be a bridge?'

The officer peers at it, blinking his eyebrows out of the way.

'It's nothing of the kind. So much for your expertise.'

'Quite right, officer,' Trump says. 'There's nothing of interest here. Only memories of days long gone – aye, me. What's the use of keeping such souvenirs? They might as well be destroyed.'

And he starts to tear them up. The policeman is disconcerted by this.

'Pray don't do that, sir.'

Trump continues tearing, sighing as he does so.

'Empty fantasies. Vain seemings. What meaning can they have for me now? Only pain…'

The officer is now frantic.

'Stop at once! I forbid you to continue. I shall take these – prints – with me.' He grabs the loose sheets of paper, attempts clumsily to enfold them in their wrapper, and hands them to one of his colleagues. Then he clears his throat.

Now, with your permission,' – he seems unaware of the irony of this – 'we shall search the premises.'

All the policemen leave the room through the door into the small scullery at the rear, and then disperse to various parts of the house. They thunder up the narrow stairs, into the little bedroom, and reach the attic, which is not locked now. There is nothing to detain them in any of these spaces, which a glance is enough to show them are quite empty. A shallow cupboard let into the wall of the bedroom is the only point of interest, for its door is jammed and they take half a minute to prize it open and subject its meagre contents to a brief scrutiny. Trump winces as he hears the splintering of wood, then gives Chaz an enormous wink. The two of them remain frozen in their seats until the policemen return. When they reappear, the men look baffled and deflated.

'We have found no suspicious harticles,' their spokesman announces. 'For the time being, there is no reason for you to come with us to the Station. But I should warn you that we may require your attendance there presently. For now, good-night, gents.' And, clutching his package, he leads his men out of the front door, making noise in proportion to their disappointment. After a few moments of astonished immobility, Trump and Chaz embrace rapturously. Then Chaz breaks away.

'But, Ben – what did you do with the – ?'

'Too dangerous to have in the house. I pushed 'em down the drain under the pump. They truly are *water*-colours now.'

Chaz, furious, raises his fist, then drops it again feebly. For the moment, it seems, there is no more to be said. After all the varied anguish that the day has brought him, he falls on to a chair and buries his head in his hands on the table-top, sobbing loudly.

Chapter 23

THE AFTERNOON is gratifyingly propitious for Thomas Griffith's *conversazione*. His handsome villa in Beulah Hill is bathed in sunshine worthy of its cream Italianate stucco. It has a large and well-tended garden, with a broad lawn surrounded by tall trees, ample shrubs, and beds of colourful flowers coming into full bloom. Over the lawn daisies sparkle like little stars in the brilliant light. Griffith's friends are dispersed across the grass – Pickersgill, Roberts, Landseer, Leslie, Jones, and Eastlake, who is there with Elizabeth and Harriet, together with many more luminaries of the artistic and literary world, all talking noisily. Servants with trays of lemonade and things to eat are circulating discreetly.

Griffith comes out of the house by French doors that open on to a paved terrace at the top of the lawn, and walks across to where Harriet is, as usual, bored by the conversation. She has wandered off towards a little lake and is watching the mallards enjoying the sunshine. Griffith produces a letter from his coat pocket and flourishes it as he comes up to her.

'Harriet, my dear. This came to my address in town. It's for you.' She snatches it from him without a word. 'I hope it is not a – an improper communication?' His eyes twinkle, but he half turns to see that Elizabeth Rigby is not looking in their direction.

'Please don't tell them, Mr Griffith. I swear it's nothing bad. But they would forbid me, I know, if they found out.'

'If they found out that you were receiving letters – from a young gentleman? Love letters?'

'Oh no! They're – it's nothing like that. I promise. Oh, please!'

'Well, it's none of my business. But I shouldn't wish to act as Mercury between you and some unknown admirer, someone not approved by those responsible for you.'

'I assure you that I'm in no danger on that score.' She turns away from him, so that her back is to the party on the other side of the lawn, and her only witnesses are the mallards. She tears open the letter, and reads it avidly. Then she carefully folds it and pushes it into a pocket in her skirt. Griffith watches all this with kindly concern, not presuming to come too close, and anxious not to appear to be prying.

'It's really nothing, nothing at all,' she says, turning back to him. 'I beg you not to mention it. Or – any other letters that may be sent to your gallery for me.'

'Is it to become a regular occurrence, then?'

'No. But there may be one or two more.'

'You put me in a delicate position, my dear. But I will do as you ask, provided you agree to one thing that I shall ask in my turn.' She looks slightly alarmed at this. He gently takes her hand. 'Will you tell me directly you think you are involved in anything you are unable to – to manage on your own? I will undertake complete discretion. And one caveat,' he adds before she can reply. 'If the letters begin to reach me in too large numbers, I shall demand to be told of their substance. For your own sake, my dear Harriet. You may trust me! Older people are not all gorgons and grampuses!'

She can't help laughing.

'You are so kind.' She kisses his cheek, and he blushes. 'Thank you, dear Mr Griffith, thank you!'

He walks away to his other guests. She takes advantage of being alone again to peruse the letter once more. She is so engrossed in it that she fails to notice that Elizabeth and Eastlake have broken away from the others to admire the herbaceous border and their stroll has brought them quite close to her. Always on the *qui vive*, Elizabeth spots her charge, and the piece of paper, and quitting Eastlake comes rapidly over the lawn towards her. There's no chance of Harriet's hiding the letter, but she instinctively crams it into a pocket. As Elizabeth stares at her she reddens and is conscious that the hastily crumpled-up paper is making a bulge in her dress.

'What is that you have there, Harriet dear? It looks like a letter!'

'Oh no, really, it's nothing. Nothing.'

'How did you come by it?' Elizabeth asks sweetly.

'Mr Griffith brought it to me.'

'Is it from him?'

'No.'

'Then, from whom does it come? I sincerely trust it is not a communication from either of the two young men I have so strictly warned you against?'

Harriet cannot reply. She casts down her eyes and hopes she is not blushing too furiously.

'It is, I see. Give it me, at once. It shall be burned.'

'No! I'll burn it myself.' She flattens the bulge in her skirt with one spread hand.

'But I wish to read it.'

'No!'

'You are contrary, Harriet. What shall I say to Mr Leslie – to your uncle, if he enquires? You are receiving the attentions of not one but two entirely unsuitable young men, neither of whom has presumed to ask our permission to court you. One of them is even suspected of being a thief, and is known to be a teller of untruths.'

Harriet flares up. 'You don't know that!'

'I am disappointed in you, my girl. I am afraid I must demand to see that letter.'

'Please, no!'

'I am sorry, my dear. You must let me have that letter. I am answerable to your family far away in the United States of America. Think of them!'

After a long inner struggle against the inevitable, Harriet silently hands her the letter. Elizabeth reads it as the girl stalwartly stops herself from crying.

' "Dear Miss, I shall be honoured if you will communicate with me at the above address. Meanwhile, be assured that I shall do all in my power to obey your command. Believe me Miss your ever devoted servant, J. " – what? "Pound"? – what is this? "Your command"? Who is this person?'

Harriet makes no attempt to explain, but remains biting her lip to hold back the tears.

'Well, I shall ensure that no further correspondence takes place. You shall not have the opportunity to make a note of the address he gives.' She tears the letter up, and stuffs the fragments into her reticule. 'And Mr Griffith must be warned. I am surprised at his acting as go-between – quite irresponsible. Now come and join us for some tea.'

She turns back up the lawn. Harriet waits for a moment, and her lips move imperceptibly as she recites to herself:

'2nd floor, number 48 Goswell-road, London, N.'

As she sweeps along, Elizabeth passes a group of Academicians talking earnestly. Pickersgill has evidently had his ear to the ground.

'The police have arrested a woman,' he recounts in a half-whisper, ' – and they say she claims to be his own daughter.'

'Take no notice of scandal, Pick,' George Jones advises him. 'Turner has never trodden the common path, for he's not a common man. Leave him to his own ways, for they harm nobody.'

'Yet you want to know his hiding-place as much as any of us, Jones.'

'Aye, for I love him and would be grieved if anything were to occur without my being able to help. He's getting old now, and has been ill, as you know. The Academy has always been his Masonic Lodge, as it were, and like brother Masons we should not fail him when he needs us.'

'He don't need us,' laughs Pick. 'It's we who need him. With the President sick and incapacitated, we need to be able to call on him at a moment's notice. How can we when he goes to ground for such long periods – spirits himself out of time and place?'

'If only that boy hadn't run off,' Leslie says. 'I'm persuaded that he would in time have got to know Turner's secret, and could have been induced to part with it.'

'That's a fantasy, Leslie,' Jones says. 'The boy's gone – a thief, apparently. We must use our own resources. Come now, are we such ninnies that we can't solve a simple mystery attaching to one of our own number?'

Leslie says, 'If only it were as simple as discovering the meaning of his pictures!' and they all laugh.

Roberts chips in, with his Scots accent: 'It's no the laddie we need – a girrul would be much more suitable. He's a soft spot for a bonnie lass. If we could introduce a braw young leddy to his household, might she not act as a convenient sort of spy for us?'

'But she could not be told of her mission,' Jones points out. 'It would be vital that she should act in all innocence. We must proceed cautiously.'

'Well,' says Leslie, spotting Harriet approaching. 'Here she is. A young lady who has already made a deep impression on him. Hattie, I believe you like Mr Turner's wonderful paintings?'

'Yes!' she responds eagerly. 'Our visit to his gallery was something I'll never forget.'

'And I understand you have – ah, returned there? Should you like to go there again under more suitable auspices?'

'Oh please, Mr Leslie!'

125

Jones says judicially, 'We'll see what we can do.'

'It may be,' resumes Leslie, 'that we shall be able to arrange for you to spend some time there – without a companion. Without, that is, Miss Rigby as a companion. She would hardly wish to sit there all day while you made copies of the pictures, do you think? I know you would like to do that.'

'Mr Turner hates anyone copying his work,' Harriet objects, though with evident regret. It's clear that she finds the idea attractive.

'So he does,' says Leslie. 'But I feel sure that for *you* he would happily make an exception, especially since you would then be able to send the copies to your uncle and so help him to choose a new acquisition. That would surely appeal to his business sense. Look, here he comes – with young Ruskin. I believe the old fellow really loves that boy for his book about him – the most magnificent tribute anyone could pay to an artist. An astonishing performance – I couldn't believe he was so young. He writes like a sixty-year-old, and a philosopher at that.'

Turner and Ruskin are crossing the lawn with Griffith. Turner looks old and frail but is obviously delighted by the reverent if voluble conversation of Ruskin, whose rufous fringe flaps excitedly as he expatiates on his latest enthusiasm, the medieval sculptures on the Doges' Palace at Venice. Griffith introduces Ruskin to Harriet and he is immediately enthralled, and spends the rest of the afternoon torn between the two shrines, Turner and Harriet, switching from the character of mature sage to that of adolescent lover with disconcerting and sometimes ludicrous suddenness.

'Turner,' Jones says to him, taking him slightly aside, 'I know you disapprove of copyists in your gallery, but I think you might make an exception for this delightful young lady, whom I believe you already know. Her passion is making water-colours and it is only equalled by her admiration for your work. Might you...?'

Turner looks unhappy.

'Hm. I let a youngster into me gallery the other week, and before I can turn round he's off with a water-colour of mine. Stole it, he did. And didn't he let you in without asking me, Miss? It wasn't you aided and abetted him in taking it?'

'I am really most awfully sorry, Mr Turner. Mr Sherrell didn't know I was coming. I wanted to ask you about my uncle's picture.'

Leslie comes to her assistance. 'You did say, Turner, that you might paint one, if Hattie were to ask.'

'Ah – yes. I think I'd had too much rum in my milk at the time.'

'But you wouldn't imply that Miss Lenox could ever be guilty of such conduct?' Jones asks, judicial again.

'O' course not. It's only that I'm – well, I'm not so young as I was, and I don't like to think of my things getting cast adrift. I want to keep 'em together.'

'But Mr Turner, sir,' Harriet says, boldly addressing the Master, 'I'm sure, indeed I am, that Frank – that the young man didn't steal your picture.'

They all turn to stare at her. Then Ruskin articulates his feelings.

'Your instincts, my dear Miss Lenox, are of the finest, I'm persuaded. How could one so fresh and springlike be mistaken in anything?'

'Oh Ruskin,' Leslie protests, 'I wouldn't go quite so far as that. She's not infallible, you know.' Then he adds, with a little bow to Harriet, 'With respect, my dear.'

But Ruskin knows he is right.

'I believe she is,' he says solemnly. 'Infallible as the orbit of the moon in its circularity; as the ash-sprays in their symmetry… Beauty is truth, you remember, as Keats told us.'

Turner cuts across this incipient sermon.

'Tell you what, I wish she'd paint a few pictures for me to send in to the exhibition this year. What with this burglary and one thing and another, I've nothing ready.'

'That's not like you, Turner,' Leslie says. 'But you mustn't tax yourself. You've been very sick.'

'Miss Lenox would cheer you up, I've no doubt,' Jones suggests.

Ruskin is pawing the ground in his eagerness to speak.

'I wonder if I might beseech the favour of a visit too, while she is there? I'm sure you yourself would not have time to attend her, Turner.'

'What?' Leslie puts in. 'Act as Hattie's guide and mentor? A capital notion!'

Elizabeth and Eastlake have joined them.

'Alone?' she says. 'Would that be quite proper? I should be happier if one of us were to accompany them.'

'Hannah will always be there,' Turner explains. 'I'll tell her to keep an eye on 'em. Well, Ruskin, if you don't mind – I may leave the young lady in your charge, may I?'

Ruskin is ecstatic. 'Yes, sir! Indeed you may!'

Eastlake murmurs in a low aside to Elizabeth: 'Now there's a serious young man who ought to be encouraged.' To which she nods in energetic agreement.

Harriet is delighted at the proposed arrangement, and is prepared to tolerate Ruskin, though she finds him decidedly odd. But she can't quite forgive Miss Rigby's interfering assumption that she always knows best and must have the last word on every subject — at least, every subject that involves Miss Lenox.

Chapter 24

JABEZ TEPPER, attorney, has come to the Marylebone police station early, and is being interviewed by the Inspector. He is a dapper, fresh-faced man about thirty, with a manner that suggests he will not be patronised or kept waiting. To one side, George-Anna stands between two policemen, looking as though she has not slept, which is the case. Tepper glances only momentarily at her before turning to the Inspector to attend to his questions.

The Inspector intones his catechism: 'You are Mr Jebez Tepper, attorney, of Bream's Buildings, Fetter-lane?'

'Yes.'

'This woman has asked for your recognizances. She is known to you?'

'Yes.'

'She is known to you as Miss Georgiana Danby?'

'Yes.'

'She claims to bear some relationship to yourself. What is the nature of that relationship?'

Tepper clears his throat. 'She is – er – the daughter of a cousin of mine. A second cousin of mine.'

'Not a close relation?'

'Not strictly. But I have close dealings with my second cousin. I act as his attorney.'

'Do you act as this woman's attorney?'

'I do not. But I am willing to vouch for her.'

'You will go bail for her?'

'What? Is she accused of any crime?'

'Not as yet. However, she is suspected of being accessory to a crime.'

'To what crime?

'To the theft of a work of art.'

'A work of art! And who might be the owner of this work of art?'

'We understand the owner is the artist of the work in question. A Mr J.M.W. Turner, Royal Academician.'

Tepper, who has maintained his stern and intense concentration on the Inspector to this point, suddenly breaks into a smile and turns, keeping his hands clasped in front of him, to give George a wry look.

'Then I hope bail will not be necessary.'

'Is that so, Mr Tepper? We shall see. By the bye, we were speaking of your connection with this lady. Who is your second cousin, Mr Tepper?'

Tepper, who has been so forthright hitherto, is strangely reluctant to answer this simple question. After a moment, he replies.

I don't think it necessary to say more than that he, too, is named Turner.'

The Inspector looks hard at him. 'Now there's a thing,' he mutters to himself. 'And this Mr Turner is the father of the person who has called you as character witness? Can you explain why she is known as Miss Danby?'

'I don't think such an explanation is necessary or relevant.'

'Do you insinuate that there are circumstances regarding this woman that you – and she perhaps – would wish to hide from the police? What is the relationship, if any, between the father of this woman, who you tell me is a Mr Turner, and the Mr Turner who has suffered the larceny we are investigating? The coincidence of names, you will allow, is striking.'

'There are no circumstances relevant to your investigation that I would wish to conceal. I state only that my recognizances are all that you require to set Miss Danby at liberty. Those I willingly give. The rest is obfuscation.'

'Is what, sir?'

Tepper has undergone the interrogation with equanimity to this point. Now he raises his voice a little, and speaks very firmly.

'If there is money to be tendered, let me have the amount. If there is a document that I must sign, let me sign it and then let us be done.'

This cows the Inspector somewhat. He grunts and pushes forward the paper. 'If you would oblige me with these details, sir. And your signature here.'

Tepper writes as he is directed. The Inspector reads through what he has written, then makes a signal to the policemen in attendance. They release George, who runs to Tepper and almost collapses into his arms. The Inspector wipes his brow, and looks irritated. He turns to speak to his colleagues.

'Since we seem to have advanced not at all with Miss Danby, we must try Mr Trump again. Mr Trump and his companion,' he refers to his notes, 'his suspicious companion Mr O'Reilly. We shall commence, I think, by paying Mr O'Reilly a visit.'

George is listening with all too obvious attention to these proposals. Tepper takes her firmly by the elbow, and begins to walk out of the office.

'Come, cousin. We must leave this place.'

'Quickly! Quickly!' she breathes, and pulls him along with her as she rushes out.

He takes her to the reassuring comfort of his own offices in Fetter-lane. He ushers her through a very solid door into his outer office, a room populated by clerks seated on high stools, at tall-legged desks with wooden panels acting as screens between them. His own room, beyond, is cosily set up with newish-looking brass-studded green leather upholstery and a bookcase of leather-bound works of legal reference. He sits George in an armchair and a servant brings her tea, which she drinks thirstily.

'I have no doubt,' Tepper says, watching her, 'that your father will be here before long, expecting me to act for him in this matter. If he does, I shall need to know what your role has been in this supposed theft. Do you wish to tell me now?'

'There's nothing to tell!'

'Forgive me, but there must be something.'

'Oh, yes, there's a great deal – a great deal! But nothing to do with any thieving. Any thieving that I know of.' Ben Trump would never stoop to robbery, surely?

Very gently, Tepper persuades her that, relevant or not, he needs to know whatever facts she can give him. She rehearses the events of the past few days, wondering now at how a few trivial encounters have built into a confused and frightening story. He listens attentively, and makes notes.

'It's likely your father will take no action until the police have found their suspect. You say you hardly know the young man, but would judge him guiltless. That is something you may have to affirm in a court of law. But let us wait, and hope the matter blows over. Knowing your father, I'm inclined to think that if the lad is apprehended, and proves to be in possession of the stolen work, he will be content to take it back without courting the public exposure that a prosecution would bring. Especially if the case involved calling yourself as a witness.'

George considers this analysis and thinks it a wise one. She nods slowly, with a growing sense of relief. But there is something more to be done.

'Now – you must go home and rest,' Tepper tells her. 'What an ordeal! And your mother will be worrying about you.'

George is already on her feet.

'Send to her, cousin, and tell her I'm free, and safe. But I can't go there yet. There's someone I must find. Someone who's in danger. I'll come back when I've done what I must do.'

'If anyone's in danger, let me see to it. You should recover your strength. Then you may help your friends if you wish.'

'It's not work for you. He'd never talk to you. Only I can do it. I must go...'

'Please...' He has stood up too, and tries to restrain her with an outstretched arm.

But she is determined, and puts on her bonnet and shawl with resolution. He attempts once more to prevent her leaving, barring her way. It is a battle of two determined people, and Tepper isn't used to being baulked. But George is driven by unexpected passion. He sees the fire in her eyes, where he would expect to find only fatigue and despondency, and at last realises that he isn't strong enough to rein her in. Pushing past him, she walks through the rows of clerks in the outer office to the big door. One of the clerks gets up and opens it for her. Tepper has abandoned any hope of stopping her, though he has the greatest misgivings as to what she is doing. He stands looking after her retreating figure with an expression of helpless dismay.

Chapter 25

THE EXPERIENCE of his night under Waterloo Bridge has wrought a change on Frank's frame of mind. As dawn breaks in on the hidden city of outcasts, pitilessly exposing their wretchedness, he knows that he must not allow himself to drift into such a life. It's vital that he should return to Queen Ann-street and face whatever wrath awaits him, fortified in the knowledge that he is innocent. The image of that policeman proudly polishing his whistle has something to do with it too: how could he be seriously frightened of a force composed of such very human beings?

He is attending to the child's requirements according to the pastry-cook's instructions, and making himself more or less decent prior to ascending to the upper world of daily affairs, when he notices a pale-eyed woman looking at him. Her face wears so pathetic an expression of weariness and emptiness that he stares back, arrested by sheer compassion for this lost soul among such a congregation of lost souls. He smiles at her.

'Ach, there's nothin' to be smilin' for,' she says, and then inconsistently gives him a little nervous grin of her own. 'Unless it's the day you're movin' on to another o' these elegant doss-houses.'

'Doss-house!' he echoes, and laughs.

'Well, and what would you be callin' it, my dear? For some of us it's a mortuary. For some, a lying-in ward. Whatever it is, it's no workhouse. And maybe we should be grateful for that small mercy.'

'But cannot some of you go to the workhouse?'

'Bless you, boy, there's not one of us here that's a resident of any parish in London. If we were residents, we shouldn't be down here, should we? But – you're not from over the water, are ye? You speak like no Irishman.'

'No. I – I'm English.'

'English, now! One of the Lords of Creation! And here you are, English, and sharing our shelter – very condescending, I will say.' She looks sternly at him, and she points with a thin, nervous forefinger. 'How did you come by that babby?'

'It's not mine – I –'

'Not yours? Who did you take it from?'

'I found him. I don't know what to do with him.'

'You won't be doin' with it yourself?'

'I can't – I must find him a home somewhere.'

'That's fine, my barney. I'll take him for ye. I lost a child, only the other day. I'll have him instead.'

She moves towards them with such speed that Frank is quite shocked, her arms outstretched, her mouth distended in a wide grimace of delight.

'Let me have 'im, I say. I'll be glad to take him off ye.'

Frank is torn between revulsion and compassion. It would be so easy to surrender the baby and be relieved of a terrible responsibility, while giving this pathetic young woman something to love, to nurture. Yet that seems too easy a solution. To condemn the new life to an existence of squalor and deprivation – surely that would not be right?

She seems to read his thoughts, and what she says jolts him into a feeling of guilt.

'I know what ye're thinkin'. If you care for the child, you won't be leavin' it with a creature like me, in a place like this. But Heaven's my witness, I'll be a good mother to the brat, I will indeed. Come, give him to me.' And she begins to pull at Frank's arms. Her mouth clenches with the effort, her blackened nails dig into his wrists. He only hugs the baby tighter and recoils, horrified by the intensity of her attack.

'No – no,' he protests. As he tries to push her off, he remembers the baker's gesture to him yesterday morning – shooing away a pest. Feeling him weaken a little she renews her assault, goaded to frenzy by the prospect of possessing an infant of her own. He struggles to free himself, and almost overbalances on the brim of the stone shelf, teetering above the black river, now at high tide and lapping close at his feet. He has a sudden vision of dropping the child into that foul murk. Should he hand it over to her, rather than risk that? But at this moment another voice intervenes.

'Mother of God! What are you about, Siobhan? Leave the lad alone will ye?' An older woman has somehow insinuated herself between them. Tall and strong, she easily disengages Siobhan's claw-like grip from Frank's wrists, giving her a violent shove.

'You don't want to oblige Siobhan, at all events,' she tells him. 'Poor colleen, she's half crazed since they took her babby away. But she couldn't care for't, and she couldn't care for that blessed thing o' yours, neither.' She pauses, and looks at Frank with a quizzical expression. 'Now, say, are ye joyful to have charge of your little brother? Or is it a good home for him you're lookin' for?'

Frank, too taken aback to speak, can only nod at this last suggestion.

'Well, this is a cruel town for orphans, that's the truth,' she tells him. 'But there's one place ye can go – a kind, true, good place where a child will be taken in and loved and cared for.'

'Yes – I've heard tell of a public orphanage, but I don't know where it is.'

'Well, you're a lucky young man. You're talkin' to just the very person to tell you exactly. Oh yes! I could take you there blindfold, me boy.'

And she tells him about the Foundling Hospital, an asylum where young women can leave their babies quite anonymously, never questioned, never embarrassed or betrayed, and know that the abandoned mites will be fed and clothed, and in due course educated and trained for employment in some craft or trade. He can scarcely get a word in to ask her how to find this magical place, and when he does, she gives him interminable directions, so involved that he fears he will never remember them. At last, even though he still doesn't quite understand, to staunch the flood of her talk he gives her a heel of bread that is still in his pocket, and while her mouth is full thanks her firmly and hurries away.

In departing, he almost trips against a handsome, bony-faced young man with flowing dark locks under a wide-brimmed hat, sitting on a low wall and peering intently over the top of a large sketching-block at a group of the vagrants who are sitting and lying disconsolately under the arch of the bridge. He is wielding a stick of red chalk with dexterity, his long cheeks drawn in as if in sympathy with their misery. Frank can't resist pausing to look over his shoulder. It's an accomplished drawing, and he feels instinctively that he's in the presence of another fine artist. Sensing his interest, the draughtsman raises his chalk, poised for a moment in the air, and leans slightly backwards, as though to give Frank a better view. Rather grandly, he announces:

'Pestilence and Famine – the Hibernian Apocalypse. A grand subject. So poignant, so moving.'

He's probably talking to himself, but Frank instinctively wants to voice an objection. 'Oh, but these people are not grand.' Then, plucking up courage: 'If you're going to paint them, give them a simple title. "Under a dry arch" would do, wouldn't it?'

'I want to give them a dignity they don't obviously possess,' the young man explains. 'But perhaps you are right. There's much dignity in a plain description. I'll think about it.'

And he returns to his task with a concentration that seems to repel any further intrusion. After a few moments, torn between fascination and shyness, Frank walks on. He makes further enquiries of puzzled and sometimes embarrassingly inquisitive strangers, and eventually finds his way north from the river, across the Strand, through Holborn to Lincoln's Inn. In the end he comes upon the Foundling Hospital almost by chance: a four-square red brick building, partly screened by a protecting wall and standing self-possessed in its reassuring, neatly kept little park. There are small children playing there, in neatly kept uniform suits, overlooked by a benign-looking woman who is talking to two gentlemen. The child will indeed be going to a good home.

Confronted with the prospect of imminent separation, he realises that he will be sorry to part with the creature he's cared for these two days, a baby that doesn't so much as bear a name, and which he hasn't thought to give one. Should he christen it before he abandons it? His Irish friend, in the course of her babbling monologue, mentioned that it was common for the young mothers to pin notes to their babies' gowns, mentioning a name and any other details they wished to communicate, even sometimes small sums of money. She'd heard tell of an orphan being left there with a hundred guineas in a bag round its neck!

No. He'll do nothing like that. He has no money, and no right to name the child. All he can do is consign it to the care of this heaven-sent asylum.

Now Frank wishes it were night-time again. He doesn't want to be seen wandering round the walls of the Hospital, searching for one of the little wickets into which he must thrust this bundle of life he has so oddly become associated with. He can't bring himself to do it in broad daylight. He tells himself he should simply go up to the benevolent-looking woman and tell her he has found the baby, ask her to take it and look after it. But she's most unlikely to believe him. What terrible story will she invent to explain the improbable situation of a young man seeking to deposit a baby? It's the mothers who do that. A young man in that position must have done away with his girl – with the mother. Of course, she might have died giving birth – but the idea of inventing such a story simply to exonerate himself is almost worse in his mind than being mistaken for a murderer.

He looks at the gentlemen talking to the woman in the park. One of them is obviously an official of the institution, but the other – now he looks more closely – seems vaguely familiar. A tall grey-haired man – it can't be – but perhaps it is: one of those Academical friends of Mr Turner's – Mr Jones, was it? What on earth might he be doing here? That clinches it: he must wait until nightfall, and clandestinely deposit the brat, running no risk of being recognised.

It will be as well to find out just where he needs to go, and so a promenade of reconnaissance is in order. He skirts the park, hoping the lady and gentlemen have not spotted him, and makes a circuit of the building. At last he finds the principal entrance, and identifies in the wall near it the little wickets or hatches, discreetly covered by hinged flaps, into which over the past century so many terrified and guilty young women have pushed their offspring, loved or unloved, with desperate prayers for their future.

Another day on the London streets, and this time Frank is less enchanted by the experience. The drizzle of last evening cleared long before daybreak and the weather is hot again. He is hungry, dirty and tired after his uncomfortable night, and haunted by the reality of a London he'd heard of but never before witnessed. In comparison, the plain little house of Ben Trump over by the Docks is a decent, civilised domicile. Still, he shudders as he thinks of it, and is reminded of the treatment he received there. His train of thought leads him back yet again to the danger he faces from the police, and it strikes him that once he has left the baby here he will no longer be the anonymous vagrant of the last few hours, but Frank Sherrell once again. He'll pass the night somehow or other, under the protection of the dark, and at first light will go to Queen Ann-street and demand a hearing of Mr Turner.

The operation of leaving the baby in the wicket is unexpectedly simple – almost shockingly quick. A jerk at the flap, a gentle push, and the child disappears for ever. He finds himself almost involuntarily

137

uttering a brief prayer for its safety, and adds his heartfelt thanks for the protection the infant has unwittingly provided today.

As rapidly as he decently can, he walks away from the scene of what he can't help thinking of as a betrayal of the helpless baby. Then he notices that the great front door of the Hospital is open. Brilliant gaslight floods out into the dark courtyard in front of it. Frank can't resist going up to peer inside. The reputation of the place as an example of charitable works emboldens him – no one, surely, is likely to reprimand him, even if he is gently told off for coming too close?

A porter or some such official comes out on to the steps and peers into the dusk. He can hardly see anything out there, dazzled as he is by the light indoors, and he disappears inside again. Fearful that he may close the door, Frank hurries up and positions himself so that he can get a clear view into the hall. The man has vanished, and the hall is empty.

There's a polished stone floor, and at the back a grand staircase leading up to some rooms above. Propped against the wall at the bottom of the stairs stands a large picture. Frank supposes that someone is about to carry it up to one of the grand rooms on the first floor, where he has noticed, through the windows, chandeliers sparkling against ornamental plaster ceilings. It's a picture for a grand room – a whole-length portrait. A portly, jolly old man is sitting in a great armchair, smiling out at the whole world. There's actually a world there in front of him – a great globe on a stand, with the oceans painted on it. And behind him the sea itself, stretching into the distance, with ships sailing away over the horizon. The jolly old man looks as though he's just sat down for a moment and unbuttoned his coat, to get his breath, and will be up again and off on his charitable business. The book and papers at his feet are so real it seems you could pick them up and read them. The whole picture is so lifelike, Frank catches himself thinking that he must be ready to run when the old gentleman decides to come outside.

But he doesn't move. Instead, the porter comes back to close the doors, and sees Frank transfixed on the step.

'Ah, you've noticed the picture of our founder, young man,' he says genially. 'Come in and look more closely, if you like.' Frank shakes his head nervously. He doesn't want to be noticeable in any way. Suppose this man discovered that a baby had just been left there? Suppose the police came to question him about whom he'd seen today?

138

But the man goes on talking.

'Maybe you've heard of him?' he asks. 'His name was Captain Thomas Coram. He was a merchant, whose ships plied the thriving trade routes with the American colonies – this was in the days when they still were our colonies! When he discovered how many small children were left to perish in the hard streets of this city of ours, he resolved to build an asylum for them. That was in seventeen-hundred and forty – and here we are, still caring for the poor desolate things to this day! I hope it wasn't your fate to be abandoned by your own mother?'

But Frank doesn't answer. He is lost in contemplation of the rubicund old Captain, who sits and smiles and surveys the splendid building in which his dream of an orphanage for the lost children of London has been realised.

Chapter 26

IT IS EARLY MORNING in Queen Ann-street, the light still cool and thin, though it will be another hot day later. After a third uncomfortable night, under a tree in a square not far from Captain Coram's hospital, Frank has at last steeled himself to come back. He has managed to find his way from Holborn to Marylebone, and now walks cautiously up to within a few yards of Turner's house, then stops. Having prepared himself mentally and taken a deep breath, he drops quietly down the area steps. That dank defile is enjoying a rare period of comparative drought: there is no moss on the flags and the puddles have dried up. He pauses before knocking on the basement door, at first timidly, then, getting no answer, louder. After a while, Hannah answers it.

'Frank, lad! You!' She has got used to him and in any case is too astonished to throw her apron over her face.

'I didn't steal that picture – I didn't, I didn't!' he bursts out.

''Course you didn't. I knew that. But he got a bee in 'is bonnet about it.'

'Is he here?' She shakes her head. 'I must find him! When will he be back?'

'You know I don't know. Could be tomorrow – could be a week or two. He's not sending to the Academy this year, so there's nothing to bring him home.'

'I shan't be able to rest till I know he doesn't suspect me. I must find him.'

She looks at him, shaking her head over and over again. Then, after a pause she suggests: 'You could try them at the Academy.'

'I suppose I should. But I don't know who to ask.'

'The porter will know where they all are, if anyone does. But come in for a bite o' breakfast.'

'No, thanks – I must find him!'

'You come inside,' she insists, patting the knee of her gown, as though she were coaxing one of the Manx cats. 'You need feeding, and

140

I doubt you could make use of a splash o' water over your face. You're none too clean, if I may say so. And however you got that bruise, it needs ointment.'

He knows she is right, and after a further struggle with his sense of urgency, follows her into the dim, cool kitchen. He last saw it – or didn't see it – when those men bundled him through under a sack, three – or was it four, or five? – nights ago. As she watches him munch bread smeared with goose dripping, he describes what happened. She is incredulous, can't offer any explanations, but promises him he can count on her complete support if it should come to an argument with Mr Turner.

After he has eaten, he sits back for a moment in the kitchen chair, and as she watches him, drops almost immediately into a dead sleep. She tut-tuts and leaves him quiet there, to recoup his energies. The cats eddy round her feet as she goes about her chores, and one of them lies across Frank's immobile shoes. He doesn't stir for an hour, then wakes suddenly, with a sense of panic urgency. Hannah suggests he changes back into his own clothes, but he's now in a hurry, with no time for further self-indulgence. Besides, it will be useful, perhaps, to retain what's left of his disguise. So he leaves his bundle with her, and with brief thanks for her kindness is off again, up the area steps and away down the street, almost at a run.

It takes him twenty minutes to reach Trafalgar Square, that big new open space which is so unlike London, an almost continental gesture of national pride in a great naval victory. He finds the entrance of the Academy premises in a part of the equally new National Gallery building, which has been erected overlooking the square, on the site of the old royal mews. It is all very grand. There's a huge mahogany door in a finely moulded Portland stone frame, and beside it a brass bell-pull, set into a plate engraved with the august name: 'Royal Academy'. Frank pulls it and there is a distant jangle. As he stands waiting for a response, two men in aprons come up, carting a vast picture wrapped in thick cloths. One of them orders Frank imperiously,

'Pull that bell for us, youngster, vill you? I can't get a hand free.'

'I've pulled it already,' Frank tells him.

'Vell, where are they, then? 'Ow long do we 'ave to stand here 'olding this veight? Put it down, Tommy?' The other man nods and they laboriously lower the picture to the ground. Just as they finish doing so, the great door is opened, and a thin-faced, balding man pokes his head out. He is the Academy's porter. The two carriers start to pick their picture up again. The porter looks vaguely at the group.

'Yes?' he says, as though they were pedlars trying to sell him trinkets.

Simultaneously the two men and Frank begin demanding admittance, in their varying styles. The porter puts his hands to his ears.

'One at a time, please. Now, you, lad. What is it?' The two carriers slowly lower their burden again. Another man arrives, carrying two much smaller pictures, also wrapped up and tied elaborately with twine knotted in many places. Frank explains as succinctly as he can:

'I'm looking for Mr Turner.'

'Would that be the Turner who is the Secretary's temporary assistant? Or I believe one of the librarian's clerks is called Turner, too. Which?'

'Mr Turner the painter, please.'

'Oh – Mr *Turner!* And what, pray, do you want with him, young man? He's not here at the minute, I can tell you that. Normally he'd very likely be here by this hour. But he's not submitting this year. Getting old, you know. Past it altogether, I'd have said, though I'm as loyal as any man to the Academicians. He's a stalwart old gentleman and won't give in easily, of that you may be sure. No, I can't tell you where he might be. But you could try his home address. I know that by heart – number 47 Queen Ann-street. There. That should put you on to him.'

'He's not there, I've already asked. He doesn't go there much now.'

'Ah, then he's spirited himself off to his mysterious hideaway, his Queen Mab's Cave. Last year he sent in a picture of that, did you know? A real haunt of faërie it was – though, goodness, I couldn't make much of it myself.' He pauses, as though to recollect where he'd reached in his discourse before he was diverted by this snippet of art criticism. 'He's as likely to be there as anywhere, and that's my free opinion, and I can guarantee the rest of the gentlemen here will say the same. He keeps 'em all guessing.'

Frank is beginning to weary of this disquisition, and his despairing look registers with the porter, who tries another suggestion.

'What about his agent, the dealer, Mr Griffith? He might know, if anyone does. In Pall-Mall. Or try Turner's club, just opposite – the Athenaeum.' Frank is about to thank him for these words of advice,

142

but the porter has not finished. 'Now I come to think about it, he was here yesterday and most agitated, about a water-colour of his that had been purloined. Maybe he's with the police. It was a youngster like you he was after, as I recall. You wouldn't be him, would you?' He thinks this a whimsical and not entirely unamusing joke. 'No – sorry I can't help you. Good-day. And now, you men. This ain't the entry for works of art – take 'em round the back. Go on – off with you!'

Scowling and cursing, the picture-carriers gather up their loads and depart.

Frank has made a careful mental note of the places the porter suggested. Pall-Mall is no distance from Trafalgar Square and he is shortly ringing frantically on the bell of Griffith's shop. But the door is locked, and there's no answer. He presses his face to the windows to see whether anyone is around. While he is thus occupied, John Pound comes up behind him, dressed at last in the full panoply of his new wardrobe, and carrying a letter which he is going to push through the letter-box.

'I say, you there,' he says languidly to Frank. 'What are you doing? Trying to break into the place?'

'Of course not,' Frank rejoins, stung. 'I'm looking for someone, but the shop seems to be shut.'

'Who might that be?' John asks with hauteur.

'Mr – never mind. But – do you work here?'

'Work here?' John echoes, and laughs derisively. The very idea of his working. 'But I do know certain people, of course…'

'Do you know Mr Griffith?'

'Er – met the fellow.'

'And Mr Turner?'

John is suddenly very defensive.

'What do you want with him?'

'A private matter,' Frank says, realising that he will be unwise to divulge too much to this character.

'He won't be here today, I should say. He has a lot on his mind, has Mr Turner.'

'I know.'

'*You* know?' Scorn is blended interestingly with unaffected astonishment in John's hitherto carefully controlled tone. 'And may I presume to ask what your name might be?'

'Sherrell.'

John looks hard at him, allowing his eye to travel up to the top of Frank's dishevelled head and down to his scuffed shoes. He notes the nasty bruise on one cheek, the ragged clothes. Rumour was correct, then. The lad is a rogue. But he keeps these thoughts to himself.

'Sherrell, eh? Well, well! How very apposite!' He looks at the letter he is carrying. 'So – you – are – the miscreant who stole one of Mr Turner's water-colours. More than one, I think?'

'It's a mistake – a dreadful mistake! I didn't –' Frank pulls up short. 'What do you know about it?'

'More than you might imagine. I am – I have the privilege to be intimate with Mr Turner.'

'I don't believe you.'

'I don't care what you believe. At any rate, I can prove to you that I have legitimate business here, while you are no doubt bent on further larceny.' He brandishes the letter. 'You see, I am in correspondence with someone at this address. And I think I ought to summon the police to have you arrested.'

He looks about him, as if for a policeman. But Frank has caught sight of the name on the envelope.

'Wait!' he cries. 'Why are you writing to Miss Lenox?'

John brings himself up to his full height, which is not inconsiderable.

'I – know the young lady well. We are in frequent communication. She has condescended to admit my – my addresses. But that's none of your business.' He looks round again to ascertain that no police are in sight. 'Hi! Police!'

While John is absorbed in his play-acting, Frank grabs the letter from his waving hand and runs off. John is taken completely off guard, and a moment elapses before he can set off after him.

'Hi! Give that back! Thief! Police! Help!'

He gives chase, and the two of them, John in his smart new clothes pounding after Frank, who looks like the thief he considers him to be, threading the crowds on the thronged pavements. The dense traffic is a constant threat if one steps into the road. Drivers flourish horsewhips as much to deter pedestrians as to encourage nags. As Frank and John run they dodge whips, horses and vehicles alike, and negotiate stray dogs and swung walking-sticks, and crinolines almost as wide as the pavement, and sweepers' brooms, vendors' baskets and barrows. They stumble against the bins that hold horse-dung on the street-corners and briefly play a deadly earnest game of tag round one of them.

Oddly enough, whenever there is someone close by who might be asked to help stop the runaway, John is slow to take advantage of the fact. After that first outburst, he prefers to conduct his pursuit in a silence broken only by his increasingly noisy gasps for air. Frank darts into side-streets, and on into ever more obscure alleys. One of these turns out to be a dead end, leading only to a high wall of heaped rubble beside a deep trench dug into the clay. On top of the towering piles of masonry, and down below in the trench, a dozen navvies are at work amid thick clouds of dust and a deafening clangour, demolishing a long terrace of old houses. They must be clearing space for the new railroad that is being carved through the heart of the city. Swinging their pick-axes and crowbars with determined concentration, they take no notice of Frank as he skips over piles of fallen bricks, looking for an escape route. He sidles into an empty courtyard among the partially destroyed buildings and considers concealing himself in a decomposing shed, its doorway hung with sacking and flanked by mounds of rubbish. But in another few minutes that too will be a heap of rubble; besides, to hide smacks of cowardice. Instead, he rounds on John, who has lumbered up, quite out of breath now, and positions himself with fists clenched, defensive. John stops, unwilling to risk fisticuffs. He is red in the face, perspiring and panting hoarsely. He would rather sue for peace.

'Give me my letter, and I'll leave you alone.'

He can hardly be heard above the clamour of the pick-axes. Frank sees that his opponent is a weakling, putting on a mere show of physical aggression. He laughs at him.

'I don't want to be left alone. I want to give you a thrashing. Come on!'

He makes a sudden charge, and John jumps aside to avoid him. Frank shifts his position until John is the one who is cornered, with a blank wall behind him, a large heap of dung and a puddle of horse-piss on either side. They stand tense, facing one another, teeth bared like two enraged dogs. Suddenly John produces his long kitchen knife.

'Very well, then,' he says, grinning ferociously. 'You bully. Come on. I'll show you.'

He lunges at Frank, a poorly timed thrust that enables Frank to dodge the knife and grab his wrist. John, caught at close range, begins dancing about on his toes, imitating what he has seen prize-fighters do, and launching occasional jabs with his free hand. He brings it, bunched into a fist, up under Frank's chin, jolting his head painfully backward and knocking his cap off his head. He follows up this lucky hit with a carefully-aimed slap on the bruised flesh of his cheek. Frank winces, but manages to keep his grip still on the hand that holds the knife. He knows he mustn't let go of that, and with one hand occupied hooks a foot round John's ankle. John loses his balance and plunges forwards, falling on to Frank, who pushes him off with a hand over his face. John instinctively bites his palm, and Frank involuntarily pulls it away. John, regaining a precarious equilibrium, tries to force his other arm down, bringing the knife close to Frank's chest.

Both of them are straining at the limit of their strength, but Frank is clearly the fitter of the two. John's fine clothes don't help: his neckcloth has partly unwound and is hampering his movements. Eventually, his arm judders with the sustained effort, his grip weakens and the knife falls to the ground. Reacting quickly, Frank steps on it. John tries to punch him in the groin but Frank intercepts the blow, and knocks him backwards so that his head bangs against the wall. Frank picks up the knife, which he tucks into his belt. Then he pushes his dazed opponent into the dung-heap, and in extracting himself from it John slips into the puddle. He is well and truly beaten and bruised by this time. Frank stands over him for a few seconds, unable to resist a moment of triumph, then darts off and disappears. John opens his mouth for one last yell of protest.

'You've still got my letter! Give me back my letter!'

Chapter 27

FRANK ROUNDS several corners before he judges that his antagonist is unlikely to find him, then stops and recovers his breath. He pulls the letter out of his pocket, flattens its creased pages and reads it. He notes the address: 2nd floor, 48 Goswell-road. Then he puts his head under a pump, shakes himself dry and sets off again.

The Goswell-road is a long way off, and it takes him a good while, and many enquiries, to find it. At first he thinks it too fine a street to contain the domicile of someone who, as he could see, was not the grand gentleman that he pretended. But the road climbs a long gentle hill and changes character as he walks along it, and becomes a varied neighbourhood with small shops and lodging-houses among the more substantial family dwellings. A narrow lane branches from it, and on the corner is a greengrocer's stall, with a canvas awning over mounds of fruit and rows of plants in pots. Next to it, at the end of a terrace, is a house with grubby children playing round the door and in the area. Frank emerges from the alley next to the shop and peers cautiously round a bank of vegetables in boxes and spring flowers in pyramids of baskets. The shop-woman is buxom, with a long striped apron and a chip bonnet. Frank pretends to be examining the tulips.

'Penny an armful, young gentleman,' she tells him. 'Just what your sweetheart would like. How many will you take?'

'Can you tell me which is number 50, Goswell-road, please?

'Why, you are beside it, my dear. The other side of this alley. Forty-eight that side and fifty t'other side. The odd numbers are opposite. A very convenient new scheme, if you want my opinion. Who are you looking for?'

'Oh – I'd been told there was an excellent greengrocer by number 50. Thank you, I'll know for the future, and – you'll see me again, as soon as I need a pound of strawberries!'

He sidles off, smiling ingratiatingly at the woman, and comes face to face with the barrage of small children. They bring him to a halt. He crosses the road, and stands looking covertly at the house. A flustered maid emerges from its front door, and calls the children inside. They gradually disappear. The door is shut. He crosses again, and tries the handle, making sure that the greengrocer woman hasn't seen him. The door opens easily and silently.

Inside, there is a long narrow hall, empty yet filled with the children's cries, which seem to be coming from the basement. Frank swiftly climbs the first flight on to the landing, and looks around. No one about. The doors he passes are all closed. He takes courage and presses on, up another flight.

He mutters to himself, 'Second floor.'

On the next landing there are two doors, both shut. He very gently turns a handle. The door opens with a loud squeak. He jumps, and waits, then, when no one appears, he ventures gingerly inside. It is a small back room, its window looking over outriggers and serried yards, flagged, with outside privies, pumps, pails and occasional patches of soil sparsely planted. He imagines that further down the street, at the smarter end that he has just passed, the gardens are well tended and full, at this season, of blooming flowers and bushes coming into fresh green leaf. Here there is little evidence of any love for natural things. Perhaps the woman in the next-door shop supplies all the substitutes for growing beauty that these people require. The room itself is very roughly furnished and in a frightful mess, with an unmade bed and a pile of clothes tumbled on the floor.

Frank slips out again and goes to the door at the other end of the landing. This opens into a larger, brighter room, also very rudimentary in its furnishings, with a few chairs and a lean sofa with its stuffing showing. There is a stained and scratched table against the wall opposite the modest cast-iron fireplace, which has a tarnished mirror over it. Everywhere clothes are strewn – expensive jackets, neckties, waistcoats, shirts, some neatly folded, most thrown pell-mell into heaps. Frank examines some of these, and gasps as he finds under one pile a largish canvas with painted on it a misty landscape in brown and yellow, quite obviously one of Mr Turner's. It is partly attached by panel-pins to a broken stretcher, from which it hangs in sad folds. Frank cannot bear to see such a thing badly treated, and his instinct is immediately to perform first aid.

The urgent job is to remove the panel pins, and free the canvas from the stretcher so that it can be rolled up and kept safely. It's not a difficult task, and he sets about it, oblivious now of the situation he is in. He remembers the knife he has just acquired, and inserts the blade under one of the pins to ease it out. As he is doing so, he hears footsteps on the stairs. He freezes, and considers his position. What harm can the absurd young man do him? Especially now Frank has his knife. But Frank now knows his antagonist is a criminal – apparently the very thief whose robberies he has been blamed for. There may be some advantage in being able to watch unsuspected while this unpleasant character incriminates himself further. Frank darts behind the sofa, and holds his breath. A number of blankets, coats and pairs of trousers draped over the sofa create a very adequate hide from which he can observe what transpires. Someone is stealthily turning the door-handle, and in a moment is creeping into the room.

Then Frank realises that he has left the knife wedged under the pin. He starts to move, in a last-minute attempt to claim it, but it's too late. The door opens. He is astonished to see that the new arrival is not his supercilious opponent, but the affected little man who kept watch on him for Ben Trump.

Chaz has decided to take the bull by the horns. The more he has pondered the question – and he's done little else since that nightmare morning – the more it's become clear to him that his situation is insupportable. On careful consideration he has come to believe that the old mother for whom John professed such concern was an invention. He has also concluded that his blackmailer's position is almost as precarious as his own: the water-colours he bought from the loathsome youth were, of course, purloined. Why should he be frightened of someone who is clearly a thief? But he, Chaz, is now implicated in receipt of stolen goods, and it will be impossible to bring the miscreant to justice without embroiling himself. He must devise a means to remove once and for all the threat that now hangs over him with no prospect of remission. Desperate measures are required, and he will probably have to enlist the services of Ben Trump. Another kidnapping, perhaps – or something more, as it were, permanent? At any rate, Trump owes him a favour. And Ben has shown him the way in this respect, at least: first, reconnoitre the territory.

From his hiding place Frank watches Grimshaw as he moves about, surveying the room, staring from the window, opening the door and contemplating the landing, the stairwell, leaning over the banister to listen to the sounds of the family downstairs. Then he sets about rummaging in drawers and among the piles of clothes, throwing garments aside, careless of how they will look to their owner when he returns. Eventually he unearths and stoops to pick up a loose brown-

149

paper parcel, which he takes to the table. He thumbs through its contents, making appreciative noises with his tongue, and after much hesitation abstracts a water-colour from the pile and examines it minutely. But then he thinks of the already overwhelming danger he is in, and pushes it firmly back into its parcel. The less evidence of his association with these plaguey water-colours, the better. Ben's action in pushing those works of art down the drain was the only prudent course.

He replaces the parcel in its hiding-place and is about to leave when he catches sight of the damaged canvas. His curiosity is aroused; he can't resist examining the picture. Frank watches the expressions that pass over his face. But there can be no question, now, of making off with an oil painting. On the other hand, the knife might come in useful... Chaz prises it out from under the panel pin, and holds it in the air, his eyes glistening. Suddenly, he is a theatrical villain, about to wreak the vengeance he has so long craved.

His eyes narrow to slits and dart sideways to left and right. He strikes an attitude, one hand aloft, the other thrust behind him, the fingers spread. Then, stealthily, he walks with exaggerated strides across the cramped space of the little room, forward leg crooked, back leg taut. He flourishes the knife, sneering manically and uttering intermittent cries. He lunges forward as though to pierce the bosom of his hapless foe. A triumphant laugh issues from his lips, and with a jerk he mimes the action of withdrawing the blade from his victim, and wiping the blood from it. On that tiny stage he is reliving a scene from a forgotten drama of long ago, a moment from a time when he was not a lonely and laughable elderly man but a budding theatrical talent, with the future before him. Frank follows all this with fascination, wondering how the scene will end. But as suddenly as he was transformed into an assassin, Chaz is reminded of where he is and what he is doing, and is once more his seedy present self. He hastily pockets the knife, then goes back to the door, peers out, and tiptoes away down the stairs.

As he does so, the cries of the children start up again. A woman's voice can be heard: 'Who's that?' then, 'What are you doing, mister?' followed by further hubbub. Frank is breathing again, fast, with sheer relief. He was an idiot to forget the knife. If he had been detected, the little man in the wig would surely have used it on him, if only out of shock. And now he has no weapon. But he knows – or thinks he does – that his adversary no longer has one either. He goes to the window and looks out into the street, where he can see Grimshaw fleeing, a hand pressed down on his toupée to keep it in place – he seems to have lost his hat – and his coat-tails flying. On the landing, he listens to the noise coming up from below, which at this moment is augmented as the children see someone coming.

"'Ere 'e is, Mother! 'Ere's Mr Pound! Mr Pound! Mr Pound! You've 'ad a visitor! Hey, ain't you all muddy!'

Frank can hear Pound talking to them, and to their mother. She is heard promising a bowl of hot water. This is brought up and placed in the middle of the floor by a harassed maidservant – the same maid who seems to have charge of the unruly children. John follows, rushing first into one room, then the other. By this time Frank has hidden himself again, though much more nervously now: Pound might look anywhere in his suspicion. His first act, indeed, is to go to the various folders of drawings that he has secreted around the room, riffling through them apparently uncertain whether anything is missing or not. He catches sight of the canvas on its broken stretcher, and looks at it puzzled, as though he can't remember whether that was how he left it. After this survey he starts to wash and change.

He picks out various articles of apparel from the piles scattered about and disappears to the other room at the far end of the landing. Frank considers taking a chance and slipping away while John is occupied with his toilet, but now that he's here, he doesn't want to lose the opportunity he sees presenting itself. He will bide his time, and await what happens.

When John reappears he is fully dressed once more, very dandified with an exaggeratedly large necktie and coloured waistcoat, set off by check trousers. He seems to have got over his humiliation completely, and is as cocky as a solitary individual who believes himself alone can be. He goes to adjust the tie in the mirror over the fireplace, alternately whistling jauntily and scowling into the glass as he fiddles with the folds. As he is doing this, he catches sight of Frank's reflection immediately behind him. His whistling ceases abruptly. There's a moment of silence as Frank waits, half amused, half apprehensive, for John to take in his situation. Then he turns to face him, to remonstrate and bluster.

Frank listens to the tirade for a moment or two, then coolly interrupts him.

'You know where Mr Turner lives, don't you?'

151

'I shan't tell you, you vicious urchin. It's a secret. No one's allowed to know. Now, get out!'

'We'll see. But if you won't tell me, I've means to inform him who took his water-colour – his water-colours, I see – and his oil paintings, too.' He indicates the canvas on the table.

'You wouldn't do that!'

'Of course. To get myself out of the mess you've put me in. Why not?'

'But then he'd guess that I –'

'That's as may be. Perhaps you can charm him better than I could. But if you do as I ask I won't tell him what I know. That's between him and you.'

John clenches his fists, but he is shaking.

'I don't trust you. I've told you already: Go away!'

'I'm not interested in whether you trust me or not. But I think you'll agree I'm more likely to obey you – if you obey me. Of course, I can always challenge you to another fight.'

He puts up his fists, which make a considerably more convincing show of sturdy purpose than John's. John blenches, and Frank fixes him with a steady eye.

'All I want is to be taken to Mr Turner. Will you do that?'

There is a great deal more bluster, but gradually, reluctantly, John yields to the persuasion of Frank's stern resolve, and to the proven efficiency of his fists. Sullenly, he goes to the door and leads the way downstairs.

Chapter 28

IN SARAH'S parlour in Lisson-grove, she and Trump are engaged in anxious, breathless discussion. He has made the journey there in the grip of a fearful foreboding, only to find her preoccupied, brooding on her own woes, hardly prepared to listen to his anguished pleas for help. He grasps her frail arm and shakes it more vigorously than he ought.

'You must do something, Sarah, for the sake of our old friendship.'

She pulls her arm free, and shakes her head despairingly.

'What can I do? I'm worried sick about Georgie. Help me get her out, since you've pushed her into this confounded mess.'

'I? I pushed her? I'm innocent, I tell you! I'm hounded and persecuted, near my wits' end with worrying over money – what a sordid occupation, for a man of my talents!' His tone softens and he strokes her thin forearm. 'Sarah, love – don't forget your old lover.' But she shakes him off angrily.

'Fool! D'you think I imagine you care for me? Decrepit creature that I've become. And do you think you're any more spry? Why pretend, Ben? I'm old and half drunk, and you're old enough too. Old enough to know better. To keep your affairs in order, and survive as best you can. I can't help you, I tell you.'

'You can reason with him.'

'I've told you, I can't.' She takes his two wrists and stands facing him, confronting him with her wrinkled skin, blear eyes and rotting teeth. As she does so she looks up steeply into his face. Yes, she thinks, he is still a very attractive man. 'Look at me, Ben. Stop pretending there's any beauty left here. Why – he was tired of it long before it passed! Will he notice me now? He – who makes his own beauty anew every day of his life? What power can a mere woman have over him? That's what I never understood before. If I were eighteen again, he'd be bored with me after half an hour. I know it

153

now. I've learned it the hard way. You can't get round an artist like that.'

Trump listens to this with growing impatience. As she subsides, her little moment of revelation over, he raises a fist and threatens her with it.

'You mean it, don't you? You won't help me.'

'I can't, and that's all. Don't bully me!' He lowers his fist and hunches his shoulders resentfully. 'Face up to it like a man, Ben!'

'But how? I can't go on. I've but a penny left in the world.'

'Then get yourself a penny whistle, and blow it in the streets. There's worse ways to earn your bread, and your rent-money, when you're really up against it.'

He stares at her in disbelief. How can his old friend, his old lover – how can she care so little? Then he sees her as she has described herself: wizened, shrunken, dried up. How can such a hag, such a shell of womanhood, feel for him, or feel for anyone? He gives utterance to a great howl of frustration and rage, and storms out of the house. For a while after he has gone she stands there, not moving, staring at the space he has vacated as though he might rematerialize in front of her, and perhaps give her a chance to unsay that last callous remark. Then, slowly, she pours herself a large tumblerful of gin and returns to slump into her chair by the fire.

After some time she has another visitor. It's a messenger from Jabez Tepper's office, an eager youth, fresh-faced like his master, whose cheerful appearance seems the physical embodiment of his message. He has come to tell Sarah that her daughter, Miss George-Anna Danby, has been released from custody, and wishes her to know that she is safe and sound. She also wishes to inform her that urgent business will prevent her returning home to Lisson-grove for a while.

Sarah hears the news with a dull, unresponsive stare. The ruddy-faced youth is disconcerted to find his well-meant effort so glumly received. What's the point of hurrying across London with tidings of release from a police cell, if they don't cause rejoicing among the recipients? The messenger leaves without a further word from Sarah, and wends his way back to Bream's Buildings, Fetter-lane, in a state of disillusionment with an ungrateful world.

Chapter 29

FRANK AND JOHN walk steadily for an hour, a little apart, John in front, sulky and uncommunicative, Frank attempting to make conversation, to cajole him into divulging information. John will have none of that, and continually glances to right and left, in hopes of discovering a convenient escape route, but Frank is so close behind him that there are few chances to give him the slip. When they have left Clerkenwell and Marylebone behind, they cross Hyde Park and pass through the village of Knightsbridge on the way to Chelsea. There are market gardens and large country houses, beginning to be swallowed up in the inexorably expanding townscape.

At last they reach the river, and follow the towpath past Chelsea church and along the bank to Sophia's house. As he opens the little garden gate, John gives Frank a stern look before going in. Frank hovers outside, gazing with wonder on the unpretentious little dwelling, the neatly tended garden, the cinder path, the plain house-front and the iron balcony high up over all. So this is the carefully guarded secret! This is the great man's private retreat. And Frank vows there and then that, whatever happens, he will not betray Turner's hideaway to anyone – not to Mr Eastlake, or Mr Jones, or even to Hannah.

When John enters the house he can hear his mother and her companion in the kitchen. He waits a bit outside the door, listening. Sophia is polishing spoons and forks. Turner is sitting by the little window, holding a pencil poised over a scrap of paper. He is muttering something – some odd words that don't make sense at first. Then they resolve themselves into something like a poem.

> 'Come my Sophy, let us play,
> Dally all the livelong day.
> You and I, my sweetest joy,
> Playing, loving all the day.'

'That won't do, dear,' Sophia says. 'You've had "day" already.'

'Aye,' he agrees. 'It's not coming right.'

155

He breaks off, dissatisfied, and looks out of the window at the caged blackbird, as though seeking inspiration from its dulcet warbling. Then he throws down his pencil in defeat.

'You're too old for all those sentiments, Bill, if you ask me. Anyone'd think I was a young girl!'

'You are to me, me darling.'

He is about to get up and go to her when John interrupts them, all swagger. He has been in two minds about going in, but can't resist showing himself off in his new attire. But instead of the awed approval he hoped for, his mother evinces only shocked surprise.

'Johnny! My, what clothes you're wearing! Wherever did you get them?'

Turner has a more austere comment.

'What's all this foppery about, John?'

'You told me you'd believe me when I had a smart suit of clothes. Well, you can believe me now.'

'I'd like to, I'm sure, but my notion of smart isn't – effeminate.'

'But that's wonderful, Johnny,' Sophia exclaims quickly. 'You are clever. And what have you been doing?'

'That's my affair.'

'It's your mother's affair too, lad.'

'Aye,' she joins in. 'I want to be proud of my son, but how can I be that if I don't know what he's up to?'

'Give your mother an honest account of yourself, John.'

'If you're going to tyrannise me, I'll be off again.'

'Oh, Johnny!'

Seeing that he is to be pestered for details of his new life, John makes to leave. Sophia pursues him and takes his arm. Turner gets out of his chair and follows them to the door.

'Bill,' she says. 'You persuade him. He owes us some explanation.'

'Now, young man,' Turner says to him. 'Tell your mother what you've been doing. And where you get your new clothes from.' At that moment, he notices Frank hovering in the road at the end of the garden. He points. 'Who's that? By God, it's Sherrell! Come here, you rascal. Come here, at once.'

Frank walks up to the door where all three of them are standing. He doesn't wait for Turner's wrath to descend on him.

'I've come to say, I didn't steal your picture, Mr Turner, truly I didn't.'

Turner stares at him, speechless for a moment, and scratching his head in astonishment. Then he finds words.

'I'd like to know who did, then.'

Frank can't help glancing at John, but looks away quickly.

'I – don't – know, sir. But it was not me, I swear.'

John cannot resist putting his own gloss on the disavowal. 'Oh no! of course you wouldn't admit to a thing like that, you scoundrel!'

It is a disastrous intervention.

'Now that's a very interestin' question, John,' Turner says, a hand on his chin. 'I can't think why Frank should have come all this way to Chelsea to see me, if he was the culprit. Who does that leave, hey?' His hand goes out to grasp John's collar. 'Who, then? Who? My God, has it taken me so long to see?'

'What, Bill?' Sophia asks anxiously. 'What do you mean?'

'Of course! There's only one person who could possibly have taken me drawings. And there's only one way this lazy rogue could 'a got himself a new suit of clothes.'

'No, Bill, no!'

'John,' he says solemnly to her son. 'Tell your mother honestly now. Did you take that water-colour?'

John tries to stare him down, but his eyes falter, and he turns to look at his mother. He is still defiant. Then he looks at Frank, who is silently fixing him with a sad, almost pathetic expression. His glance drops and he shuffles uneasily.

'Oh, I can't credit it! You young monster!' Sophia weeps.

'I don't care. You've got all the goree you could ever spend, and you're mean with it. You look after *him* – you bought this house for him. But you don't care about *me*, though I am your son. I have to look after myself. And you don't like it when I do.' He sees they are both still stony-faced, and starts another line of argument. 'Beside, I was set to it by Mr Grimshaw. He's the one you should blame. I'm only young and knew no better.'

Turner looks on at this performance with disgust. Sophia takes his arm.

'Bill, you hear him? He's young and easily led. I'll swear he'd never have done it of his own accord. There's some villain behind it, I vow. Who's this Mr Grimshaw, then?'

Turner looks affectionately at her, but his smile doesn't last long.

'I fear this one's a villain in the making. You're a fool to spoil him the way you do. And I'm a fool to have been taken in so long.'

'Don't say that, Bill. Forgive him. For my sake.'

'Hmph! I'll let it be for now. But you'd better send him out to work in good earnest. Then I'll maybe see my way to forgiving him. If there's good in him, let him show it. There's a good living to be had from engraving, now. Why don't you try that, John? I can get ye apprenticed in a good shop. And you can make a start by taking off that ridiculous fancy dress. Go on, upstairs with you, and get into some decent manly clothes.'

John slouches off, hang-dog.

Through these last exchanges Frank has been making himself unobtrusive, quietly getting to know the blackbird, stroking its feathers through the bars of the cage.

'And you, boy. I don't know.' Turner puts a hand on Frank's shoulder and looks down, quite shame-faced. 'I'm sorry I ever suspected you. A barber's brother! I should have known better. Did you know my father was a barber? And an honester, more hard-working man I never knew.'

Frank, watching his face attentively, sees an unexpected tear drop on to the weather-worn cheek from the corner of Turner's grey eye. The old man wipes it off with a forefinger.

'But what did ye mean by bringing that girl into my house without my permission? And then – to tell a great lie to Mr Eastlake about it! Well, I can think of only one good reason for that. You're a fool, but why should I blame ye? I half fell in love with her meself. And that *is* folly! Ye see what old age does to a man? I must be losing me faculties to have been so dull. Ye'll forgive me, won't ye? And come back to help me in Queen Ann-street?'

Frank nods eagerly.

'I've something important to tell you, sir. Some gentlemen came to see you, and asked if you would be willing –'

'What's that? Willing to do what?'

'To be President of the Academy, sir.'

'No–o, no. They didn't ask that. They'd never ask that. Of *me*. Look at me – look at my life –.' He gestures towards Sophia and the poky room inside the front door. 'You've got their message wrong, lad.'

Frank recollects. ''Twas Acting President, I think, sir.'

'Aye. There you are. Acting President. Their dirty work done for 'em when they can't find another willing. That was the message, correct this time.' He sounds very bitter, and Sophia takes his arm again, soothingly.

'I'm sorry, sir.'

'It's I should be sorry. All me own fault. But I'm no courtier. I follow me own road, and this is where it's led me. I've been happy enough. But there's one thing, Frank. You mustn't tell a soul of this – of John, and Sophy here, and me – you know what they call me hereabouts? Admiral Booth.' He chuckles, and puts his arm round Sophia. That's who I am in Chelsea. A sea-faring man, Admiral Booth. And, as you haven't yet been properly introduced, this is Mrs Booth. So – mum!'

As Frank and Sophia chat, getting to know each other, they quickly discover that they have Margate in common.

'That was where I got to know Billy,' she tells him. 'I ran a boarding house up on the cliff there, looking out over the harbour. I don't know who has it now – perhaps you do? He thought it was a good place to stay, with its views over the sea. Drew them in all weathers, sunrises and calms and storms, at all times of the year – whenever he could get away from his life in town, or wasn't travelling abroad. A home from home it was for him, he said. He'd come down from London on the steamer, it was very convenient. And one day, when I'd decided a landlady's life wasn't for me no longer, I got this little house on the river, and we set ourselves up together. He put that iron balcony up there on the roof so that, if he couldn't have the Margate sunrises any more, he could make do with Thames sunsets. It's a comfortable arrangement.'

Frank can see that it is, and is inwardly grateful to the motherly Sophia Booth for her care of the great man.

When John comes downstairs again, more soberly clad, his mother asks him a question that has been nagging at her ever since the revelations of an hour ago.

'By the way, Johnnie. Have you by any chance seen a kitchen knife of mine, went missing a while ago? I'm sure we can't find it anywhere here.'

He is about to deny all knowledge, but catches Frank's eye, and lowers his head, mumbling something unintelligible. Frank says nothing.

159

'I wonder where it can have got to,' she says. 'It's been lost a fortnight or more.' Then she cocks her head on one side, listening. She goes to the door again, and looks down-river. The water stretches away to the east, glimmering under a heavy sky. Over the City itself, the sky is quite black, and shafts of lightning are cracking out of a huge purplish cloud. They can all hear the distant sound of thunder.

Chapter 30

A FLIGHT of stone steps leads down to the Thames, which slaps dark and muddy against it, the tide coming in. The late afternoon light is partly obscured by a large black cloud that has drifted over the sun, sending a shiver of chill through the air, and mottling the sparkle of reflections on the oily water. Beyond the steps the narrow perspective of Fish-hill leads up into the City. Halfway along it is the front of Grimshaw's little emporium. In the street a few people are scurrying towards shelter before the storm breaks. Soon there is almost no one about, but at the top end of Fish-hill, silhouetted against brighter light beyond, a man is coming down over the cobbles towards the shop. He walks purposefully but with an air of grim despondency. Is he making for the river? What are his intentions – towards himself – or others?

He stamps up to the shop and peers through its window. Now he is clearly visible: it is Ben Trump. The proprietor is not to be discerned between the prints wafered to the window-panes, or behind the piles of books and papers. Trump traces a few circles in the dirt on the glass, and applies an eye to them. Then he tries the handle of the door. It is not locked. He looks up at the narrow sky between the buildings and sees that the great cloud covers most of it. There are a few splashes of rain. He opens the door and goes in. The door-bell jangles as is its wont, and Ben freezes. But no one comes.

The shop is in its customary muddle. Trump starts hunting for something among the piles of paper. At last he finds a cardboard folder, and inside it, a water-colour. He smiles to himself as he takes this out of the folder and puts it under his jacket, creasing it as he does so. He is trying to rearrange the drawing so that it won't suffer any further damage when Chaz comes in from the street, hurrying to escape from what has developed into a downpour. Behind him the narrow thoroughfare is briefly lit by spasms of lightning, and thunder rolls menacingly. He pushes the door firmly to, excluding the noise and rain, then turns to see Ben Trump.

161

'Ben! Just the man I want to see. I have an idea – a most important proposal, and I need your help.'

He notices Ben's lowering expression, his clenched jaw.

'But – what are you doing here, at this unlikely hour?'

'Never you mind what.'

A colossal flash of lightning cracks outside, and a moment later there is a second, shattering peal of thunder.

'What are you up to, Ben? What have you got there?'

'What's that to you?'

'I have every right to know what you are doing in my shop. And you appear to be trying to conceal something. I've a right to know what that is.'

Trump's face is darkening ominously.

'Had you by any chance come to buy a work of art from me?' Chaz asks with sarcasm, pointing to the corner of the sheet that is protruding from Trump's coat.

Trump removes the hand that is holding the drawing in place, so that the water-colour drops to the floor. He steps on it as he goes for Chaz's throat. The two men struggle, papers flying around them, boxes and portfolios and piles of books falling in avalanches. Chaz gasps, whines and squeals, and pummels with his fists, but Trump, taller and stronger, pins him to the floor with his hands round his neck. Chaz's hands feebly pull at the taut wrists, but little by little they slacken and drop. The convulsions of his body become weaker until they are a mere shudder; and then he lies still, his face darkened as though by a great shadow, and his mouth slightly open.

As Trump kneels over him, contemplating what he has done, he notices that a large knife has fallen out of Chaz's pocket. It had not occurred to the little man that such a useful means of self-defence was in his possession. Trump begins to wish it had. If Chaz had shown the knife, they might have made peace and this terrible thing would not have happened. He is about to pick the knife up when the door-bell jangles deafeningly, as it seems to him, and he looks up to see George-Anna enter the shop. She is soaking wet.

'Is this Mr Grimshaw's?' she says. 'They told me I might find Ben Trump here –' She stops, recognizing him. 'Ben! What – ?'

He scrambles to his feet.

'Get out, woman! Get out! What do you want here?'

'I've been looking everywhere for you, Ben. All the way over to Shadwell… The police are after you!'

'The police? What do you mean? They've got nothing on me...' His eyes return to Chaz's body. George sees it now, too, illumined intermittently by the vivid flashes of lightning that flicker over it while the thunder keeps up a deafening drum-roll.

'What have you done, Ben? Is he all right?' She kneels over the body on the floor, and seeing no movement starts hesitantly to touch his clothes, his neck.

She screams.

'He's – he's dead! Ben, he's dead! You've –' She can't get any more words out. She covers her face with her hands, sobbing. 'I can't help you now, Ben. I'm sorry. I can't. I can't!'

He grabs her wrists roughly and pulls her hands away from her face.

'What do you mean you can't help me? You've got to help me, George!' He puts a ruthless emphasis on each word in turn. But she only goes on crying, staring at him through her tears and shaking her head. 'Selfish bitch!' he shouts at her.

'I'm sorry,' she gasps again between sobs, shaking her head from side to side in hopeless misery.

He sees the knife still lying on the floor and grabs it impulsively.

'Selfish bitch!' he yells again, plunging the long blade into her stomach. She looks astonished, clasps the handle and continues to hold it as he pulls it out, dripping red.

'Why, Ben? – Why did you do that, Ben?' she asks, puzzled, her voice choked and faint.

He stands back, drawing a forearm across his brow as he looks down at her in a kind of puzzlement.

'George, George!' he says, suddenly gentle. 'That wasn't what I meant. You and I should have been singing partners. You were always meant to be the mezzo-soprano to my tenor. But you wouldn't, would you? Too good for me, you were. Like your mother – your god-forsaken – bitch of a mother.' He crouches down and takes her failing body in his arms, holding her tenderly as she sinks to the floor, blood pouring from her wound and staining her dress. 'No one would help a poor musician who'd fallen on hard times. The artist, left to rot by the people he's lived to please. It's always the same. Always the same.'

He is talking to George as though she still heard him. But she will not be listening to his complaints any longer. He is silent for a long while, then begins to sing, softly, looking down at her blanched face and staring eyes.

'He kissed her cold corpus a thousand times o'er,
And called her 'is dear Dinah though she was no more,
Then he swallered up the p'ison and sang a short stave,
And Villikins and 'is Dinah lie both in one grave,
Singing tooral-i, ooral-i, ooral-i-ay.'

His voice fades into shocked silence as he realises what he is doing. But he goes on sitting there, pondering his own misery, and it is only slowly that he awakens to the full enormity of his situation. He is covered with blood. He extricates himself from under George's body, letting it fall anyhow to the floor. Almost suffocated by a rising sense of panic, he tries to heave Chaz's corpse away. With enormous effort he eventually manages to haul it upstairs, and lays it on the unmade bed. Using Chaz's cracked old ewer and basin he attempts to wash, and to scrub away some of the blood that has got on to Chaz's body, and on to the bedclothes. He realises that the staircase too is now dripping with blood. He takes a full pail of water and frantically sluices it down the wooden stairs. Books, prints and drawings float in the pool it creates. The water floods across the floor and begins to seep round George's body, steadily reddening as it flows. He looks at it for a long time, his heart pounding so hard that he can hear it. His temples are throbbing with its insistent beat.

He looks out of the shop door. The wet surface of the street reflects a little light from the sky which is still thickly covered with cloud although the rain has now stopped. The rolling of the thunder is growing fainter in the distance. There's no one about. That is something; but the risk of being seen is still great. He decides to wait until night, and hopes that no one will come by. There is a key in the street door and he turns it. Then he goes to Chaz's chair and sits there, waiting. But as he sits brooding in the dark shop his position becomes clearer to him. The police are looking for him, George has said. He probably doesn't have very long. Can he afford to wait for the luxury of darkness? Every few minutes he goes to the window, afraid of being seen, but desperately anxious for night to fall. Damn these long summer evenings.

Sick with anxiety, he dithers. And then he realises that time has passed unnoticed, preoccupied as he was. Darkness is indeed falling. He waits some moments longer, then decides. He crouches over George, pulls an arm over his shoulder, then stands, bringing the body up with him. Thus awkwardly, carrying her like a postman with a heavy mail bag, he stumbles out and down the empty street towards the river.

The tide is high now. At the stone stairs, he staggers a few steps down and lets go. The body falls into the black water with a quiet splash, then gradually drifts out to where light catches it and glints on the ripples round it as it slowly turns and is taken off downstream by the ebbing current.

Chapter 31

HE STANDS ON the steps, watching the dark mass bobbing among the oily ripples until he can barely make it out, and then goes on standing there, as though in a profound reverie. As though he were meditating on life and death, on the unbearable sadness of things. In harsh fact, his mind is a blank, unable to comprehend either what he has done or what it means for him. When at last he turns and makes his way slowly up the hill, he goes to the door of Grimshaw's shop as if he expects Chaz to welcome him with a cheerful greeting and a glass of something warming. It's only as he turns the handle and goes into the dark room, with its wet floor and drifting wads of soaked paper, that he is abruptly reminded where he is.

Gripped once more by panic he stares, immobile, into the darkness and imagines the room above, with the body on its sordid bed. In his mind's eye he sees it bleeding, gouts of blood gushing over the dirty sheets, across the floor and down the narrow staircase. He looks down into more darkness and imagines the swirl of filthy water engulfing his feet, a reddened flood of guilt that will soak and stain him wherever he goes. He lifts one foot after another, convinced that each will stick to the planking as though glued there by the power of the coagulated blood. He feels trapped, imprisoned with the evidence of his crimes, and wants to scream aloud for delivery from this nightmare. But then he realises that his feet are not fixed; his legs are free, and if he chooses, he can go.

And yet he cannot. No congealing blood is needed to detain him. His own terror roots him to the spot. Where can he go? If the police are looking for him, they will find him wherever he flees. Yet it's impossible to remain here, with Chaz upstairs, gazing sightlessly at the dusty ceiling, his blackened face swelling, throbbing, colonising every last corner of the loathsome darkness. And he must be on the move, to give himself at least the illusion of escaping. That's it – escape by running, running and running until no one can follow. Defeat them all

166

by sheer perseverance, by will-power! And the sooner he starts off, the greater chance he has of eluding his pursuers.

Now it's so dark he has no idea how much blood is on his clothes, or what he looks like. He ought to wash, and change his coat. He'll go home, use the pump in his own yard, and take a clean suit of clothes from his own cupboard. He can be away again in a few minutes. Away, out into Essex, or farther – the other end of England, why not? Or, better still, a boat to Holland. He might get away on the dawn tide: there are a myriad boats in the docks a minute from his house. Any one of them can spirit him away from this plaguey London for ever.

But if he's going to escape by water, why not take advantage of the landing here? Wasn't there a dinghy moored down by the steps – the steps where he's just now...?

Buoyed up by a plan of action at last, he slips out of the shop and slinks, on tiptoe almost, as he thinks, to the river. His first instinct is to scan the dark water for a sign of what he threw into it a little while ago. But he can make out nothing. It's as much as he can do to discern the small boat jolting against the stones at his feet. He feels its prow, and runs a hand along the thin wet hawser that holds it to an iron ring let into the quay. He uses both hands to wrest apart the saturated fibres that have tightened into a hard knot. He remembers the knife, still lying there in the shop – it would be easy to cut this knot with that. Here, at last, is a proper use for that sharp blade! The time he would save! – and he could then throw the cursed thing into the river and do away with a damning piece of evidence. But the thought of returning to that place, and scrabbling in the darkness, in the blood-dyed water, for the ill-starred weapon is too daunting to his stretched imagination. He would rather go on tearing away at the tangled rope, loosening it little by little. There's a soothing distraction in that trivial, repetitive action. And eventually – after something like half an hour – there's a little triumph in feeling it come apart in his hands.

He climbs down into the dinghy, swaying as his bulk makes the craft buck on the water. He gropes in the bottom for a paddle, and to his relief finds a pair of oars. Awkwardly, and cursing at their unwieldy weight, he fits these to the rowlocks, then begins to pull out from the steps. It's a huge relief to be moving, to be aware of his whole body moving evenly with the steady motion of the oars.

He steers himself out among moored boats, the high swelling hulls of ships, the striped gunwales of lighters and ferries, trailing hawsers and black floating corks. The oil-dark water slaps at his craft, reflecting in broken flashes the riding-lights that twinkle among halyards overhead. His head clears, and his conscious mind is filled with a jaunty refrain:

'Singing *too*-ra-lie, *oo*-ra-lie, *too*-ra-lie, *oo*-ra-lie, *too*-ra-lie, *oo*-ra-lie...'

The cockney song has become a shanty that keeps time with the rhythm of his pulling.

At one moment he thinks he sees a solid shape in the water, and his imagination is once again ignited. A flare of horror illumines a vision of George's body tangled in ropes at the foot of a ladder leading up the side of a ship. He dips an oar more sharply into the water, and turns his craft towards it. He might still find it, take it on board, and give it over to the police with the story of how he happened to be afloat in the small hours and found this poor woman – no, there would be too much to explain. They wouldn't believe him. Not for a minute. Abruptly he steers away again. Besides, it's not her. Only his fevered brain. And no, no – he couldn't look at her now.

With renewed determination he bends to his task, and keeps on down-river, past the serene pale colonnade of the Customs House, past the looming bulk of the old grey Tower, past the entrance to St Katharine's Dock, and on past the straggling clusters of old houses at Wapping. He is tired now, and thinks of landing at Wapping Stairs, but something tells him he should stay afloat. The river is not his habitat. No one will think of looking for him as long as he remains surrounded by the alien medium of water. Now that he's fairly escaped from Fish-hill, why not float on down the Thames to the sea? The farther off the better.

But another thought enters his head – there's no order to them, they jostle and throng and press for attention, until he prefers to shut them out willy-nilly. This one, though, sticks like a burr in his brain until he has to let go of the oars and hear it out.

You know someone in Wapping, a good friend, someone who will listen to you, understand you, maybe lend you some clean duds, give you food for what may be a long voyage...

It's still quite dark. He can creep ashore, find Sammy O'Reilly and be back on the water long before dawn. He pulls in to the stairs and makes fast. Then, hastily, silently, he threads his way through the streets of Wapping until he's standing in front of Sammy's place of abode. It's even smaller than Ben's, and when you think of Sammy's great size, that makes it much smaller. Beside a chandler's shop, under a lean-to roof of broken tiles and rags of felt patched together anyhow, a crude plank door let into a roughly nailed wall of planking is flanked by a tiny square of glass in a warped frame of laths. Ben surveys the ensemble. Yes, this is the façade of Sammy O'Reilly's narrow dwelling. There's no upstairs, no front parlour, no room for anything beside the door and the exiguous window. And Sammy lives here with a woman – what species of woman, whether wife or kept whore, or maybe even sister, Ben has no idea. Ben knows, though, that behind the cramped front the premises extend back many yards, a long corridor or tunnel clinging to the side of the chandler's shop, that serves Sammy for parlour, kitchen, and sleeping quarters. Now, if Sammy is fast asleep at the rear of this tube of a house, he's going to prove difficult to awaken.

Ben tries the handle on the door. It's loose, but to his surprise it opens at once. The ill-matched timbers of the door let out a grating squawk, and he is inside, in darkness.

He quickly closes the door. How to locate and rouse his friend without attracting the notice of the female? He begins to work his way forward in the pitch blackness. Almost at once his shin collides with an object and he emits a howl of pain. The object, for its part, shrieks too, the protesting cry of a table leg being pushed over a rough floor.

'Who's that?' a nervous woman's voice issues from the depths.

'Only me – Ben Trump,' he tells her in a low half-whisper.

He hears a rustling, a thump or two, and the shuffling of feet in loose slippers. A candle is lit, and peering down the long perspective, he sees her framed in the apertures between hanging draperies of clothing and bedlinen, opening after opening, like a peep-show. She pushes them aside so that, one by one, they are set swaying in the light, and comes towards her visitor. A blowsy, half-asleep frump, fat and comfortable, Ben thinks, if you were in the mood for her.

'Ben Trump! What are you doin'? Aren't you safe at home? The p'lice have been 'ere, lookin' for Sammy. They said they was lookin' for a short stout cove, name of Samuel O'Reilly – short, my Sammy! Where did they get that notion from? I told 'em I didn't rekernize anyone o' that description.'

Ben thinks he knows how the confusion occurred, but he says nothing.

'Anyways. Sam weren't here. He went to find you, hours ago. Have you seen 'im? He had summat to say, very important 'e said.'

'He's gone to Shadwell? When did he go?'

'I tell you, hours back. I thought he'd a' been home again long since, but maybe it were a providence 'e was out. He must be waitin' for you there. It was urgent, that I do know.'

Trump stands there, once again plunged into indecision. To go home, find Sammy – or perhaps miss Sammy on the way? Or return to the river and the comparative safety of the dinghy? The idea of the dinghy has become a picture of security, a safe haven in his mind's eye. He wants to be there, in the gently moving boat, away from buildings and people and urgent messages.

'Go and find him, Ben. He won't leave till you get there.'

'You know that?' But what if the police have followed him there?

'I know Sam. He'll be waiting for you. Go on!'

She shoos him off, as though this midnight meeting were the most ordinary thing in the world. She turns away to her bed before he has got through the door. Obediently, he takes himself away, back down to the river, and puts off again. At once, he lapses into the narcotic bliss of drifting smoothly downriver, unconnected with the city, with its noise and pain and violence. He'll make no contact with the dangerous land, but quietly glide away on the tide into oblivion.

But as Shadwell Dock comes into view, a familiar constellation of silhouettes against the sky, he realises that the summer dawn is coming up. The luxury of his invisible flight is almost over. Before long the rising sun will shoot its light along the corridor of the Thames, and all will be exposed to scrutiny. Already there are more boats on the water, early ferrymen, lightermen, dockside workers, vagrants stirring from uneasy sleep, dark blots in darker shadows gradually becoming visible, three-dimensional members of the living world. And Sammy is waiting for him – Sammy who may yet be able to help him. Trump hastily pulls in to the shore, and is about to secure the hawser when a thought strikes him. Why leave a clue to his whereabouts? A dinghy from Fish-hill come down-river to Shadwell at the dead of night? He throws down the rope without making it fast, and with a kick nudges the boat away from the quay. With luck, it will drift off into the oblivion he wishes for himself.

He hurries through the village of Shadwell, and ascends the long street that contains his own home. There is plenty of noise coming from the docks that extend round Shadwell Basin behind the high wall, and in the street too there is the bustle of working people beginning their day's labours. They hurry along, still half asleep, or talking among themselves, taking no notice of the tall man striding up the hill, away from the river. There are lights in the Ship and Bladebone, where porters who have toiled all night are refreshing themselves. And there is his house, quiet, undisturbed: he can almost persuade himself that he has indeed escaped, eluded the police, and reached sanctuary.

Chapter 32

AS HE COMES UP to his door, it opens and Sammy bursts out, with a great cry.

'Ben! Where was yer? Where was yer yesterd'y?'

'Quiet, Sam!' he hisses. 'Don't make a sound!'

He pushes the big man back inside and pulls the door shut. Then, as Sammy watches, he sinks on to a chair, his legs folding under him weakly, arms dangling, head lolling, eyes closed, mouth open. And then Sammy sees, to his consternation, that Ben is crying. Great tears course down his exhausted cheeks. And as he takes in this phenomenal sight he notices blood on the cheeks too, then sees that there is blood on Ben's shirt, on his sleeves and trousers.

'You been in a fight, Ben?' he asks solicitously. 'Shall yer wash yerself?'

He goes out into the yard to pump some water into a pail. When he brings it in, Ben is still slumped there, apparently incapable of rallying himself. To be helpful, Sammy cups his hand in the water, and brings it out to dash in Ben's face. Ben lets out a yell.

'Idiot! What did you do that for? Leave me alone!'

'Are yer hurt, Ben? What did they do to yer?'

He gets no reply. After a few minutes Trump levers himself out of the chair, and stumbles up the narrow stairs to throw himself, utterly spent, on his bed. Sammy follows him up and stands looking down at him uncomprehendingly, still holding the pail.

'I – can't stop, Sam. I – must go – on. Don't let me sleep –'

But Sammy disobediently allows Ben to drop into a heavy sleep, and himself sinks on to a chair, to keep vigil over his weary friend. It's an hour or more later when Ben wakes, and, half opening his eyes, sees him sitting there like a faithful dog. He leaps off the bed.

'What the Devil do you think you're doing? I told you not to let me sleep! I must be off. Out of my way!'

'Ho, no, Ben. You got to explain. I waited all night for yer. I came to tell yer that woman was a-lookin' for yer, yesterd'y. But you

wasn't here, and I didn't know where to find yer. So I waited, and –
here I am.'

Trump is giving himself a perfunctory wash in the pail. He looks
Sammy over as if to find proof that he is not here, as he claims.

'Well – did yer see 'er?'

But Trump is in too much of a hurry hauling a shirt over his
head to make a reply. In a few moments he is ready to set off again.

'Did yer meet the woman, Ben?'

At the head of the stairs Trump turns to him, as though he has
only just heard him.

'What – woman?'

'She came once before, to see you 'bout somethin'. Was when
you 'ad that youngster up in the attic. Wanted so urgent to see you, she
did, yesterd'y.'

'You spoke to her?' he asks fiercely. 'When was that?'

His tired, frantic brain thinks it has found a way out. He goes
back into the bedroom, and sits heavily on the bed. He points to the
chair, and Sammy sits in it again.

'Tell me exactly when you saw the woman, Sammy.'

Sammy gazes vaguely at the wall. 'Exactly' is a term he finds
uncongenial. Ben watches his face as he vainly chases the idea of an
exact time of day round the inside of his head. At last he rubs his
forehead, and groans.

'Ah, Ben, I can't do "exactly". I can do "maybe", per'aps. Maybe
I saw her 'round dinner-time yesterd'y.'

'Dinner-time, maybe? And when's that?'

There is another pause as Sammy's brain engages with the
problem.

'Now, you saw me yesterday too, didn't you, Sammy? When
would you say that was? Dinner-time? Or later?'

He searches Sammy's face for inklings of recognition.

'Do you remember the thunder-storm?'

Sammy's face clears.

'Thunder! I should say I do! That was a cracker!'

'It was. And where were you at that time?'

After a moment to consider, Sammy answers distinctly.

'I was here. I was a-waitin' for yer, and the woman she come and
ask for yer.'

'In the thunder-storm?'

A long cogitative silence. Then Sammy nods, grinning with satisfaction.

'You met the woman here during the thunder-storm? Are you sure?'

Sammy looks wounded, as though his integrity has been impugned.

'And how long did she stay?'

'Aw, not long. Only till the rain stopped.'

'She was here until the rain stopped. And then she went – where?'

But Sammy cannot sustain such intensive investigation any longer. He passes a hand across his brow once more.

'Aw, Ben. Don't grill me so. I'm not made for grillin'.'

Trump relaxes a little.

'Sorry, Sam. But it's important. You see I need you to remember. I don't need any exact time. But if you could say you saw me here with that woman during the thunder-storm –'

'You – and her?' Sam doesn't follow.

'We were here together, weren't we? You, and me, and her. And then she went away, and you and I sat down together –'

Sam thoughtfully rotates a finger in his ear.

'That's not what I remember.'

'Really, Sammy? Are you sure?'

Here is something Sammy can affirm positively. He is proud that his memory is so clear.

'She came 'ere. But you weren't at home. No. That's certain. Then she went away. The thunder –' He trails off, as though the memory were fading as he tries to capture it.

'Now what I think, Sam,' Trump says confidentially, 'what *I* think, is that you could easily remember us all being here together. That would be just perfect.'

'But I don't. No. It wa'n't like that.'

For a moment Ben wants to put his hands round Sammy's trunk-like throat and throttle him. That pulls him up short. He sees that he must tell this last remaining friend everything. At the thought, his spirit rises in him and yearns to unburden itself of its ghastly secret. Alibi or no alibi, he must confide in someone. And so there, in the poky bedroom of his poky house, he tells his gruesome story. Sammy sits transfixed, gripping the front of his chair-seat between his huge thighs as if he would be blown away by fierce winds if he let go. At the conclusion, there is a long pause.

'Well, Sammy? Would you help your old friend by telling the police what they need to know?'

'The – police?' Sammy shudders.

'They'll be asking all sorts of questions. All you have to do is tell them that. We were both here – during the thunder-storm – with the woman. You remember it vividly! Don't you recall how the lightning lit up her face?'

Sam is more bewildered than ever. Ben sees that his hope of help – his last hope – is doomed to disappointment.

'So. That's not how you remember it.'

Sammy slowly shakes his head. Ben heaves a sigh. It was too much to expect. He stands up again.

'Well. Now you know why I must be gone. When I've had a crust of bread – for I'm ravenous – I'll take my leave of you, Sammy, and who knows when we'll meet again.'

He puts a hand on Sammy's shoulder, and tries to look him in the eye. This huge lout, this blundering bully, this overgrown clown with scarcely a brain to call his own, Sammy O'Reilly seems to Ben Trump now like a noble piece of work, a real man, honest, loyal, replete with simple virtues. He puts his other hand in Sammy's great paw and shakes it.

'Good-bye,' he tells him in a quiet voice. He is about to descend the creaking stairs when he hears his name being shouted outside, and there is a violent knock on the street door below.

Chapter 33

EARLY ON THE morning after the great thunder-storm over the City, the sun is shining on a very different stretch of the river. It is a bright, breezy day, freshened by the recent storm; fleecy clouds are scudding across a blue sky. Turner and Frank are in a small steam-boat plying between Chelsea and Wapping. There are several other commuters on board, sitting round the gunwales out of the way of the brown smoke that blows across them in the wind. The chugging engine propels them swiftly downstream. Turner has found a secluded corner where he can talk without being overheard. He tells Frank how much he admires the wonderful things that man has achieved with steam – the railways, which rush people from one distant part of the country to another in mere hours, and these boats that are transforming the life of London's inhabitants, taking them speedily to their work or their play regardless of the set of the wind. He points out the regular swirls of the foaming wake of the boat, the effects of light sparkling on the disturbed surface of the river, the patterns of the clouds. Frank looks eagerly at everything, not so much because he hasn't observed such things for himself, but because the great man loves them, and on that account they are doubly wonderful.

'Aye,' the painter tells him. 'It's all there, in the world about you, me lad. You may think you want to learn from my pictures. But what are they, if not to show people what's there before their eyes?'

'I think artists always say that,' Frank suggests, conscious that he is being rather cheeky. 'They don't mean it.'

'Mean it? I never meant anything more seriously in me life! Make no mistake, that's what ye must do. Look – look – look. And then – put it all down. The more you look, the more ye'll see. But what makes a landskip painter, eh? It's not 'is love of nature, nor 'is clever ideas neither. It's his hard work. What's the good of looking, if ye won't learn how to paint what ye see? Some o' them – my brethren, my fellow Academicians – they can draw and paint like nobody's business, but they have fancy ideas about what's there in front o' them.'

176

'But I thought,' Frank says, timidly now, 'I thought that your pictures were all fantasies. Dreams. Wonderful dreams. And nightmares, sometimes.'

'And do you think that's not what the world's like, boy? Ye're young yet, and no mistake. That's why I tell 'ee to keep your eyes open. Your mind too. Oh, yes – you'll never see clearly with a closed mind. *They* only paint what they think people want to hang in their dinin'-rooms. But no artist ever learnt anything that way. And so he never taught anyone else anything neither.'

Frank is bewildered.

'But the Academicians – you respect them, don't you?'

'I love them. I wish I could help 'em. I want to help 'em to see better.' Seeing Frank staring so attentively into his face he breaks off, laughing.

'I never said that to anyone before – d'you know that? I've always kept me thoughts to meself. What's the good of trying to explain them? But you, youngster – maybe you're young enough, maybe you can understand, in time.'

Abruptly, as though he had caught himself indulging in a forbidden activity, he changes the subject, or it seems to Frank that he does.

'You know where we're a-going? We're going to visit some little properties of mine. In Shadwell. Hard by the docks. Properties, you'll say, what's a painter doing with properties? He's no business with such things. His job is to paint. But do you know, lad? I keep those properties for one reason only. To make sure that when I die – and that won't be long now – I can do something for all those brothers of mine – all my brothers in Art. They're my fam'ly, you know. Oh, Sophy, she's a good sort, but *she* understands. She knows it ain't really the Presidency I wanted. I only wanted to look after me brothers. And I shall. That's what I've saved for all me life. So as I can look after those poor painters who didn't have my luck. I'm a-going to build 'em such a family house! With a gallery attached – all me pictures in it. How about that?' He turns to Frank, grinning with satisfaction at his vision.

'You see, I've got more property, way over in Twickenham. And there, when I'm gone, they'll build an asylum for 'em, with the money I'll be able to leave. Some of it's from me paintings. But more's from rents. I charge rents so that my poor brothers will be able to live out their days in peace, by the river. That's the place to be. That's what

177

Sophy's done for me, you see – got me a nice comfortable home by the water, where I can be at peace.'

He stops talking, and sinks into a reverie, leaving Frank to ponder what he has said. He looks at Mr Turner's weather-browned face, and remembers the jolly sea-merchant who built the Foundling Hospital. Like him, Turner is sitting there looking relaxed, with his greatcoat open, and he has a book on his lap – the sketchbook he always carries. He is like a reincarnation of the good angel of that other asylum, and, with sudden insight, Frank sees that his ideas are just as admirable, equally full of love for his fellow creatures. With another jolt of recognition he sees, too, that it is the same compassion that fills his pictures: those fantastic landscapes of his are ecstatic hymns to the human race in all its variety and complexity, and to its sublime home, the created world.

When they step ashore, Turner takes Frank on his round of inspection. Their first port of call is the Ship and Bladebone tavern, which, the painter tells his apprentice, is a 'little property' he is particularly fond of. The publican and Meg make a great fuss of him, and are flatteringly friendly to Frank.

'So, Frank, would you credit that I'm the landlord of this little ale-house?' Turner asks with a smile that betokens his delight in being there. 'I bought it as a pair o' dockside cottages, and thought as how I could make 'em useful. What could be more useful than a grogshop, eh?' He slaps Frank on the back and laughs. 'Very handy I know I've found it, doing me rounds as rent-gatherer. Leave that to others nowadays, I do. It's a young man's job. And some of the tenants need firm handling. Today, now, I'm here to speak with a man who hasn't paid me a farthing for six months. And he's still pleading for more time! Well, 'twouldn't be businesslike to leave it any longer. Where would all me poor brothers be, if I let meself become bankrupt? But he's a tricky customer, and I'm right glad to have you by me, boy. Not that I expect trouble, but it's as well to show you don't mean to be bullied. Seen him lately, Mr Baxter?'

'"Oo? Ben Trump? Nay, 'e's a stranger to us, though 'e do live next door, as you may say. I don't know what 'e gets up to these days. Shady doin's, I'll be bound. What'll ye drink, sir? A pint o' porter for Mr Turner, Meg.'

'No, thank 'ee. Stomach won't take it these days. A glass o' milk will do nicely, with a drop o' rum in it.'

'Meg, fetch a glass of rum and milk for Mr Turner.'

'And one for the boy, too,' Turner adds.

'Perhaps 'e'd like some hale?' suggests the publican.

Frank nods.

'Ale, Frank? Well, you're young. A pint of ale for the lad, Mr Baxter.'

'A pint o' porter, Meg, and Mr Turner's rum and milk. What are you starin' at, Meg?'

'Why, ain't that the young man as come out of the necessary-house t'other day?'

'Gracious Meg! What are you thinkin' of? Mr Turner's young friend!'

'Yes, it is!' Meg affirms with excitement. 'Why, you give me a turn, you did. And left in a mighty 'urry, too. With that poor lady all covered wi' blood. Who'd a' thought you was a friend o' Mr Turner's, eh?'

'A woman covered with blood?' Turner asks. ' I don't like the notion of my Ship being a place of violence. Who was she, Mr Baxter?'

'Meg!' the publican reproves the girl. 'Shut your prattlin' mouth, for 'eaven's sake. This 'ere's a young gentleman,' he surveys Frank's rough clothes with a certain prim distaste, but suppresses his inward criticisms in the light of Frank's evident friendship with the landlord. 'I don't believe *he* ever came out of no necessary-house. Don't know 'oo she was, Mr Turner, sir. Just came, and went. But the lad – 'e must know.'

'Her name was Danby. George-Anna Danby,' Frank says quietly.

Turner looks startled, but then recollects.

'Aye, she came to speak with a tenant o' mine. The very man we've come to see today. But what was she doing, covered with blood?'

'I think – she'd been hit by Mr Trump, sir. Or one of his cronies. There were several of them here.'

Turner stands up.

'The villain! Come, lad. We're late for our appointment.'

'He's a dangerous man,' Frank warns him. 'You must be careful, sir.'

'Careful – aye, careful to come away with my money.'

They are about to leave when Meg reappears, flustered and excited.

'Ooh,' she cries. 'There's a great to-do outside in the street. Policeming everywhere. They're comin' along from the river, and from the City, both ways. Crowds of 'em! Let's go and look.'

'Come, Frank,' Turner says. 'We must get on to Trump's. No good flinching. The job's to be done, and no man got respect by shirking his duty.'

On the way to Trump's cottage they have to dodge a thickening horde of people, gathering to watch the drama as a posse of police advance along the road under the high docks wall. When they get there, Turner calls out and knocks on the door. There is no reply for some time, but at last Trump puts his head out of the upstairs window, apprehensively. When he sees Turner, he draws it in again with a fierce 'No!'

Then he cries out, 'Sammy!' and the giant they have both seen before emerges from the front door.

'That's him!' Trump says. 'I think you can handle him, Sam.'

Sam squares up for a fight, but looks more than a little uncertain about tackling a venerable old man in a crumpled top hat. This is not his usual assignment.

'Now see here, Trump,' Turner calls out, ignoring O'Reilly. 'This is my house, and ye're six months in arrears with the rent. I've tried waiting, as you asked me. I've tried reasoning with you. Now, I'm sorry, but I'm warning you. If ye won't pay me now, the police will be on you.'

Frank glances round. 'They're here already,' he observes.

Trump has reappeared at the front door.

'Where are you, Sammy? What's holding you?'

Then he looks along the road and sees the police approaching. Sammy has seen them as well, and has begun to sweat and shiver as though the plague had struck him.

'I don't want no part in this,' he mutters. 'Leave me out of it.' And he walks away, hands in pockets, trying to look unconcerned, as if he had nothing to do with Trump. But a few hundred yards down the road he meets the line of policemen. He tries swagger and bluster, then resorts to his elbows, upon which they gather round him in force, pinion his arms and arrest him without ceremony. He is a known criminal, in any event; and his name and place of abode have been in their hands in connection with Trump ever since Chaz volunteered them. They will deal with him in due course.

Trump watches his friend's capture with horror, then suddenly dives between Turner and Frank, parting them with a gesture of his arms like a swimmer entering the water, and sprints off. He is pulled up short by the realisation that there are police at both ends of the street. For a few moments he stands at a loss, as the two bodies of men approach from opposite ends of the long wall.

'What's this?' Turner says. 'I haven't summoned 'em yet!'

'They wouldn't send so many men to round up one defaulting rent-payer, would they?' Frank points out. 'Just look at them all!'

Trump, wild with desperation, tries to scramble up the wall, his only escape route.

It's almost impossible to find a toe-hold in that regular brickwork, and he slips and slithers, hanging by a hand from a large rusty iron peg that chance has placed where he can reach it. As the first group of police arrive and stretch their arms up to grab him, he just manages to haul himself out of their reach. He finds a foot-hold and after further scrabbling at the mortar between the bare bricks succeeds in shinning over the top. The police are halted briefly, but quickly find their own ways to follow him.

Trump lets himself drop on the other side. It's even further than he imagined and he has to pause for some moments to recover from the jolt. Then he starts to run. He dodges along the ranges of dockyard buildings, tripping over cables, rounding bollards, crates and bales of merchandise. A burly stevedore tries to bar his way; he punches him in the belly, winding him, and rushes on. He skirts basins, leaps over canals, runs cat-like across narrow girders bridging inlets of water, and all the time the tall masts of the ships with their lattices of rigging hang over his head like a phantasmagoric labyrinth high in the air, into which he could clamber and disappear for ever, if only he knew how.

The police spread out across the area to cover and anticipate his route. Crazed with panic, he heads for the tall warehouses fronting the river, and runs into one of them. The idea of escaping upwards suggested by the encircling ships has somehow lodged itself in his fevered mind, and it seems logical to seek a safe haven above. For a moment as he enters the great building he has a treacherous sense of security, of being protected by the huge bales of goods – he hasn't time to notice what sort of goods – piled on either side of a long gangway. But he can hear the police outside, close on him now, and he darts forward along a corridor between the high cliffs of merchandise. At the far end is a dark place, an opening in the wall of bales, where he thinks he can hide. But the running feet are approaching still, and there is nothing for it but to take a narrow cast-iron stair to the next storey. There he is again lulled for a moment into a false belief that he is safe. But what he can climb, the police can too. Remorselessly they pursue him from floor to floor, as he shins up iron ladders and races across resonant expanses of wide planking. Every gangway leads nowhere but to the far end of each floor, where there are yet more stairs taking him higher and higher up the warehouse.

At last he is trapped in a vast upper storey, with tall openings outside which gantries are mounted for hauling goods up from the wharf. Seeing police crossing the huge floor-space, closing in on him, shutting off every route of escape, sheer terror compels him to leap out on to a chain that hangs from one of the gantries. He hauls himself up, link by rusty link, until he is able to cling to the steel beam that projects from the top of the warehouse wall. It offers a refuge of sorts, and he summons a last effort of strength to hoist himself on to it. He looks at the great block and tackle suspended from the beam. They might serve as a means of lowering himself to the ground like a bundle of dry goods. But, seated precariously there, he is too terrified to look down either to right or to left; he can only see the dark-uniformed men gathering in the apertures of the warehouse to watch him. And he can see from their faces that they know he has nowhere to escape to now. They are simply waiting for him to end it all.

But their chief has no desire to see the quarry destroyed. He would like his criminal captured alive and able to answer questions. Panting and cursing, he has followed his men up to this height, and has pushed his way to the front of the line of constables on the edge of the platform opposite the gantry. One of his men hands him a loud hailer.

'Benjamin Trump!' he calls in a pompous voice that echoes across the dock. 'I arrest you in Her Majesty's name! Come inside this minute!'

He has a momentary sense that he sounds like a nursemaid summoning a disobedient child from play. Trump has not dared to look round to see who is speaking; he is too frightened of losing his balance. Then the voice booms out again, louder and more emphatic.

'For the last time – Trump!'

And an absurd voice in Ben's skull calls out silently to him, like an echo:

'... the last Trump.'

His dangling feet feel the links of the chain between them, and he endeavours to steady himself by twining them round his ankles. But in doing so he loses his hand-grip on the steel bar, and topples sideways, scrabbling for a hold, missing, and then finding himself hanging by his tangled ankles, head down, over the eighty-foot drop to the wharf below. His body jerks and writhes with the effort of righting himself, but in the process he becomes utterly exhausted, and is forced to let himself hang there, to regain his strength. But his ankles cannot maintain their grip for long, and he can feel them gradually loosening, the links of the chain slipping inexorably between them. He tries to pull himself up, to reach out for the beam, but that has the effect only of further weakening the grip of his ankles. He hardly dares twist his head to see that the police have gathered there on the wharf underneath him. Even if he could find a safe way down, he would be surrounded. A fatalistic blankness invades his brain. Then his ankles finally surrender their hold, and with a shriek that resounds through the dock and across the surface of the wide Thames, he falls spinning into an inlet of dirty water.

Chapter 34

TURNER HAS followed with Frank, at his own pace, to witness the chase, and is standing on the wharf near the warehouse that saw Trump's demise. A policeman is talking earnestly to him, in a low voice. The two of them turn and walk away, and the policeman puts his hand on Turner's shoulder. Frank is absorbed, horrified, in the last agonies of Trump, and only later looks around for Turner. Not seeing him anywhere about, he goes off to find him.

He is not in the Ship and Bladebone. They haven't seen Mr Turner since he and Frank left together an hour or more ago. Mr Baxter very much wants to share with Frank his excitement over the police chase, and to ask Frank's opinion of what happened. Meg stares at him with unquenched fascination from behind the bar. But Frank is too preoccupied to chat, and leaves to pursue his quest.

It is a long time later that he finds himself in a quiet creek farther down the river, which ripples lazily in heavy sunshine. The breezy morning has given way to a sultry afternoon. At the river's edge, dirty water laps the mud. Beyond there is marshland, sparsely populated by a few weatherboarded huts blackened with tar. Seagulls are wheeling and crying. He approaches the water across tussocks of marsh-grass littered with long-discarded nets, lobster-pots, wooden crates, oyster shells and other jetsam.

Then he sees Turner, sitting on a whitened stump of driftwood, top-hatted, his coat-tails dragging in the mud. As Frank gets nearer, he sees that he has his sketchbook in his hand. Before him on the mud is – Frank stares in disbelief – a body, a woman's body. A policeman is standing nearby, waiting, it seems, for the artist to finish his sketch. Has he turned police draughtsman? As Frank edges closer he sees that Turner is indeed drawing the corpse. Tears are pouring down his face. And then Frank sees that the body is that of George-Anna.

Turner at last puts away his book, gets up and sees Frank. He totters towards him and leans heavily on his arm. Two more policemen appear and between them they begin to lift George-Anna's

184

body off the mud and carry it towards a waiting cart. Turner is still weeping, and makes no attempt to brush away the tears. Frank, who knows that there is nothing to be said, leads him gently away.

They find a hackney carriage that takes them to Lisson-grove, a long and jolting journey. Slowly they mount the steps to Sarah's door and Frank knocks. A light flickers in the hall – for it is evening by now – and Sarah opens the door. Peering out at them she asks, 'Who is it?' She is obviously drunk.

'Sarah,' says Turner. 'Did they come? The police?'

She is nonplussed. They stare at each other for some time.

'Sarah,' Turner says again. 'It's me – Billy.'

'What are you doing here? Get away! At a time like this!' She comes down the step to him, and deliberately strikes him in the face. He totters backwards, and is caught by Frank. When he has recovered, he renews his attempt to engage her in conversation.

'They told you?'

'What?'

'About – George-Anna?' He makes to touch her arm. She recoils from him, but he pushes her gently indoors.

'I don't want you here – I never wanted to see you again!' Sarah yells.

He speaks to her with great tenderness in his voice.

'Sarah – I'm sorry.'

'You were never so tender to me – never! What's the good now?'

'She was our daughter.'

'*Our* daughter is it, now! You left her to me when she needed you. What sort of a father did you make for her?'

Turner looks toward Frank, who is hovering uneasily on the edge of the scene.

'You go along, lad. Leave us.'

Sarah adds, 'Aye, go – and take him with you.'

'Can we not share this, Sarah? 'Tis too terrible for one alone.'

'You never shared anything, Billy, never! Your feelings, your passion, your genius – everything – you kept them to yourself and left me outside. What can you do to help me now – now you've killed her?'

Frank is unable to prevent himself crying out, 'No! You don't understand!'

'I understand very well. You think I'm drunk, no doubt. But my wits are clear. What was she doing out there in the docks?'

Turner takes her hand, and she lets him hold it.

'She was murdered by that rascal Trump. They told you he's dead too?'

'Aye. And who made him a rascal? Who but you, and your everlasting demands for his money.' She pulls her hand away from his. 'You drove him to despair.'

'Ha! So, to your roundabout way of thinking, I killed me own daughter! And you say your wits are clear.'

'Don't you lay claim to her! My daughter, mine alone! You cast her aside, you cast me aside –'

'Aye, you're right, Sarah. And now I can't even comfort you when you most need it. It's too late, ain't it? I'm a useless wretch. But not for much longer. I shall be followin' George all too soon.'

'I wish you would.'

He flinches as she inflicts yet another wound. He stares hard at her, and shakes his head, turning again to Frank.

'She's right. It's too late. A lifetime too late.'

He puts out his hand to touch her arm again, but she turns away resolutely, and goes to slump into her chair. He stands in the doorway, watching her pour another glass of gin. The two men turn to go. As they reach the outer door, Turner stops once more.

'Frank, lad. Stay here with her a while. Keep her company. Come on to Queen Ann-street when she's calmer.'

Frank hesitates, but Turner pushes him back into the room, and quietly closes the door behind him as he descends the steps into the street. Frank goes over to Sarah, and waits for her to acknowledge his presence, but she sits frowning into the fire, holding her tumbler in both hands as though it might warm them. Very quietly, he pulls an upright chair into the glow and sits opposite her, waiting and thinking.

Chapter 35

IN THE HALL OF Turner's Queen Ann-street house the morning light is shining on the painter, who stands at the foot of the stairs with Frank and Ruskin. The three of them are looking at a canvas that Frank is unrolling over one of the stiff little hall chairs. It is the picture that he found in John's room in the Goswell-road. Ruskin, having examined it earnestly for a while, falls on one knee to inspect it more closely. Turner speaks to Frank over his head.

'I owe you a lot, lad,' he says. 'The young rascal had taken dozens of things – and this! I'd forgotten about it.' He notices that the canvas is very dusty, and gives it a perfunctory wipe with his handkerchief. The dust is puffed into Ruskin's face, and he sneezes. Turner laughs. 'Do you think it would be the picture our young lady's looking for? To send to 'er uncle in Ameriky?'

'She's upstairs,' Frank says.

'We'd better get 'er opinion. Go and ask her, boy.'

Frank goes up the stairs, taking a letter – John Pound's letter – out of his pocket. He looks doubtfully at it, reaches the gallery door and is about to go in when he stops and gazes, rather as he did on his first morning there. In a beam of sunlight, seated in front of the Vision of Italy, with a sketchbook and water-colour box, Harriet is working with intense concentration.

She turns and sees him, then stands up, knocking over paint-box and pot of water. Frank holds out the letter, but doesn't move. They stand facing each other for a long time; then, unconsciously, he drops the letter. They take a step towards each other, and she sees the bruises on his face. Her mouth opens in alarm, and she puts out a hand to touch the sore flesh, very softly and gently. He knows she should do no such thing, and instinctively takes her wrist to draw it away. But the sensation of her cool fingers on his cheek is electric, too thrilling to be interrupted. He stands there, holding her wrist, and gazing into her troubled blue-grey eyes. Still they neither of them speak, but he reciprocates her action with a tentative movement to

187

touch her rippling golden hair, to stroke it. It's something he has dreamed of doing often enough, and now it seems quite natural. She doesn't prevent him, and the concern in her eyes dissolves into a beatific rapture.

Very slowly, but with an irresistible inevitability, their incipient caress draws them closer, and they embrace, first hesitantly, then with passion. Round them the pictures incandesce, glow, spin and burst in a glorious celebration of their excitement. The cats, who have emerged from their nesting places all over the house and followed Frank into the gallery, gather in an inquisitive circle round the couple, who are oblivious of them and of everything else. When their ecstasy is at its most intense, the door is pushed open silently and Ruskin looks into the room. They have been much too preoccupied to hear the creak of the stairs as he came up, and now, unnoticed, he stands stunned by what he sees. He watches them, incapable of movement, for some time; then, mute with shock and embarrassment, he retires.

As he descends the stairs, the street door opens and Eastlake comes into the hall with Elizabeth on his arm. Leslie is just behind them. Turner greets them warmly.

'My dear Turner,' Eastlake says expansively. 'What a glorious morning! That storm the other day has cleared the air wonderfully, and we are now going to enjoy a perfect summer, I do believe. And you look far better. How good to think all is well with you.'

Elizabeth interrupts him: 'Harriet – wilful girl – insisted on coming here at crack of dawn, refused to wait for us, putting me to the trouble of sending her in a cab with my own maid. I trust they have arrived safely – and I hope that, once here, she is being useful?'

'And your missing water-colour is recovered, we hear?' Eastlake resumes.

Turner nods corroboratively to Elizabeth, and replies to him cordially, though there is a certain restraint in his voice.

'Aye. And several others – paintings and all – that I'd never even missed. Perhaps if I'd painted less, I'd remember more. But it's no matter. I've lost more important things.' He pauses. 'All my life, art has been my only treasure – my darling. It's late to learn it, but now I realise there's other things too. It's not till you lose 'em that you realise what they meant to you.'

Eastlake is puzzled by all this, but takes his hand, sensing that something is wrong.

'Of course, my dear old friend, I understand. But the water-colour mattered too. Any slight thing of yours is *our* treasure, our national treasure. Don't say you don't know that!'

'Tush, Eastlake,' Turner mutters, dismissing the matter. ''Twas a scrap.'

'We have come with joyful tidings, Turner. Ruskin, good day! Listen. You must be the first to know. We – Miss Rigby and I –'

Ruskin can't help trying to finish his sentence.

'Are – to – be – ?'

'Yes. Married, very soon.'

Turner offers his hand.

'Congratulations, Eastlake. My felicitations, Miss Rigby.' He bows to her. Her customary expression of intellectual imperviousness to mere emotion is softened into a beguiling smile.

'And now, young fellow,' Eastlake continues, turning to Ruskin, 'we have set you an example. Is there not a charming young lady – not unconnected with Mr Leslie here – with whom you have formed a – an association? Something more, perhaps, than a passing attraction...?'

Ruskin blushes and stammers, and tries to turn the conversation. But Eastlake is in a bluff and hearty mood.

'Come, no false modesty, now.'

Ruskin finds words at last.

'I should not dream of answering for the young lady I think you have in mind. And she, I am sure, would not wish me to.'

'What! Are you sure?'

Despite his embarrassment, Ruskin can't help being amused by the authority with which Eastlake seems to understand other people's lives.

'Yes, I am very sure,' he replies. And he pronounces this with all the conviction that he is accustomed to wield in print.

Turner has observed the exchange with wry insight.

'He knows how to interpret the messages sent out by Beauty, Eastlake. He's a dab at that game. You'd better believe 'im!'

He slaps both men on the back.

'But now, some of us at least have something to celebrate. Where's Frank?'

He calls up the stairs, but Frank doesn't appear. Turner leads the way into the dining-room. It is as austere as the rest of the house, and dominated by a large ugly sideboard. Even in mid-summer it's a cold, inhospitable place. Two of the Manx cats appear to have made a nest for themselves on the table in the centre of the room. He shoos them off with a casual sweep of his arm.

'Hannah!'

The little housekeeper comes out of the kitchen, where she has been entertaining Miss Rigby's maid. Turner is unwontedly kind to her.

'Hannah, my dear, fetch the brown sherry.'

She goes back to the kitchen to bring a tray, then burrows in the sideboard and retrieves a bottle of sherry and six extremely small glasses. She puts these on the tray, and takes it to the table, then stands waiting for further instructions. Turner indicates with a flick of his forefinger that she is to pour. She does so, but the forefinger is poised to arrest her movement before she can fill any of the glasses to the brim. When they are all satisfactorily half-full, Turner takes one, and uses his forefinger again to indicate that each of them should do the same. Elizabeth picks up her glass, followed by Eastlake, Leslie and Ruskin. There are two glasses left on the tray, each with its modest charge of brown sherry. Elizabeth is about to raise hers when she notices that they are unclaimed.

'What – ? Where are – ?' she begins. But before she can get any further Turner chinks his glass against hers, and proposes a jovial toast.

'To – Mr and Mrs Eastlake,' he says. Charles draws Elizabeth's arm closer to his waistcoat and looks happily proprietorial. She simpers with uncharacteristic coyness. 'And,' Turner goes on, 'it's not indiscreet, I think, to predict that before long we shall be drinking the health of *Sir Charles* and *Lady* Eastlake.' The couple revise their expressions to ones of amused disbelief. ' – And, of course, to all the rest of us,' Turner concludes, 'including – absent friends, particularly those two upstairs.'

He nods in the direction of the untouched glasses. The Eastlakes must again modify their expressions, and Turner notes with a half-smile that they are having difficulty suppressing their disapproval, which cannot be permitted to show itself on this occasion of unalloyed gladness. They rearrange their faces to register complete delight. Leslie seems to have no misgivings, and is beaming with pleasure. Turner is their host and, today at any rate, they must accept his hospitality on his terms.

'To absent friends,' Leslie takes him up, and Eastlake echoes him. Elizabeth can't bring herself to repeat the phrase, but she touches her glass to his, and gives the company a strained smile as she notices some questionable smears round the rim. Ruskin makes no attempt to smile, and seems lost in thought, knitting his fair brows as he sniffs his glass. Looking round at them, Turner reflects on his contrasting private grief. How different and alone we are, he thinks, in meeting life's sorrows. And look here, now – don't we all have our own very different ways of celebrating its joys, as well?

A sudden thought strikes him. He remembers the pledge he made to Eastlake on the condition that his suspicions of Frank should prove wrong. He realises that he owes the future President of the Royal Academy a barber's libation of scented oil, and turns to Eastlake with the intention of reminding him of that promise. But another thought makes him pause, and he lets the idea drop. Eastlake will garner enough tributes in the course of time, having no need of being anointed with Sherrell's unguent. He pauses on this idea, then with another smile and nod to them all drinks down his sherry. They all do the same.

Postscript

TURNER died in December 1851 and was buried in St Paul's Cathedral. His relatives, whom he had ignored through most of his life, contested his will. This included a direction to build almshouses for indigent artists on land he had bought in Twickenham, near the small country villa he had designed and built for himself in 1812 and used until 1825. In 1856 the Court of Chancery decreed that all his assets, amounting to some £140,000, should be allocated to the family, while his paintings, drawings, watercolours and sketchbooks, without distinction between finished and unfinished, should go to the National Gallery in London. He had hoped for a special room there, to be called 'Turner's Gallery', in which his finished pictures, some hundred works, might be hung in rotating displays. (At one stage, he thought of adding a picture gallery to the Twickenham almshouses.)

The National Gallery in Trafalgar Square did not have room to show more of his works than a single view of Venice that had been bequeathed by Robert Vernon, a collector of contemporary British painting. The pressure on space was relieved when the National Gallery of British Art was opened on Millbank in 1897, with money given by Sir Henry Tate, and throughout the twentieth century substantial displays of Turner's paintings could be seen there. In January 1928 the Thames flooded the basement of the Tate Gallery, destroying or damaging many works. To avoid a repetition of this catastrophe, the works on paper were removed to higher ground at the British Museum in Bloomsbury. Selections of them, as well as of the paintings at the Tate, were often sent on tour not only in Britain but all over the world. In 1987 an extension to the Tate, the Clore Gallery, was built to show all of what was misleadingly known as 'the Turner Bequest'. The British Museum returned the works on paper, which were made available to the public in a specialised Print Room, open five days a week. It is to be hoped that that service, at present only partially maintained, will be fully restored as soon as possible

The National Gallery retained a small representative group of British masterpieces, including pictures by Turner, which were regularly exchanged from the Tate's holdings, so that different works might be seen there at different times; but in 1998 a catalogue of the British paintings at the National Gallery fixed those currently on show as part of the Gallery's permanent collection, putting an end to that flexibility. Apart from these examples, which include *Calais Pier*, *The Fighting Temeraire*, and *Rain, Steam, and Speed*, the bulk of the Turner Bequest is to be seen at Tate Britain on Millbank, principally in the Clore Gallery.

Printed in Poland
by Amazon Fulfillment
Poland Sp. z o.o., Wrocław

52484843R00116